Dear Reader,

Thank you for reading *The Protective One*! I hope you enjoy E.A. and Will's story. Though I liked a lot of things about this book, my favorite parts were the chapters that took place at a county fair. Ah, fairs! Have you ever been to one?

When I was a teenager, my father took me to the State Fair of Texas. Everything there was magical! I loved seeing and hearing "Big Tex," the rides, all the baby animals, and, of course, all the food!

When it came time to write this book, I knew I wanted several scenes to take place at a much smaller venue, and I needed some help! That's when I reached out to a group of about sixty women, all former members of my Buggy Bunch street team. After telling them that I needed small, tiny details about state fairs, we began a three- or four-day discussion filled with all things "fair." These women were a wealth of knowledge and memories! It was so fun to read all about showing livestock, everyone's favorite rides, the fair food, the dust, the cute boys . . . all of it made me smile. What started out as a rather urgent need to get some quick details so I could write a book ended up being an opportunity to get to know some ladies a little bit better.

I'll always be grateful for their help and their stories.

If you've never been part of a writer's street team, I hope you'll consider joining one in the future. You'll not only get some free books, you'll help a very grateful author. And you might just meet some other reader buddies along the way, too!

I put out a call for interested people every fall on my Shelley Shepard Gray Author Page on Facebook. Join me there! I'll look forward to getting to know you.

In the meantime, thank you for giving my books a try. It really does mean so much to me.

With blessings,
Shelley

Also available from
Shelley Shepard Gray and Gallery Books

THE WALNUT CREEK SERIES

Friends to the End*
The Patient One
The Loyal One
A Precious Gift*

*ebook only

THE
PROTECTIVE
ONE

Shelley Shepard Gray

GALLERY BOOKS

New York London Toronto Sydney New Delhi

Gallery Books
An Imprint of Simon & Schuster, Inc.
1230 Avenue of the Americas
New York, NY 10020

First Gallery Books trade paperback edition January 2020

GALLERY BOOKS and colophon are registered trademarks of Simon & Schuster, Inc.

For information about special discounts for bulk purchases, please contact Simon & Schuster Special Sales at 1-866-506-1949 or business@simonandschuster.com.

The Simon & Schuster Speakers Bureau can bring authors to your live event. For more information or to book an event, contact the Simon & Schuster Speakers Bureau at 1-866-248-3049 or visit our website at www.simonspeakers.com.

Interior design by Erika Genova

Manufactured in the United States of America

10 9 8 7 6 5 4 3 2

Library of Congress Cataloging-in-Publication Data is available.

ISBN 978-1-9821-0091-9
ISBN 978-1-9821-0092-6 (ebook)

This book is dedicated to my BBA Facebook group—
a large group of longtime readers who jumped in wholeheartedly
when I needed some help for this book.

You have been my protection,
like a strong tower against my enemies.
—Psalm 61:3

God adds to the beauty of His world by creating true friends.
—Amish Proverb

PROLOGUE

*F*unerals and marriages. Elizabeth Anne had once heard her mother proclaim that these two events always brought people together.

As she stood off to the side in the vestibule of Marie Hartman's—now Marie Byler's—church, E.A. reckoned her mother had been right. She might have been standing by herself, but she wasn't alone. The space was filled with longtime friends and both John's and Marie's families. And in the midst of all of them she could easily spy the rest of her best friends in the world, known as the Eight.

This time, they'd all come together for a wedding or two of their own. But not too long ago, they'd gathered together for a far more heart-wrenching occasion: Andy Warner's funeral.

That day had been painful in so many ways. They'd each been grief-stricken by Andy's sudden death and perhaps were feeling far more alone, because his funeral had accomplished what their best intentions never had: it had brought all of them together for the first time in years.

Still remembering that stark sense of loss like it was yesterday, E.A. shivered. It had been July. Scorching hot, and they'd all been wearing black. But as she'd stood with the rest of the Eight on Andy's parents' front lawn, she'd been chilled. Only seven of them stood together. They would never be a true "Eight" ever again.

It hadn't surprised her that everyone else felt the same way. Standing there on that lawn, they'd all vowed to stay in better touch. Yes, a lot of those promises had stemmed from guilt, because Andy had committed suicide.

However, those promises had also come from someplace else. Someplace deep and true. A place that had as much to do with true long-lasting friendships as private losses. With the fact that their friendship had transcended everyone else's expectations about how so many different people could remain so close for years and years.

It was during that moment on the lawn that they'd all promised to each other to be better friends. And, amazingly, in the past eighteen months, that had happened. Marie had moved back to Walnut Creek. John B. and Will had stopped putting their careers first and now never said no to group gatherings. All of them had let their guards down and shared secrets that they'd previously only kept to themselves.

And now, here they were, celebrating a wedding. Marie, their very own English homecoming queen, had just married John Byler, who'd grown up Amish.

It seemed that love really did conquer all.

Now E.A. was cooling her heels in the vestibule before it was time to go into the reception. Looking down at her pale pink bridesmaid dress, she couldn't help but frown again. Though it was a pretty dress, and rather modest, she never would have picked it. No freckle-faced redhead would ever willingly choose to wear pink.

"What's got you looking so irritated, E.A.?" Katie asked as she walked toward her with her husband, Harley. Harley was wearing a black coat and black trousers, looking like a slightly spiffier version of his usual self. Katie was wearing a dark blue dress that she'd sewn herself. Harley and Katie were both Amish, and while they were also in the bridal party, Marie had been respectful of their preferences for conservative dress.

Though it was vain and selfish, E.A. couldn't help but look at Katie's gown with longing. The blue dress matched Katie's eyes. It would have matched her eyes, too.

"Oh, *nee*. Was I truly looking that irritated?" She really hoped Marie's mother hadn't seen her looking like that. Mrs. Hartman had a lot of expectations about this day, and that included how her daughter's bridesmaids acted.

"A little bit," Harley murmured. His lips twitched—it was obvious he was fighting off a smile.

"Sorry. It wasn't about anything important. I was just thinking about how much I hate to wear pink."

Katie gave her a sympathetic look. "You look nice in that color." When E.A. raised her eyebrows, Katie blushed. "I mean, it ain't *that* bad."

"Come on. This color is somehow managing to make me look both washed-out and sunburned at the same time."

"It could've been worse. It could've been orange."

And just like that, all of E.A.'s sudden worries about being on Mrs. Hartman's radar vanished. She burst out laughing. "You've got me there. An orange dress would have looked worse." Folding her arms over her chest, she asked, "So, what's going on? Does Mrs. Hartman need us to do something?" Marie's mother hadn't been shy about telling the bridal party what to do.

"Oh, *nee*. Nothing like that." After sharing a small smile with her husband, Katie said, "Harley and I came over here to ask you something."

"What is it?"

Harley answered, "Elizabeth Anne, me and the guys were just talking about who was going to give a proper wedding toast for John and Marie." He paused.

When he didn't say anything more, E.A. looked at Harley curiously. "All right . . . that makes sense. So, who is going to speak?"

"Well, now . . . " He cleared his throat. "You see, we started talking. After a bit, we came to a decision."

"Yes?"

He folded his hands behind his back. "We think you should do the honors."

Her? No way. She was good at organizing things. But standing up in front of everyone and giving a speech? It honestly made her feel a little ill. Hoping to keep her expression neutral, E.A. said, "Katie, you are Marie's matron of honor. Plus, everyone knows how good you are at telling stories. Shouldn't you do it?"

Katie looked sympathetic but stayed unwavering. "I would, but everyone is thinking of a specific tale to tell, you see."

"A specific story? Wow. So, um, which one are you all thinking of?" she asked, though it was all an act. There was only one really good story she could tell about Marie and John.

Harley grinned. "You know which one I'm referring to. The night Marie got her crown."

She'd been afraid of that. That episode didn't exactly put her in the best light. Sometimes she didn't think it put any of them in the best light. However, it really was a perfect tale to highlight Marie's and John's longtime affection for each other.

"Do you really think it's the best story to share on their wedding day?"

"Yep."

Even though she was dallying, E.A. added, "Even in front of their parents?"

Make that "in front of all the Eights' parents." Oh, her mom was going to be so mad.

"Come on. You know we're right." Katie, all five foot two inches of her, looked up at E.A. "Please?"

What could she do?

"All right."

Katie started to smile. "Really?"

"Really." Thinking about standing in front of two hundred people, telling an embarrassing story while also wearing an unflattering pink dress, didn't exactly make her feel good, but this day wasn't about her, anyway. It was about Marie and John. And the Eights' long-standing friendship. "I can't promise that I'll do a great job, but I'll try my best."

"You'll do fine, E.A.," Harley said.

Katie grabbed her hand. "Come on. Let's go tell the others."

E.A. let herself be tugged. But even though her feet were moving, the rest of her wanted to hedge a bit. "Do we really need to go right this minute?"

"Oh, for sure." Harley nodded. "Sorry, E.A. The reception is about to start."

Elizabeth Anne let herself be dragged down the narrow hallway to the large fellowship hall where the reception was being held. Catching sight of Logan and Will, she gave them a little thumbs-up.

Logan grinned and put both of his thumbs in the air. Throwing one arm around Logan's shoulders, Will smiled broadly at her.

Suddenly, all her doubts and fears drifted away.

It didn't matter what she was wearing, or how good she was at speaking in front of large groups of people.

All that mattered was the memory of one night, almost eight years ago, when she'd gotten a frantic phone call from Marie. And how she, in turn, had done something that turned one quiet night into an adventure none of them would ever forget.

Now she simply had to hope that she wouldn't leave a single part of it out. If she was going to tell this story, one thing was certain: she had to do it right.

ONE

"Hi, everyone. My name is Elizabeth Anne Schmidt, but most everybody calls me E.A. I thought I'd share a favorite story with you about Marie and John B.

"I think the first thing you ought to know is that our Marie here was named homecoming queen her junior year of high school. You should also probably know that until that evening, John B. had no idea that such things even happened."

JULY

*T*here were more fireflies dotting the fields around her house than Elizabeth Anne could count. But still she tried. She'd once read that people believed wishing on them, like on the stars, might make dreams come true. She'd always thought such a notion was foolish.

But lately?

Well, lately, Elizabeth Anne was beginning to think she'd

been going through life a little too *resolutely*. Perhaps she would be happier if she took more time to daydream and wish on fireflies.

She was a twenty-four-year-old Mennonite, had a job at the fabric store that was rather boring, and was anticipating a proposal from a man who had never made her pulse race or her heart sing.

Though having both employment and a beau should have given her a feeling of fulfillment, she felt empty. Like a firefly that had no light.

But maybe, just maybe, she wasn't the kind of woman destined for fierce longings or challenging jobs. Were some women simply more romantic and apt to blush and fuss more than others? Perhaps the problem was that she'd never felt such things. Perhaps she wasn't capable of such.

She sighed. The action rocked the swing a bit, jarring the man sitting next to her.

"Elizabeth Anne, you've sure been quiet for a while," David blurted from her side. Looking her over like a doctor might look at a sprained ankle, he continued, "Is everything all right? Are you ill?"

"Am I ill? Oh, *nee*." She was simply bored.

Folding his hands over his chest, David sighed. "Well, then . . . what have you been thinking about?" Impatience was in his voice now. "You know it's only proper for us to sit together on the porch swing for thirty minutes. We should make the most of our time."

Elizabeth Anne almost rolled her eyes. Because *that*, she feared, was the problem. Here they were, a courting couple sitting alone on a porch swing on an early summer evening. The air was warm and comfortable, fireflies were twinkling in the distance, and the faint scent of honeysuckle floated in the breeze.

No one else was around, and even if someone were, no one in her family would so much as blink if David had his arm around her shoulders. Not even if they were kissing. They'd been court-ing a long time now.

But they weren't doing any of that. Nothing even close to it. And they never had.

"I'm sorry." Looking at handsome, wholesome David, with his brown hair, brown eyes, full cheeks, and rather thin lips, E.A. wished yet again that there was some kind of spark between them. "I was just looking at the fireflies."

"What about them?" He turned his head to stare out at the soybean field that seemed to go for miles on either side of them. As if they were pleased to have his attention, the hundreds of fireflies danced and sparked. The sight was mesmerizing.

"I read once that people used to make wishes on them," she said softly, hoping to instill a bit of whimsy in their conversation.

He looked back at her and wrinkled his nose. "Wishes?"

"*Jah.* You know, like on stars." When he still gaped at her, she cleared her throat. "Do you think that's true?"

Turning to the field again, he shrugged. "I have no idea. Hon-estly, Elizabeth Anne, I've given up trying to understand why other people do the things they do."

Elizabeth Anne. David always called her by her full name. Never E.A. like her best friends. Or her parents, or her sister, Annie. Even her teachers had called her E.A. on occasion.

She didn't think calling her any sort of pet name had ever entered David's mind. Ever.

Thinking about that, about how David didn't see anything

in the distance but a bunch of bugs, she pressed her lips together. "Hmm."

His voice sharpened. "Come now. You know I'm right. Why, lots of folks do strange things, things that people like you and me couldn't even begin to contemplate."

"I guess that's true," she replied, though she wasn't sure if his statement actually *was* true. Especially since she was contemplating all sorts of things at the moment.

Staring back at the dancing fireflies, she ventured, "You know what? Maybe we should play a game."

"Out here in the dark?"

"It's not all that dark."

"It's too dark to play any sort of game." He sounded shocked. So shocked she couldn't help but egg him on a bit.

"David, how about the two of us make some wishes right now?"

"Um . . ."

"Come on, it will be fun. I mean, look at all those lights! Why, it looks like Christmas in July. Don't you think it's the perfect night to make a wish or two?"

"*Nee.*"

"No?" That was it?

"Elizabeth Anne, you and I both know that no good ever comes from making wishes that won't come true. It's best to concentrate on what is possible." Before she could comment, he continued, "That's what I've always admired about you. You don't waste your time dreaming about things that could never happen to a girl like you."

"A girl like me?" Why did that sound extremely unflattering?

"*Jah.*" He waved a hand. "You are smart."

She knew she was. She'd been smart enough to graduate at the top of her high school class. Yes, the Lord had truly blessed her with a good mind.

But being smart wasn't only what she was. Did he see that?

He kept talking. "You are also strong. *Jah*, you have fortitude."

She was at sea. "I don't know what you are talking about."

"Sure you do." While she gaped at him, he nodded. "You never contemplate selfish acts."

Everything he was saying sounded awfully old-fashioned. "David, what is on your mind?"

He crossed one leg over another, like a proper old man from the Victorian age. "Come now, you know who I'm thinking of."

His look, even in the dim light, was pointed. She shifted uncomfortably. "I'm sorry, but I don't think I know what you are referring to."

David pushed off the swing and stood in front of her. "Not what. Who."

"Hmm?"

"Of course, I'm talking about that man."

"What man?" She was becoming exasperated.

"That man you used to know," he said impatiently.

She decided to match his tone. "Stop speaking in riddles."

"Fine. I'm talking about Andy Warner."

He was speaking of Andy? A chill entered her body and settled in. Wrapping her arms around her middle, E.A. took a deep, fortifying breath. Anything to stop the sudden rush of tears that had just filled her eyes.

"David, Andy was my *friend*, not just some man I used to know." Actually, he'd been so much more than that. He'd been the Eights' leader, and their instigator. More than once he'd been her protector.

He'd been that way with everyone.

Sadness filled her as she thought of the boy he'd been. Oh, he'd been so many things. Loud and handsome and caustic. Yet, so very kind, too. He'd been a jumble of emotions and personality traits. He'd been complicated.

Just like she was.

Propping his hands on his hips, David looked at her directly. "Well, Andy Warner might have been your friend—"

"No, he *was* my friend," she said firmly. "Andy was one of my best friends."

He grunted. "All I'm trying to say is that he must not have felt the same way about you."

Elizabeth Anne gaped at him, shocked. "Of course he did. Why would you say that?" What she meant to say was *How could you say such a thing to me?*

"Come now. He killed himself. That's the most selfish, weak act a person can do."

"Don't say that." One, two tears slid down her cheeks. "You don't know."

"All I'm saying is that no man who cares about his friends, who *really* cares about his friends, would take his own life."

Her temper flared. "You need to stop," she ordered, her voice thick with emotion. "You didn't know Andy at all. You have no idea what you're talking about."

He stood up straighter, almost as if he were a parent delivering a lecture to a recalcitrant child. "I'm sorry if my words made you upset, but you know I'm right, Elizabeth Anne. All I'm doing is pointing out the truth."

"No, you're spouting off your wrong opinions like you have a right to say them."

"I do. I have every right."

Not about Andy. Looking at him directly, E.A. wondered why she'd ever thought David could be the man for her. Getting to her feet, she said, "I think it's time for you to go."

But he didn't budge an inch. "Are you really going to get upset with me about this?"

Yes. Yes, she was. She was finally going to get upset with him about a lot of things. About the way he timed his visits. How he only called her by her full name. And never tried to get to know her other friends. Or held her hand.

But most of all, she was going to make him leave because she was finally admitting to herself that she deserved better. Someone much better.

"Yes, I am," she said finally. "I do believe I'm going to be very upset with you."

He sighed, like he thought she was being overly dramatic and would soon collapse in a fit of vapors or something. "I see. Well, then, I guess I should be going." He stood and walked down the front steps. "I certainly hope you will be in better spirits when I come calling next Saturday night."

A quick vision entered her head—a vision of the two of them sitting on this blasted front porch swing again and again. Never doing anything but talking about the weather and their jobs. Never noticing the fireflies. Never being anything more.

She couldn't do it.

"David, don't come back next Saturday night."

He turned around. "Say again?"

"I said for you not to come calling on me next Saturday."

Feeling relieved that the decision was made, she continued, "In fact, I think it would be best if you didn't come back here again."

His eyebrows rose so high, they hid under the brim of his hat. "You're going to stay mad at me for that long?"

"No. I'm going to finally move on. We're done."

He looked incredulous. Went so far as to reach out a hand to almost touch her. "We can't be done, Elizabeth Anne. What about all the time we've put into this?"

"This isn't about time spent courting, David. This is about the fact that we are too different. I mean, you don't even understand how much Andy meant to me." And how hard it had been to lose him.

His expression hardened. "What will our parents say? They're counting on this match."

But she didn't want to be in a "match." She wanted to be in love. Realizing that David would never understand that, she muttered, "They will have to be disappointed then." Just as she was.

"But—"

"Good night and goodbye," she said over her shoulder.

Even though he was still staring at her in shock, practically frozen, she strode inside.

She was fuming. She was so mad, her skin felt clammy and a bead of sweat was running down her brow.

"Has it been thirty minutes already?" Daed asked as Elizabeth closed the door firmly.

She took a deep breath and attempted to answer her sweet father in a calm tone of voice. "*Jah.*"

"Ah. Well, yes. I guess it has, indeed, been David's allotted thirty minutes." Her father, who everyone said looked a bit like Santa Claus, smiled at her.

Reluctantly, she smiled back at him.

After folding the latest issue of the *Budget* on his lap, he looked at her over the rims of his reading glasses. "Well, how was your beau tonight?"

For a moment, E.A. contemplated sharing with her father what had happened. Thought about explaining her feelings and how she knew there had to be someone better suited for her than David.

But if she did that, Daed would call for her mother, Mamm would rush in, and then the three of them would have a "cozy discussion" that would last for at least an hour. There was no way she was up for that.

"He was the same as always," she finally said as she started up the stairs.

"Elizabeth?"

"I'm sorry, Daed, I've got to, um, go to the bathroom." He looked taken aback, but nodded, leaving her alone with her thoughts as she climbed the steep stairs to her attic bedroom.

Yes, David had been the same. Not very romantic, not very perceptive. It wasn't even the first time he'd mentioned how mystified he was about Andy's death and her continued mourning of him.

She was the one who'd become different. Someone who wanted more, someone who felt she deserved more.

Or, maybe, just maybe, she'd at last become her real self. The person she'd meant to be all along.

TWO

"Anyway, from what I understand, Marie was given her crown during the middle of a football game, then she got to wear it when she went to the dance.

"She'd been supposed to go to the dance with our friend Andy, but he'd been pressured to take a daughter of one of his parents' neighbors. So she ended up going with another boy, who basically abandoned her after the dance, which left her without a ride home.

"Well, you can imagine how that must have felt. Marie got on the phone and started calling all of us in order to get a ride.

"I was the only one who picked up."

JULY

"Some days, it's hard to believe we work at the same place, Will," John Byler said as they walked out of the trailer factory.

"It's been two days since we've said much more than good morning to each other."

A number of thoughts flew through Will's head—most of them sounding rather critical even to his own ears. Though they'd been friends for most of their lives, their relationship had shifted, thanks to John's recent marriage and recent promotion.

But it wasn't like he could bring up such a thing, it would only sound selfish. "We've been blessed to have so much work. Ain't so?"

Falling into step next to him, John B. glanced at him in surprise. "Didn't expect to hear that from you."

The comment didn't sit well. "How come? You don't think I'm a hard worker?"

"*Nee* . . . I was thinking more along the lines that it isn't like you to fall back onto trite phrases."

Trite? "It ain't trite if the saying is true. Work is a good thing, for sure and for certain."

John rolled his eyes. "Come on, Will. It's you and me are talking here, not you and the bishop."

"I'm aware of that." He was also aware that John wouldn't likely be talking to the bishop after church ever again. He'd recently married his longtime crush, Marie Hartman. And while Will was glad for both of them—they really were meant for each other—he also couldn't deny that John's becoming English for Marie and their life together had been hard for him.

In some ways, Will had felt like he'd just lost his best friend.

"You're acting like there's something wrong," John said. "What is it? Is this about my new job?"

"Of course not." John was a talented artist and had recently been given a promotion of sorts. Now he worked in the offices near their boss. He also met with clients and at times even traveled for work. It was a far cry from working on the assembly line like Will did.

"Is it Marie?"

"Don't be daft. You know I love Marie." She was as much a part of the Eight as any of them.

"What is it, then?" Frustration laced John's words. "You know you can trust me, Will."

"Of course I can. But there is nothing to talk about."

"Are you sure?"

"Absolutely." And he was telling the truth. Though he was feeling restless and out of sorts, it surely wasn't anything for John to worry about. Hoping to end their awkward discussion, Will pulled out his sunglasses and placed them on his eyes.

"All right . . . but if you want to talk about things, I'm always available."

"*Danke.*"

"Have you heard from anyone lately? Marie saw Katie at the store last week, but that's about it."

"I sat with Logan at church. Tricia, too," he added with a smile.

John grinned. "Who would've ever thought that Andy's little sister would not only end up with Logan but also become Amish?"

"Not I."

"Me, neither. Is she doing any better with her Deutsch?"

"That would be no." Thinking of the many ways Tricia Warner could mangle even the simplest words, Will chuckled. "If we ever doubted Logan's love for her, those doubts would be erased now. He's as patient with her lessons as a mother hen with new chicks."

"I never thought of Logan as being a motherly sort, but I imagine the comparison is apt. So, tell me how Eli's been on the line."

"As cantankerous as ever. And he's still complaining about his wife to whoever will listen."

"What's the latest story? I can't believe I'm saying this, but I kind of miss his complaints."

Glad to have something else to talk about, Will shared Eli's latest gripes, laughing with John at the older man's penchant for finding fault with most anything. Even with his mighty patient wife.

As they walked, the sun on his shoulders and the faint breeze on his skin encouraged his worries to subside. Yes, their relationship might have shifted, but they were still *gut* friends. And the day had been a good one.

Twenty minutes later, they stood at the corner of Third and Maple to part ways. John would head left to his home with Marie, and Will would walk another mile and a half to his family's farm.

"What hours do you work tomorrow?" Will asked.

John's expression turned guarded. "Um, actually, I won't be in for the next two days. I'm going with Mr. Kerrigan to deliver a trailer and to discuss designs for another with a potential client."

"Where to?"

"Indianapolis."

Will whistled low, trying not to feel a pang of jealousy. "That's far."

"Yeah, but not too bad. It will be quicker coming back than driving out."

"Oh. Sure." He smiled tightly. "Well, have a good trip. I'll be seeing you."

John clasped his arm. "Hey, Will?"

"*Jah?*"

"I know things have changed, but I don't want us to drift further apart. Let's try to do this walk at least once a week. It's a good way for us to catch up, ain't so?"

Will wasn't sure if he agreed. A walk wasn't going to bridge the gap that had grown between them. If anything, he reckoned it would emphasize it.

But if it made John happy to pretend that they could get back to how they used to be, Will could pretend to do that, too. "Anytime we're both free, I'm game," he said. Boy, he hoped he didn't sound as lukewarm as he felt.

"*Gut,*" John replied. Looking straight ahead, he stuffed his hands into his pockets, something Will knew he didn't usually do unless he was feeling uneasy or awkward. "You know what? Maybe I'll ask Marie to round up everyone. We could have you guys over for supper or something. That would be great."

John and Marie. Logan and Tricia. Harley and Katie. Finishing off the group would be Elizabeth Anne and Kendra. And him, the lone man. That didn't hold a lot of appeal.

But still, Will nodded. "*Jah,*" he said. "That sounds *gut. Danke.*"

John slowed. "Are you sure? Because you sound kind of off all of a sudden."

"I'm sure. Now, I've got to get going," he said quickly, hoping to fend off any more questions. "I'll be seeing ya." He raised a hand. "Bye."

John raised a hand, too, but it hung kind of limply in the air, looking just as taken aback as his expression. "Bye, Will."

After he turned away, Will at last allowed his strained smile to fall. And because he was alone, he gave in to his burst of doldrums. It wasn't good, but he couldn't seem to help himself.

All around him, everyone was changing, moving forward, making decisions about their future while he, on the other hand, was stuck firmly in place. Worse, he'd been stuck there for quite some time.

He'd always been the caretaker, the good friend, the helpful member of the Eight. He'd looked out for his friends and family and tried to be there for them so they wouldn't be alone. It was all good, and now he was seeing the product of all his efforts. His friends were happy and secure, but he'd spent so much time focusing on them that he'd forgotten about himself. Now he was at loose ends while everyone else was moving forward with their jobs and falling in love. Even his siblings seemed more settled than he was.

He was now afraid that if he didn't do something different, he was going to be left behind, alone and forgotten.

Actually, he feared he already was.

THREE

"I am Mennonite, so I could drive and had access to a car. I didn't have a lot of experience driving it because I had just turned sixteen. Not that it mattered. When Marie called on the verge of tears, I didn't hesitate. In no time at all, I snuck out my window, got in my mother's car that was parked on the street, and was ready to pick up Marie and save the day.

"Well, me and Katie and John and Harley, that is."

THURSDAY

$\mathcal{T}$rying hard not to think about the odds of her being late for work, E.A. took three tentative steps, peeked to her right, and paused. Then, when she found no one about, she eased her bicycle down their driveway, and started peddling as fast as she could past David's house.

This system, which she'd now been following for five days, was her new reality.

It had already gotten old, too.

Last Saturday, when she'd finally had enough of David and told him they were over, she hadn't thought about the consequences of it. Well, not beyond no longer having to suffer through his weekly half-hour courting calls. However, she was learning that breaking up with David affected other people, too.

Her parents were now starting to ask questions about David's absence. She was going to have to tell them the truth, and that wouldn't be good.

Though they'd often teased her about David's rather awkward courting habits, she'd known they'd been pleased about the two of them being a couple.

After all, they'd lived next door and been best friends with the Brennan family for years and years. When E.A. finally got up the nerve to admit that she had broken things off, the news wasn't going to be welcomed.

Especially not by her mother, who E.A. feared was secretly planning their nuptials.

Just thinking about that conversation made her feel guilty. Hating the fact that she was letting her parents' opinions affect her own—especially since she hadn't even told them yet—E.A. pedaled the bike harder up the hill. When her thighs started burning, she wondered why she'd decided to ride her bike to work anyway. She always regretted it.

Usually, she walked. Every now and then, she drove one of their two cars. Because she was Mennonite, most people thought they were *Englischers*.

She wasn't. Though she did have a computer and a cell phone and drove a car, she was still not "plugged in" twenty-four seven. And while she'd gone to high school and had even considered going to college, her high school had been a private one that had catered to Mennonites.

In addition, she had waited to be baptized until she'd been twenty, wore dresses instead of slacks, and also wore a small covering on her head. However, those dresses weren't especially Plain. Instead, they were constructed of printed fabric. In addition, the covering on her head was really only a small piece of lace, nothing like the *kapp* her Amish friends wore.

She straddled two worlds, the English one and the Amish one, fitting into neither completely. Most of her Mennonite girlfriends relished the freedom.

She, on the other hand, felt like she was always in danger of toppling down one side or the other. When was she ever going to become more confident and satisfied with her decisions?

Maybe when she became more confident and satisfied with herself.

Tired of trying to pedal up the hill, she hopped off and walked her bicycle up the incline. Pulling it up the hill wasn't especially difficult, but guiding the bike was certainly harder than simply walking—especially on a warm summer morning. Glaring at the bike, she contemplated leaving it on someone's driveway until she got off work.

"E.A., what did that bicycle ever do to you?"

Startled, she turned to see Will Kurtz loping toward her, an amused expression on his face.

Boy, she was pleased to see him. Will could always make any day better. "What are you talking about?"

His long legs reached her easily. "Even from fifty yards away, I noticed you glaring at that bicycle like it had done something terrible to ya."

Smiling up at him, she said, "I guess I *was* glaring at it. I hate riding up this hill."

"It is a pretty steep hill. That is for sure."

Actually, it wasn't all that steep, but she knew Will would never say that. He always tried to make people feel better, not worse. "I was more upset with myself than anything," she said. "It's hot out. I should have known better than to ride it to Sew and Tell."

He held out a hand. "You want me to guide it up the hill for ya?"

That was the thing. He absolutely would do that for her. That was his way. "*Danke*, but I'm okay. We could walk together, though, if you wanted."

Will smiled easily. "I want."

And just like that, she felt her body relax. That was Will in a nutshell, she realized. He was just so very nice.

She was blessed to have him in her life.

"Thanks again," she said.

Some of the humor in his eyes faded to concern. "Hey, are you all right?"

"Oh, sure." With anyone else, she would have dropped it there, but he was easy to talk to. And, maybe he would offer her some advice, too. "I mean, I *think* I am."

"What does that mean?"

"It means I broke up with David."

"Ah." It was almost comical, the way Will was struggling to keep a straight face. "What happened? I mean, would you like to talk about it?"

She needed to. "It all started when we were sitting on my front porch on Saturday night."

His lips twitched. "For his allotted thirty minutes?"

Ugh. Had everyone been snickering about it all this time? "*Jah*. And no, I have no idea why he decided on half-hour visits in the first place."

His eyes sparkled. "Hmm."

"You aren't helping, Will."

"I'm sorry. Forgive me. Continue," he said, waving a hand in the air.

Since his other hand was still guiding her bike up the hill, she didn't chastise him. "Anyway, there we were, sitting on my porch swing like always, when I pointed out how pretty the fireflies were."

"Okay . . ."

"Then I mentioned something about making wishes, but he didn't get what I was talking about at all." She exhaled. "Somehow, all that turned into some weird conversation about people being selfish."

Will's dark eyebrows rose. "That must have been quite a conversation."

Oh, yes, it was. Remembering just how hurt she'd felt, she exclaimed, "Will, that wasn't even the worst part!"

"No?"

"Somehow we started talking about Andy. He told me that Andy's death was a selfish act. That he must not have cared about me. About any of us."

Will slowed to a stop, putting out his other hand to steady the bicycle. "He started talking badly about Andy?" When she nodded, his eyebrows pulled together. "E.A., how did you respond?"

"How do you think? I told David that Andy wasn't selfish at all. That he was a good friend." Remembering David's smug expression and how impassioned she'd been, her voice thickened with emotion. "Actually, I told him that Andy had been a *great* friend, and that he shouldn't be saying a critical word."

"*Gut.* Good for you."

He looked so impressed, she admitted, "I might not have been that eloquent, but it was along those lines."

"Ah."

"Will, you feel the same way about Andy, too, don't you?"

"Of course I do. All of us feel that way, E.A." His voice softened. "I think you said all the right things."

"*Danke.*" Taking a deep breath, she added, "I ended up breaking up with him right then and there."

"Really?"

"Oh, *jah.* There was no way I could ever marry someone who didn't feel at least a little more compassionate about Andy." Or, at the very least, more empathetic about her feelings.

"I'm proud of you, Elizabeth Anne," he murmured. "That couldn't have been easy."

It hadn't been.

But now, after speaking with him? She suddenly felt better. It was like she'd needed Will's reassurance but hadn't even realized it. "You know what? I'm really glad we ran into each other. I've been keeping that whole episode to myself, and it's been eating my insides like a bad meal. You've helped a lot."

He looked pleased. "Believe it or not, I think I needed this conversation almost as much as you did."

"Why?"

After a brief hesitation, he said, "I don't know what's going on with me, but lately I've been feeling a little unsettled." Looking straight ahead, he continued, "I don't know if it's all our friends getting married or the fact that I'm in my mid-twenties and I don't feel like I thought I would."

"Let me guess—you thought you'd have everything figured out by now?"

"Exactly."

"I feel the same way, Will. And you know me—I like to have everything figured out."

"At least you've taken care of the David issue."

She chuckled.

"Sorry, but I never liked him. He was always far too full of himself."

"You're right. He was." Sobering, she added, "I think I stayed with him for so long to make my parents proud. And that's part of the problem! Why do I still feel the need to make them proud at twenty-four years of age?"

"Because you love them. I do the same."

"You do that, too? Really?"

He nodded. "I've been feeling stuck in a rut more and more lately, like maybe I should be doing more with my life." He opened his mouth, looking prepared to say something else, then shook his head. "Sorry. I hate sounding like I have anything to complain about. I'm blessed."

Elizabeth Anne had heard so many people say that phrase, it felt rather trite. But it didn't sound that way coming from him because she knew he truly meant it.

That's the kind of man he is, she mused to herself as they reached the top of the hill. As always, so considerate. Because that was who he was. Even when he was just a boy, he'd been that way. So caring. Why, in all the years she'd known him, she'd rarely heard him complain.

She weighed her words carefully. "Will, even when we're blessed, I don't think the Lord minds when we decide to analyze our actions. Perhaps He'd say that taking stock was part of growing up."

He grinned. "Is that what I've been doing? I don't know."

Maybe it was the vulnerability she spied in his eyes. Maybe it was the fact that she was feeling confused and a little alone, and needed a friend she could count on. Whatever the reason, she made a sudden decision. "I hope we spend more time together."

"You do?" He looked a little taken aback as they came to a stop in front of Sew and Tell. Almost like he was trying to come to terms with her suddenly making a play for him. He knelt and put the bike stand down. "I mean, sure. We can do that."

She was now officially embarrassed. "I promise. I'm not making a pass at you. I just mean that it would be nice to see you more often," she said quickly as he got to his feet again and faced her. "Especially since everyone else . . ."

"Since everyone else has become a couple." He finished, reading her mind once again.

"Yes."

In typical Will fashion, he mulled it over for a few seconds then nodded. "*Jah.* I think that would be a good thing. I'll stop by your *haus* soon."

Her spirits lifted. "You will? Oh, great!" When his eyes widened again, she tried to stop sounding so much like an awkward thirteen-year-old. "I mean—"

"E.A., I've got to get to work, and your boss looks like she's ready for you to come inside. Ain't so?"

Surprised, she turned around and saw that he was exactly right. Lark was standing at the large picture window at the front of the shop and staring at her. At them. When their eyes met, Lark pointedly looked at her watch.

Ack! She was late.

"I've gotta go. Bye, Will."

Grinning, he held up a hand. "*Jah*, see ya. Have a good day, E.A. And try not to worry about that David. You're better off without him."

Smiling at him before she turned around, she realized that he was right—she did feel better off now.

But it was funny, she wasn't just thinking about David anymore. No, she was thinking about someone else. Someone with dark brown hair, matching eyes, and chiseled cheekbones who she'd known all her life.

Someone who could still surprise her from time to time.

FOUR

"I'd intended for us to pick up Marie at school, run everyone home, and then crawl back in my window so my parents would be none the wiser.

"But, like a lot of things, I suppose . . . nothing went according to plan."

"*Yes*, that's how you do it," E.A. coaxed as she helped her student guide the fabric under the sewing machine's needle. "Slow and steady wins the race, *jah*?"

"I'm doing it! Finally!" Marta Miner smiled up at her.

"You are, indeed. *Gut* job!" Elizabeth Anne stepped back to watch Marta carefully press on the Singer's pedal a little harder. With a satisfied whirl, the machine continued, making uniform stitches in an *almost* straight line. "Watch it, now. The fabric is beginning to slant . . ."

"Oh!" Marta moved the material. "There we go."

Watching her student look almost giddy with triumph, E.A.

grinned. Marta was a thirty-year-old married woman, but her expression was as gleeful as a nine-year-old's. It was so cute.

When Marta at last let her foot off the pedal, she leaned back with a sigh. "I can't believe how nerve-wracking making a straight seam is, E.A. I think I almost broke out into a sweat."

E.A. laughed as she sat down in the folding metal chair next to her favorite sewing student. "As much as I would like to agree that sewing straight seams can be difficult, this Singer makes it fairly simple. You'll get the hang of it in no time."

"The machine is amazing, that's true. But every time you take your eyes off me, my seam drifts to the right."

"We haven't been doing lessons very long, Marta. Chin up, yes?"

"I just want to do better."

"I know." Marta had come in the shop for months before finally asking about private lessons. Then she dwelled on that idea for another month or two. Now they had ten or twelve lessons under their belts, and her skills were coming along nicely. However, Marta still worried about making mistakes.

Carefully pressing her hand over Marta's, E.A. smoothed the fabric under her hand. "I fear you might be making it harder than it has to be," she said slowly. "Remember, all sewing mistakes can be fixed. That's what a seam ripper is for."

"You're right. I need to relax." Her voice lowered, almost as if she were talking to herself. "I overthink things, I'm afraid."

E.A.'s heart went out to her student. At first glance, she looked like she didn't have any worries in the world. But she now knew Marta well enough to realize that she was filled with insecurities. The woman was always doubting herself or quietly putting herself down.

Worse, it seemed Marta's husband didn't allow her to do much. He wouldn't allow her to drive and didn't like her to do many things on her own. E.A. thought it was something of a miracle that Marta had even been able to sign up for a class at Sew and Tell in the first place.

But last week, Marta had confided that her husband didn't consider his wife's once-a-week sewing lessons to be a threat. Also, since the shop was within walking distance of her house, Marta could go back and forth without a car. That was why she'd signed up to take sewing classes from E.A.

Returning to the conversation at hand, E.A. said, "Don't be so hard on yourself, Marta. Thinking through things isn't a bad thing."

Marta smiled, but the happiness didn't reach the shadows in her eyes. "You're right. It came in handy in my former life."

"What was that?"

"I was a research assistant for an author of historical novels."

Elizabeth Anne was surprised. Marta was so withdrawn she hadn't thought she did anything outside the home. "That sounds exciting. Did you enjoy it?"

"Oh, yes. I used to spend hours combing through reference books and taking notes. I did research on all sorts of subjects." Her voice warmed. "He was a great author but not great at reading for details. He was a fan of bullet points."

"I bet he really appreciated your help."

She chuckled. "He appreciated it when people gave him compliments about his thorough research. Seriously, I didn't mind, though. Like I said, I enjoyed it."

This was the most E.A. had heard Marta talk about anything. "What are some things you used to research?"

"Oh, boy. All sorts of things," she mused. Looking amused again, she said, "Once, my author's main character worked on restoring paintings. Next thing I knew, I was researching all the Dutch masters and passing on notes about Rembrandt, Hals, and Vermeer."

E.A. loved how Marta's expression had perked up. "My goodness. It sounds mighty interesting. You know what? I never thought about how an author gets all the information for all of his books."

Marta shrugged. "I promise, I didn't do all the work, just helped make things easier. It was a good job."

"To be sure."

Her voice lowered. "Sometimes I wish I hadn't quit."

"Why did you?" she asked before she could stop herself.

"My husband didn't like me working so much." Her voice quivered a bit. "It is probably good I stopped, anyway. It took a lot of time away from the house and everything I need to do for Alan."

"Ah." Realizing that Marta was looking embarrassed, E.A. smiled at her warmly. "Thank you for telling me about your job. I liked learning about it."

"It was fun to talk about, if you want to know the truth." She winced. "Sometimes I forget that I used to be so different."

That statement sounded very telling. "My mother likes to say that *Got* helps us be the person we need to be at the right time," E.A. murmured.

"Do you think that's right?"

"I think I want it to be." Thinking about David and Will and how different their group of Eight was, now that Andy had gone to Heaven, E.A. said, "To be honest, I've been thinking about my life, too."

Marta turned to face her. "Oh?"

"Yes. I've recently made some changes. I've been thinking that maybe I need to make a couple more."

"Change is hard."

"Big changes are. But maybe everything doesn't need to be a major change. There can be little ones."

"I like that way of thinking about it." Looking like she was divulging a big secret, Marta lowered her voice. "As a matter of fact, I . . . well, I've been thinking of making some big and small changes in my life, too."

"I guess it's good we found each other, then. We can cheer each other on."

"I hope so." Holding up her lopsided seam, Marta frowned. "Maybe one day I'll even be able to make a pillowcase that is usable."

"One step at a time, *jah?*" E.A. said gently. "And for the record, this one almost is."

Marta grinned. "You're right. If I happened to have a pillow that was bigger on one side than the other, this case might work perfectly." She stood up and started putting all her supplies in her little sewing kit. "You are the best teacher, E.A. Thank you for today."

"You're welcome. I enjoy our classes."

"Me, too." Looking warily at the glass door, Marta sighed. "Now, I had best be on my way. I was going to stop at the pharmacy on my way home. If I don't hurry, I'll be late."

"I'm sure you'll get home in no time," E.A. soothed. Because, really, what else could she say? But inside, she was more than a little concerned. Marta was a mess of contradictions. She was a married *Englischer* but needed as much reassurance as the most sheltered Amish teen. She was obviously smart enough to research all sorts of things, but she fretted about a trip to the pharmacy.

Picking up the small amount of fabric and the spool of thread she'd picked out, E.A. walked to the counter. "I'll get you checked out in a jiffy so you can get on your way."

"Thanks, E.A. Wish me luck."

After running Marta's credit card for her purchases and the payment for the class, she waved her out the door.

She was still gazing out the window at her student's retreating form when Lark popped her head out of her office. "Whew. Is she gone yet?"

She looked up at her boss, who was so close to E.A.'s age yet so different in looks and temperament. Today Lark was wearing a light blue dress that fit her perfectly. It was one of many that she'd made recently. "Who?"

"You know who. Your crazy student!"

"Marta isn't crazy."

"She's a constant nervous wreck. Last week, I thought she was going to burst into tears when she dropped a bolt of fabric on the floor. You'd think that she'd be a lot more relaxed. I mean, all you are teaching her to do is sew seams on the Singer. She's supposed to be taking this class for fun, right?"

"She does enjoy it. She just, well, she just worries, that's all."

"She worries a lot. Too much."

Lark spoke harshly, but she wasn't exactly wrong. Marta was a nervous, frightened sparrow at times. Elizabeth Anne wasn't exactly sure why she was so intent on championing her student, but she was.

"I'm thankful to have a student, though. Our private students help the business, *jah?*"

"That's true." Lark chuckled. "I'll give you this—you're nothing if not steady."

That didn't sound like a compliment. "Thank you, I guess."

"You know I meant that in the best of ways. Being predictable is a good thing. I kind of like that you never change."

"I have made some changes lately." After all, hadn't she just broken up with David?

"I guess you have. I mean, I was pretty shocked to see you walking with that handsome Amish guy today."

"Hmm?"

"You know. He was walking your blue bicycle and was walking with you!"

That's because he was being kind, E.A. realized.

"I'm not surprised. You two looked like you only had eyes for each other."

"Will is just one of the Eight. We're *gut* friends."

"He isn't your boyfriend?"

"No." Not that she had a boyfriend any longer.

"I haven't seen him around town. What's his name again?"

"His name is Will. Will Kurtz."

"What does he do?"

She was starting to feel uneasy about the questions. "He works at the trailer factory. Why?"

"Oh, no reason. It's just like I said . . . he's really cute. Hey, is he available?"

Lark wasn't much older than she was. She was also Mennonite like herself. E.A. had also thought Lark was dating someone pretty seriously, too. But maybe she was simply overreacting? After all, Lark actually was right. Will Kurtz was very cute.

But she didn't like the thought of Lark setting her sights on him.

Maybe that was why she said what she did. "*Nee*. Will isn't available at all. He's taken."

She knew she should feel a little bit bad for telling that fib, but she didn't. Not one bit.

FIVE

> "First of all, we couldn't see Marie anywhere. After waiting five minutes, John B. decided to go inside and find her. Well, none of us wanted to make John go in the gym all alone, so I parked the car, and all of us decided to go inside.
>
> "That was maybe our worst mistake."

FRIDAY AFTERNOON

*M*arta Miner made it home from her sewing class in less than an hour. That had to be a record. On some days, it took her almost double that amount, especially if she had to stop by the grocery store and then carry everything home.

When she and Alan had first gotten married, she'd driven all the time. Then, slowly, Alan gave her more limits. First, she could only drive to places he thought were necessary. Then, he restricted the distance from the house. Finally, he forbade her from using the car at all, and took her keys away.

She wouldn't be surprised if he'd put a tracking device or something on it so he would know if she took it out without his permission.

Not that she would ever do anything like that.

Well, not anymore. She'd learned her lesson soon after they married. Remembering how badly he'd beaten her, she hadn't been able to leave the house for almost a week, her face had looked so bad. Her mother hadn't understood why she'd canceled their planned shopping trip to the mall and had wanted to come over to check in.

Boy, it had taken a lot of lies to stop her from doing that.

Her mother, being no fool, had known something was up. She'd even put Dad on the phone, and he'd asked all sorts of questions.

When Alan discovered that they'd both talked to her, he'd reached out and suggested they give her some space. In his best cajoling tone, he reminded them that they were newlyweds and that there was nothing wrong with Marta wanting to be at home with her husband.

At least, that's what her mother had told her several weeks later. Mom hadn't sounded like she'd entirely believed Alan, but she had also stopped asking Marta out to lunch once a week, too.

Marta hadn't been able to admit that she missed those outings, either. Not without sharing the whole truth about her husband. But how could she ever tell her mother that she'd become afraid of him? It was too hard to admit.

Now that she'd survived ten years of marriage to Alan, telling lies to the rest of the world almost came easily. All she really cared about anymore was getting through each day.

Standing in the front entryway of the house, Marta forced herself to remember how things used to be.

Back when she and Alan had first married, she'd been so grateful to be out of her parents' house that it hadn't occurred to her to question any of her husband's rules. She'd just wanted to make him happy.

Then, over time—when she'd realized just how bad things could be if she made him unhappy—Marta had been merely trying to survive.

Six months ago, Alan got a promotion at work. Now he was one of the managers at the plant. Two months ago, when they'd gone out to dinner with some of the other managers and their wives, she'd had to refuse an invitation for lunch because she didn't have a way to meet the other women at the restaurant.

Alan had gotten so embarrassed that he'd yelled at her when they'd gotten home. He'd handed her keys the next day and told her to call back the woman and say that she'd changed her mind.

Yes, life with Alan had become a minefield, with her constantly worrying about making one misstep and paying the price for it.

But things were changing. After all, she'd been brave enough to take sewing classes now. And, of course, she'd begun putting aside grocery money for the last year. And skimming some of the change from Alan's pockets. She now had several hundred dollars carefully hidden so she could escape one day.

Walking into the kitchen, Marta breathed a sigh of relief. She had worked hard all morning. The moment Alan left for work, she'd put a roast in the slow cooker and had cleaned the house from top to bottom.

After her sewing class, she'd run to the pharmacy, picked up the items Alan had wanted, and neatly put them away. It had been a good day. She would have a lot of good things to tell her husband, because he would ask. He always asked what she did and how she did them. When she didn't have news to report, he would get upset or ask questions. Lots and lots of questions.

But at least he wasn't home yet.

After taking note that everything was still neat and clean in the kitchen, she took the *People* magazine she'd bought and decided to read it for a few minutes in the cozy chair in their bedroom.

Looking at the clock, she got out her egg timer and set it for fifteen minutes. Yes. She'd have fifteen minutes to read before hiding it from Alan. He hated it when she read those magazines.

After making sure she set the timer exactly right, she made a cup of hot tea, sat in her favorite chair, and happily dove into her newest purchase.

After the timer went off, she promised herself to only read one more article. And then the time got away from her.

"Marta?" his voice called out from the entryway.

Panic engulfed her as she jumped to her feet, the magazine in her hand. She froze, wondering what to do, then hastily opened a drawer and stuffed it inside.

"Marta? Where are you?"

She cleared her throat. "Here! Sorry, I'm on my way downstairs."

She forced what she hoped was a lighthearted smile on her face and walked downstairs. "How are you, Alan?"

He was standing in the middle of the kitchen, looking around like he was searching for something. He looked up when she entered and slowly smiled. "Better now. How's my girl?"

Relief infused her. He was in a good mood. Her nights were so much better when that was the case. "I'm fine. I made a roast for dinner. Would you like to eat at six like usual?"

He pressed a kiss to her cheek. "Of course." He pointedly looked around the dark kitchen. "I hope that will give you enough time to finish getting dinner ready."

"Hmm?" She looked at the Crock-Pot. Noticed that it was still set on low and that it looked to be cooking nicely.

"The potatoes, Marta?" he asked, a hint of sarcasm in his voice. "You know I like mashed potatoes with roast." With a new edge in his voice, he looked her over carefully. "Will you have time to get them done?"

"I think so."

"What?"

"Sorry. I mean, yes. Yes, of course." She kept her expression neutral but her mind was spinning. Did they even have any potatoes in the pantry? What was she going to do if they didn't?

His gaze hardened for a moment before he smiled again. "I'll leave you to it, then. I'm going to go change and answer a few emails."

"All right, Alan."

Just before he exited the kitchen, he turned back to her. "What were you doing upstairs?"

"Oh, nothing."

"Are you sure? Because it doesn't look like you were cleaning yourself up. Your hair is a mess."

As she knew he'd intended, she awkwardly ran a hand over her neat bob. "I'm sorry, Alan. I'll fix my hair after I get dinner finished."

Luckily, his phone rang. He strode out of the kitchen.

The moment he was out of sight, she rushed into the pantry. An icy trickle of sweat ran down her spine as she hunted for potatoes.

Three! They had three! Quickly, she got out the potato peeler and set to work. She had thirty minutes to peel, boil, and mash them. If she worked really hard, she'd get them done on time.

And if she didn't?

Well, Alan wouldn't be pleased with her at all. Almost as displeased as he would be if he discovered she'd spent the last hour reading a magazine instead of fixing herself up better for him.

She began to work the peeler faster as she remembered that she'd left her cup of tea on the table next to the chair in their bedroom.

Please, God, don't let him look in that drawer, she prayed as she picked up another potato.

If he discovered that and she didn't get these potatoes done, it was going to be a bad night.

A very bad one.

SIX

"When we got to the dance, the first person we noticed was Andy Warner, who was slow dancing with some brunette. The minute he saw us, he left her side, which made his date kind of angry. She didn't get any happier when he said he had to leave the dance for a while so he could help us find Marie."

SATURDAY NIGHT

"Will Kurtz is here," E.A.'s mother announced just outside her bedroom door.

Looking up from the letter she'd been writing at her desk, E.A. smiled. Will had taken her up on her invitation. "Thanks, Mamm. Tell him I'll be right down, would you?"

"Sure." She stepped back, then poked her head back in. "Not to pry, but is there a specific reason he's here?"

Frowning at her hair in the mirror, E.A. removed the small lace covering and then started pulling out pins. "Not really," she said as she ran a brush through her almost waist-length hair. "I guess he felt like stopping by. It's no big deal." Just like it was no big deal that she suddenly felt the need to fix her hair before she saw Will.

Her mother's expression cleared. "Oh. Of course." She stepped away before poking her head in E.A.'s room yet again. "Do you think he's going to be the first of the Eight to stop by? If you're expecting a crowd, I can make some popcorn."

Her mother's question didn't come from out of the blue. Ever since they'd gotten old enough, they'd all descend on one person's house or another without a moment's notice. E.A. used to ride bikes with Katie over to John B.'s and Andy's houses all the time. Their houses were the most centrally located of the group.

Even now, E.A. found herself looking at her friends' driveways whenever she was going by their houses, just to see if any of the Eight were visiting. It seemed that old habits died hard.

But this visit from Will wasn't like that. He'd come over to spend time with her, not a member of the Eight.

"Thank you, Mamm. That's sweet of you. But I don't think anyone else is coming over. It's just the two of us. We'll go sit on the front porch. So no popcorn is needed." After twisting her hair into a low knot on the nape of her head, she picked up a couple of bobby pins. "I bet Will won't stay longer than an hour or so."

Her mother smiled again but it looked strained. There was a new edge of worry in her eyes, too. "E.A., if you two are sitting on the front porch together, David might get confused."

"Confused?"

"Well, yes. It is Saturday night."

As in, it was David's chosen evening to give her thirty minutes. "David won't be coming over tonight."

"Are you sure?"

"Positive." Looking in the mirror again, she wished she'd put on her green dress, but it was too late now. "Mamm, don't worry so much."

But still, her mother lingered. "All I'm trying to say is that if Will is sitting on the porch with you, it might look like he's here courting. David could get his feelings hurt. We wouldn't want that."

Why hadn't she simply told her parents that they'd broken up? Sure, they would have had a thousand questions, but at least she wouldn't be having this conversation! "Mother, I don't know what else to tell you. I've known Will for most of my life. He's one of the Eight. You know that," she said as she placed the white covering back on her head.

"Understood. But sometimes—"

"Mamm, he's waiting, right?" After briefly putting on her favorite black flats, which looked like ballet slippers, she slipped on her rubber flip-flops instead. It was warm outside, and Will wouldn't care.

Finally satisfied with her appearance, she slipped by her mother into the hall. "I can't talk now."

Something edged into her mother's expression, telling E.A. that she wasn't fooled for a minute.

But, because she was her mother, Mamm didn't say another word and just followed E.A. down the hall.

Will was talking to her father when they got downstairs. The moment he saw her, he got to his feet.

"Hey, you," he said, his deep voice sounding a little more gravelly than usual.

"'Hey, you' back," she teased. "I'm sorry it took me a long minute."

"It was no trouble. Your father and I were talking about the county fair. It's in a couple of weeks, you know."

"Is it?" Turning to her *daed*, she said, "I didn't know you had already started making plans."

"Can't help but get ready for it," he said. "I'm anxious to see some of the livestock. I heard the Jennings family down the road are entering their pig." Turning to Will, he grinned. "Have you seen that pig? He's a good un."

"*Nee*, but I'm sure *mei daed* has. He always says Tom Jennings has a way with sows."

E.A. smiled at Will. "It looks like we've got a lot of things to catch up on. Want to come sit outside?"

"Yep. See you later, Mr. Schmidt."

"Enjoy your evening, son," Daed replied as he slipped his readers back on his eyes and picked up the last edition of the *Budget*.

E.A. led Will out to the porch. As soon as she closed the door behind them she chuckled. "Sorry about that. My father is starved for male company."

"No reason to apologize. You know I like your *daed*. I always have. I like how he always takes the time to chat with each of us about something."

"I do, too," she agreed. Her father loved being around the Eight, and over the years he'd grown to know quite a lot about their interests. He could speak to Marie about her banking job as easily as he could speak about county fairs with Will.

After glancing at the porch swing, Will wandered over to the side of the house, where there was a set of two bright red metal chairs. He sat down in one. "I know Marie and Katie enjoyed living on their own before they got married. Do you ever wish you were on your own as well?"

She sat down in the chair next to him. "Not really. I like saving money by living here. And, well, being around my parents isn't a hardship." Even though they'd had their share of teenaged arguments, they'd enjoyed a good relationship by and large. Her parents were simply good people and had a nice way about them. They encouraged E.A. and her sister to do the things the way they'd taught them but rarely forced their opinions if the girls' choices were different.

"I feel the same way about my parents, though at times I wouldn't mind getting a bit of space from Nan and Jake."

She giggled. He was always complaining about his younger siblings even though they were really nice. "So, you're already making plans to visit the fair, huh?"

"I've been thinking about it," he said, propping his bare feet on the railing. "I haven't gone in three or four years. It's time to check it out again, I suppose."

"I've never been." Though her father liked to see the animals from time to time, her parents were more of the sort to spend their free time going to a museum in the city instead of a county fair.

"What? Well, you've got to go now. It's great fun."

"Will, I can't believe you like it so much!"

"You're gonna love it. You can go on the rides, eat too much, and see the animals." Even in the dim light, she could see his brown eyes warm. "They usually have lambs, too. They're adorable."

Liking the idea of being far from her regular routine, E.A. grinned at him. "You make it sound hard to refuse."

"Because it *is* hard to refuse, especially if you've never been. It's time you went. Ain't so?"

"I guess so."

"*Gut*. We'll plan on it. Make it a date."

Make it a date. Feeling her cheeks heat, she murmured, "All right."

Will groaned. "Sorry, I just realized what I said. You know I didn't mean it like that."

"*Nee,* of course not." She knew that, too—which was why the sudden burst of disappointment felt so strange. Hoping to cover up the awkward moment, she said, "You know what? We should ask if everyone wants to go. That would be so much fun."

"*Jah.* For sure." He smiled at her again, but his voice had sounded a little flat, almost like he, too, was just as caught off guard as she was by the new tension that was buzzing between them.

Putting her feet up next to his on the railing, she asked, "Did you walk over here barefoot?"

"Nah. I had some old boots on, but I took them off when I got here. It's too hot for them."

E.A. was wearing dime-store flip-flops, her summer footwear of choice. Looking at how their feet looked together, she couldn't help but think they were a good match. Will's toenails were neatly trimmed and his skin was lightly tanned. Hers were much the same way, except far smaller.

"What are you looking at?"

Though she was tempted to lie and point out the fireflies, she didn't want to do that. Not with him. "Our feet."

He frowned. "E.A., really?" Looking embarrassed, he pulled one of his feet down.

"Will, no! Keep it up."

"I don't want you staring at my toes."

"Stop. I was just thinking about how we've had our share of running around in bare feet over the years," she improvised.

As she hoped, Will relaxed. "That's true. For a while there, my *mamm* made us all stand on the driveway so she could wash our feet before we ventured inside the house. Do you remember that?"

"I do. And I also remember that Katie and you were always the worst culprits about tracking mud inside."

"And Andy, from time to time."

She giggled. "And never, ever Harley."

Will groaned. "Harley. Boy, he used to drive me crazy. I don't know how he managed it, but that guy never got as dirty as the rest of us."

"I used to think he only worried about his parents getting mad, but then I realized that it was just him. He was born with a need to be neat."

"*Jah.*"

"And now he and Katie are married. Did you ever imagine that?"

"To be honest? *Nee.* But now that they are together, I can see that they make a fine pair. His calm temperament is a good counterpart to her constant worrying."

"They do balance each other out," she agreed. Thinking about all of them and the way they'd stuck together through thick and thin, she turned his way. "Hey, Will?"

"Hmm?"

"What do you think it is about our group that made us stay friends for so long? I barely keep in touch with half the kids I used to hang around in school."

"And you even went to that fancy private Mennonite school."

She playfully rolled her eyes. "Stop. It wasn't all that fancy. But you know what I mean, right? We've not only stayed friends, but also half of us have married each other."

"More than half, *jah?*" he joked.

"Whatever. What is it about all of us that's kept us so close?"

"I think it's trust," Will replied after a moment. "We trust each other. And though we did drift apart for a time, we connected again. We've been there for each other in good times and bad. That's not easy to do."

"No, it isn't." Though she hadn't meant to do it, Will's words made her think of Andy. He'd been struggling with his own demons but she hadn't known. She was glad they'd all vowed to keep in better contact with each other after that. It was the right thing to do.

They sat quietly for a few minutes. Will rested his elbows on his knees, looking out at the field of fireflies.

She tucked her feet under herself on the chair and watched them, thinking about Andy and Will, and how she'd never been able to sit quietly like this with David. Not even when she'd been sure they were going to marry one day.

"Let's talk about something else. How's work?"

She shrugged. "I don't know. Sometimes I feel like I can't work at the shop another day. Not even for another minute."

"It's that tedious?"

"No, it's my manager, Lark. She's a good person, I think, but not a great boss." Hating how judgmental that sounded, she added, "But that's only my opinion."

The porch lights illuminated Will's face well enough for her to see the concern in his eyes. "What does she do that's so bad?"

"Here's an example. I have this student named Marta. She's an English woman in her early thirties."

"What are you teaching her?"

"I'm teaching her to sew." Thinking of their lessons, she smiled. "We have these wonderful Singer sewing machines. I tell ya, they practically run themselves. Anyway, I guess Marta is really smart and used to do all kinds of research and stuff for books, but she's also really tentative and shy."

"That doesn't sound so strange."

"I agree, but I worry about her. Sometimes, it feels like she's almost afraid of her shadow. She needs a lot of encouragement and time to make her decisions."

"It sounds like she needs you." His voice matched his words. So sweet and caring.

"Thank you. I'd like to think that I do help her. But Lark has next to no patience with her. She talks bad about Marta behind her back and always acts as if Marta is being difficult when it takes her a long time to check out or choose fabric."

"I'm surprised. Your Marta isn't alone. I've trained all sorts of people at the trailer factory many a time. Some folks just need more time than others to pick things up. But that doesn't mean that there's anything wrong with them or that they won't do a good job."

"Exactly. In Marta's case, I think it's just difficult for her to make up her mind. She wants to do a good job." She sighed. "I know in the grand scheme of things, I shouldn't let Lark's impatience get to me, but today it did."

"Maybe she's better at paperwork."

"She is good at that." Feeling guilty, E.A. said, "If you met her, I'm sure you'd think she was nice." She sighed. "Maybe my problem with working at the sewing shop is that I'm kind of bored there unless I'm teaching classes. And yes, I know I sound ungrateful."

He smiled at her. "Complain all you want, E.A. I won't tell a soul."

E.A. giggled. "Feel free to complain, too. I'll listen to anything you have to say."

"*Danke*, but neither Jake nor Nan has done anything too annoying lately."

"If that changes, let me know."

"It will. They can't stay out of trouble for more than a day or two at a time."

Will was good medicine. Spending time with him was exactly what she needed. Someone who understood that she needed to vent.

"Elizabeth Anne, what is going on?"

Startled, they both turned to the voice.

Will got up to his feet but didn't say a word.

She decided to stay sitting. "Hello, David," she said, letting her opinion about his unannounced visit shine through. "Any special reason you decided to come over tonight?"

"It's Saturday night."

Honestly, that man thrived on his schedule so much he should have been a train conductor. "*Jah*, but we broke up."

"Only temporarily."

Grinning at her, Will sat back down.

Ignoring Will's smirk, she stood up. "Sorry, David, but we both know that isn't right. Our breakup was most definitely not temporary."

Whether it was because of her statement—or that she was

telling him such a thing in front of Will—David flushed. "I *canna* believe you are taking that tone with me."

Will snickered under his breath.

After shooting him a warning glance, she glared at David again. "I think *you* should watch *your* tone. Don't you?"

Putting one hand on his hip, David eyed Will like he'd just crawled out of the swamp. "Is he the reason for your new attitude?"

"Will, would you like to answer that or shall I?"

"Oh, I'll answer him. I'll be happy to." With a grunt of irritation, he got to his feet.

When Will crossed the short distance between them, E.A. folded her arms and waited. It wasn't very good of her to simply watch it play out, but some things couldn't be helped. Will Kurtz was as easygoing as one came, but when he was riled up?

Well, all the Eight knew then to look out.

It was almost too bad that David did not realize that Will had a temper—and that he could behave unpredictably when he was in such a mood. But as she watched Will walk toward her, E.A. felt her pulse beat a little faster. He looked ready for anything.

What was funny was that she felt that way, too.

SEVEN

"Andy felt guilty about leaving his date but he kept saying he didn't have a choice," Will called out. "But now that I think about it, John was pretty worried about Marie, too."

"*W*ell?" David prodded. "Are you behind Elizabeth Anne's sudden surliness?"

Will knew that one day in the future he was going to wonder what he'd been thinking. But right at that minute? He couldn't think of a single reason to stop the words that came out of his mouth.

"I doubt I've ever spurred on her temper, but I can't say that I mind her speaking her mind." He smiled at her. "In fact, I'm right glad that she's telling us both what she's thinking."

E.A. smiled back in such a sweet way, it was almost like she'd forgotten David was still there.

David turned on his heel "What is going on here, Elizabeth Anne?"

With a sigh, E.A. walked over to join them. "Quite a bit, actually."

"I'd like to ask you the same thing," Will said. "It's pretty obvious that you're interrupting a private conversation."

When David gaped at him, Will glared. E.A. grabbed his bicep. "Will, what in the world are you doing?"

He wasn't sure. But everything inside of him was propelling him forward. He didn't think he had a choice but to follow his instincts. "Just go along with me," he muttered under his breath. "It'll be fine." At least, he hoped so as he walked toward David.

"I'm Will Kurtz," he said as he held out his hand. "I don't believe we've ever officially met."

David looked like he was seriously considering ignoring Will's hand, but at the last minute he shook it. "David Brennan."

"And you two are neighbors?"

"We are." His chin lifted. "But I'm more than that. Elizabeth Anne and I have been courting for years."

"Is that right?" Will had no trouble allowing a thick note of surprise to linger in his voice. David was acting as if he and E.A. were something special. But whether that had once been the case or not, they certainly weren't now.

David turned to E.A. "I can't believe you're already pushing a new man right in front of my nose."

"Oh, for heaven's sakes," E.A. said. "Nothing we're doing has anything to do with you."

"If it concerns you, it does."

She shook her head. "You're wrong, David. Whatever we used to be is over."

Will almost clapped her on the back. E.A. was giving it to this guy straight.

"We were taking a break."

"No, we weren't."

"Elizabeth Anne, we were practically engaged."

She inhaled sharply. "Oh no, we weren't."

Will had had enough of the guy's never-ending pushiness.

Because of that, he decided to say something that his mother and father would not be proud of but that his best friends would grin about. "I believe 'practically engaged' is a lot like being 'practically pregnant.' Neither makes sense. You either are or you aren't."

"Will, you are not helping," E.A. hissed.

She was right. But what could he do? He was committed now. He looked at David directly in the eye, practically taunting him to say something else.

And . . . he didn't disappoint. "You are making a big mistake, Elizabeth Anne," David said. "You ain't nothing special, nothing special at all. You're gonna miss me when I've moved on. Mark my words."

Will hated the way David was talking to her. Hated the hurt in her eyes that she was trying to hide—especially because the other man couldn't have been more wrong. E.A. definitely was special—at least she was to him.

Reaching out for her hand, he wrapped his fingers through hers as he tugged her close to him. "E.A., baby, do you want me to tell him or shall I?"

Wide blue eyes stared up into his. She looked both shocked at his words and mildly amused. "I think you'd better do the explaining," she said.

Will looked back at David. "I don't think E.A. is going to be worried about you moving on at all, seeing as how she already has." He grinned evilly. "We're just days away from announcing that she's off the market."

She raised her eyebrows. "Days?"

"Definitely days," Will affirmed, almost enjoying her amusement as much as he was enjoying putting the other man in his place. Turning back to David, he said, "It's time you went on home."

Instead of turning away and admitting defeat, David puffed up his chest. "Elizabeth Anne, are you going to allow him to speak to me like that?"

She swallowed, seemed to come to a decision, and then smiled. "I'm sorry, David, but I can hardly stop him. My Will is nothing if not ardent."

After casting another dark look at them, David turned and started walking back to his house.

But his steps were slow and he kept looking back at them, as if he was waiting for them to pull apart.

What David needed was evidence, Will realized.

That meant that there was only one thing to do.

Releasing her hand, Will turned to face E.A., gently tilted her chin up, and then kissed her good and proper.

She tensed against him, but then relaxed. Placed one of her hands on his chest.

And because he'd been motivated by adrenaline, or maybe it was simply because she fit so well in his arms, Will moved his lips to her cheek, then jaw, before finding her lips again.

He knew he was kissing her in a way he'd never kissed any girl before. In a way he knew he shouldn't. But he couldn't deny it was the best kiss he'd ever had.

Minutes later, when Will lifted his head, E.A.'s eyes slowly opened. At first her expression was filled with wonder, and then shock.

After another beat, she stepped away. "What. Was. That?"

There were a lot of answers he could have given her. It was a mistake, an embarrassing burst of male ego . . . He could even lie and act like he kissed women that way all the time.

But he couldn't say any of those things. Not when her taste was still on his lips. Not when he realized that something had just happened between them that was both notable and true.

So he settled for the plain and simple truth. "It was the best kiss I've ever had." He smiled. "I know I should be waiting for you to slap my face or apologizing, but I cannot."

Looking like she was trying hard not to smile, she folded her arms across her chest. "I'm not going to hit you," she said as she walked back to the pair of chairs. "But I *am* going to tell you that I am not exactly pleased with what you just did."

He sat down next to her. "Are you mad at me?"

"Will, you just acted as if we were on our way to the altar," E.A. said. "You kissed me. A lot."

Oh, yes he had. "I haven't forgotten." Ignoring the sudden idea to take her in his arms again, he lowered his voice. "Don't be mad, E.A."

"I . . . I don't know how I feel right now. Maybe confused?"

He'd take confused, especially since he was feeling pretty confused by his actions as well. "I'm sorry for pretending we were almost engaged," he began. "But he came over here acting like he could treat you any which way he wanted. I hated that."

"So you just decided to make up a romance? Oh, Will."

"He'll get over it."

Her voice darkened. "No, he'll tell his parents, who are going to tell mine . . ." She craned her head to look in the front windows. "That is, if they didn't already watch you kiss me in the first place." She leaned her head back against the chair. "What a mess."

She was right. He'd made a real mess of her life. Feeling a little ashamed by making an already difficult time for her worse, he tried to patch things up. "E.A., we're friends. We've been friends for years. I'll talk to your parents if you want. I'll explain to them about that kiss." What he would actually say was a whole other story, though. How was he supposed to apologize for something he didn't feel very sorry about?

"Explain what? That you suddenly decided to start kissing me like we were Romeo and Juliet?" She released a ragged sigh. "No. Way."

"Are you sure?"

"Oh, yes. If you say anything to my mother, she's going to think that she's got every right to share her opinion, and I don't want that."

"Okay . . . So, um, what do you want to do?"

"Nothing."

"Nothing?"

"Nothing more." She waved a hand. "We're just going to wait. I'm not going to say anything to anybody about what just happened until I have to."

"All right. I'll keep my mouth shut, too, then. It will be like it never happened." Almost never happened, he corrected to himself. Because he knew he wasn't going to ever forget kissing her.

When E.A. looked at him again, her expression was filled with humor but something more. Maybe a new tentativeness. "Hey, Will?"

"*Jah?*"

"Can I tell you something?"

"You don't have to ask, E.A. You know that. Tell me whatever you want, whenever you want."

"That might have been your best kiss, but it was my first."

Her first kiss. He'd given her that. Not her annoying neighbor. Not any of the other guys in the Eight. Not any other man: him. "I'm glad," he said, after a second or two had slipped by.

He leaned back against his chair, noticing the fireflies twinkling in the field right across from them. "Those fireflies look like twinkling Christmas lights," he blurted. "Have you ever noticed?"

"*Jah*, Will," she said around a sweet sigh. "As a matter of fact, I have."

EIGHT

"I couldn't help but worry about Marie," John B. said as he held Marie's hand. "I kept thinking that someone should have been looking after her." Winking at everyone assembled, he added, "After all, she was wearing a very sparkly crown."

FRIDAY

Almost a whole week had passed and E.A. was still rattled by Will's visit. What a crazy, unexpected, unsettling night it had been! After he'd left, she'd found herself walking in a daze. She'd been sure her mother was going to be standing at the doorway, eager to ask her a dozen questions about Will, David's visit, and oh yes, The Kiss.

But to her surprise, her parents had already gone to bed and her sister, Annie, was more intent on finishing her homework than paying attention to her older sister's suddenly eventful love life.

Unfortunately, for the rest of the night, she hadn't been able to think of anything but her love life—or, rather, her sudden decision to act completely out of the ordinary. She was not impulsive. She loved knowing exactly what was going to happen and when.

She was not the type of woman to act so impulsively. She certainly didn't go around kissing men like that!

So why had she not said a word when Will was lying through his teeth to David? Why had she kept her hand snug in his when Will had been acting like it was impossible to stand next to her without touching?

Most importantly, why, when she'd realized what Will was about to do, had she kissed him back? Surely she was the type of girl to turn her face. Or push him away.

Wasn't she that type of woman? She'd always thought so . . . but maybe not.

Deciding she needed both advice and something to take her mind off Will Kurtz, she'd arranged a slumber party at her house for that night. To her delight, Marie, Katie, Tricia, and Kendra had all been free and been excited to have some girl time.

Her parents had seemed bemused by her plans and had even encouraged Annie to go with them to visit friends, no doubt remembering all the nights she'd either had the girls over to her house or had dragged a sleeping bag over to Marie's or Katie's house back when they'd been teenagers.

All five of them had been looking forward to it for days. By seven o'clock, they were camped out in E.A.'s living room in old pajamas, just like they were fourteen again.

They'd eaten pizza and cooked popcorn and baked cookies. Marie had brought a case of root beer and vanilla ice cream. They were eating more junk food than they had in weeks and laughing more than they had in months.

"E.A., are you ever going to tell us what is on your mind?" Tricia asked right after they'd all put on pajamas and sprawled out on a bunch of sleeping bags on the floor.

"I am. I'm just trying to figure out how to tell you."

"The easiest way is just to say it," Katie said. "Then it's out in the open."

"You're right." But still E.A. held her tongue. How in the world was she going to tell them what she'd done with Will Kurtz?

Marie, all golden hair and green eyes, looked at her strangely. "Elizabeth Anne, come on. Nothing can be that bad. Just spit it out."

"It's not that easy."

Katie grunted as she flipped onto her stomach. "Sure it is."

"All right." She took a deep breath but hesitated yet again. "Just give me a minute. I'm trying to find the right words."

"What do you need the right words for?" Katie asked. "You're starting to worry me. I've never known you to be squeamish about anything."

Kendra nodded. "I have to agree. No matter what happens, you are always the first person to make a list and a plan of action."

That was the problem. Everything she was about to tell them was completely out of character. "There's no plan of action for this."

"For what?" Tricia practically yelled.

"For telling you all that I kissed Will last weekend!"

All the girls froze. Marie's eyebrows nearly reached her hairline.

And Katie? Well, Katie started laughing.

"No way. Now you and Will are a couple?" Katie mused. "This is crazy. All of us are pairing off like we belong in an ark."

E.A. wasn't real crazy about the ark reference. She had a feeling if Noah saw her and Will together, he would kick them off the ark. "This is more complicated than that."

"How? Love isn't complicated."

"I never said a word about love." Which made her actions kind of worse.

"Oh, speak for yourself, Katie," Marie interrupted. "I've loved John for all my life and our relationship was still complicated."

"First, I don't love Will." When all the girls gaped at her, she cleared her throat. "I mean, of course I love him."

Katie grinned. "Does that mean you do or you don't?"

This was going worse than she imagined. She needed to get herself together and fast. "It means I love him as a friend." When all the girls simply stared at her, she added, "I mean, I love *all* of you as friends."

"I love you, too," Kendra said, smiling. "As a friend. Just like I love Will."

This was going from bad to worse. How was that possible? "You know what I meant."

"Absolutely," Marie murmured. "You have a lot of love in your heart."

"Yes. Exactly." Though, not quite.

"You love us all, but somehow you accidentally kissed Will," Katie said.

If E.A.'s cheeks were any hotter, she'd fear she had a fever. "You are all having too much fun at my expense. What I'm trying to say is that while what happened was unexpected, it didn't mean a thing."

"Why didn't it?" Katie asked.

"Because Will was only pretending."

"Pretending to kiss you?" Kendra asked.

"No, the kiss was real. But the circumstances were special," E.A. explained in a rush. "You see, first David was standing there, acting like a jerk. Then he kind of insinuated that I never had a mind of my own." She lowered her voice. "And then he kind of made it seem like I would never find another man to give me the time of day." She swallowed, still hating how that comment had hurt. "And that's when Will started pretending we were in love."

"Which is why he kissed you," Marie said.

"Yes. Exactly."

"I think that's strange, but I guess I could see it happening," Katie said. "Any of us would close ranks against someone giving one of the Eight a hard time. I certainly would."

"You'd be on them like a Doberman," E.A. said. She was relieved that things were finally getting cleared up.

Just as she was about to take a sip of hot tea, Marie put her cup down abruptly. "Hey, um, E.A.?"

"Yes?"

"You never said what happened next."

"Next?"

"Yes. What did David do next? Did he say anything more or did he just silently run off?"

"He didn't do anything."

Marie raised an eyebrow. "Really?"

"Well, um, I don't think David did anything. I mean, he wasn't actually standing there when we kissed."

All the girls looked at each other again. "I'm sorry, but I don't understand," Kendra said. "I thought that kiss was for show."

"It was, but Will kissed me as David was walking away."

Kendra looked like she was attempting not to grin. "So he kissed you just in case David happened to look your way while he was walking away?"

Now things were sounding stupid again. "Um . . . yes?"

Tricia, who'd been mainly just lying on the floor and listening, sat up on her elbows. "Maybe we need more information. Was it a legitimate kiss, or just a peck on the cheek?"

Oh, she'd certainly kissed him. Thinking about how her hand had been pressed to his chest, how that kiss, no, those *kisses* had been anything but small pecks, she mumbled her answer. "Legitimate."

"Ah," Tricia said, before taking a sip of her root beer float.

E.A. picked up her own drink and sipped, too. When she spied Marie and Tricia exchange glances, she felt like covering her face with her hands. Honestly, she was starting to think that this whole sleepover idea had been a mistake. She'd hoped they'd give her clarity, but instead she had a feeling that they were feeling far clearer about her and Will than she was.

Actually, all discussing Will's visit had done was make her feel even more confused. "Maybe we should talk about something else for a while."

Though Katie looked like she wanted to disagree, Marie—dear Marie—smiled and nodded. "That's a good idea. There's so much going on with all of us, we have a lot to talk about. Why, we might end up talking all night long."

"I'm fine with that," Katie said with a smile. "Harley told me to have a good time and sleep in tomorrow. He's going to take care of all the guests for me. Isn't he wonderful?"

"Oh, *jah*," Kendra said. "He must really love you a lot. Almost as much as our E.A. here loves us all."

E.A. groaned. "Am I ever going to live that down?"

"Nope," Tricia and Marie said together.

When the other girls started laughing, E.A. joined in. After all, that was what good friends were for.

NINE

"Can we stop the story now?" Marie called out from the head table. "This is getting awkward."

"No way," Harley replied. "E.A.'s just about to get to the good part."

*I*t had been so hard to get to her sewing class. Alan had woken up in a bad mood and had found fault with his breakfast, the dishes in the kitchen sink, and even the outfit she'd been wearing.

Then, when she'd made the mistake of asking him about his boss's wife, he'd gone on a terrible rant about their move to Walnut Creek almost a year ago, the problems with his boss, and how everyone in the company was working against him.

Of course, her shocked silence hadn't helped matters. When he was in that kind of mood, nothing helped to calm him. But still she had tried.

By the time he'd left for work, his coffee cup was broken,

spilled coffee stained the countertops, and she had a new set of bruises on her forearm.

She'd also been so mad, she'd been shaking. Only two years ago, she would have taken to bed, maybe even taken a sleeping pill to help her forget about her troubles. At the very least, she would have been crying uncontrollably.

But she was stronger now. What Alan did to her wasn't right. She didn't deserve it, and there was no way she was going to subject herself to even another month of his abuse.

As she bent down to pick up the broken shards from the floor, she took the time to give thanks for how far she'd come. The journey hadn't been easy. She'd started by tentatively reading books about self-worth. Then she'd begun making goals for herself . . . and putting aside grocery money.

Before they'd moved, she had confided in a woman at church. She wanted to help her, and probably would have if they hadn't moved to Walnut Creek. But instead of giving up, she started making plans again. And now she had her sewing class.

The young Mennonite woman in the shop would never have any idea how much her kindness and easy acceptance of her had meant. Because of E.A., she didn't need to hide behind pills or in sleep. No, when she was at her weekly class, she forgot about everything but her projects.

It didn't matter to her how anything she made looked, either. She wasn't trying to find beauty in her work. No, she was looking for beauty in herself. And that meant everything.

Plus, she had a singular goal now. Somehow, some way, she was going to leave Alan within the next two months. She might not be the person she used to be, but she was still someone worth fighting for.

That was why, as soon as she was sure Alan wasn't coming back home, she walked upstairs and picked up Alan's discarded suit. Searching the pockets, she smiled in triumph. There was a five-dollar bill in the breast coat pocket and seventy-five cents in his slacks.

Pleased, she carefully hung up his suit, then carried the money downstairs to the laundry room. Opening one of the boxes of dryer sheets, she removed the sheets, pulled out the Ziploc baggie hidden underneath them, and added the latest addition to her money stash. In a few more days, she would go to the drugstore and ask Brenda, the kind cashier, to exchange her latest amount for a twenty-dollar bill. Brenda always did that without asking questions.

After carefully putting the box back into the cupboard, she walked to the kitchen and finished cleaning up Alan's mess. When everything looked as perfect as possible, she went back to her bedroom, changed to a light, long-sleeved shirt to hide the new bruises, and picked up her purse. She had a class to get to.

One hour later, as she greeted her sweet, redheaded sewing teacher, Marta felt herself relax for the first time that day. E.A. was going to show her how to pin pattern pieces on fabric.

"How are you, Marta?" E.A. asked after a while. "You've seemed a little quiet today."

Marta looked up from her project. "Me? I'm fine. Not as well as you, though," she teased. "You look especially happy today."

E.A. blushed. "I guess I am."

"Did something good happen?"

"I think so." E.A. hesitated, then said, "My friend Will and I . . . well, I think our relationship is changing."

She sounded so hopeful that Marta smiled encouragingly. "For the better, I hope?"

"Oh, *jah*. I mean, I think so."

E.A. was acting so cute. Like an eager schoolgirl. It almost made Marta believe in love again. "I'm happy for you," Marta said sincerely.

"Thank you." E.A. smiled again. "To tell you the truth, I'm not really sure what we're doing. Sometimes it feels as if I can't wait to see him—even though I might have seen him the day before." She bit her lip, then added, "But at other times, I feel so flustered whenever he's near that I almost want to avoid him. Is that normal, do you think?"

"I think so." When E.A. still looked skeptical, Marta laughed. "Don't worry, dear. We've all been there at one time or another. Love is like that."

E.A. stared at her in wonder before shaking her head, as if to clear it. "I'm sorry. You're here to learn to sew, not discuss my love life." She folded her hands in her lap. "Now, I think we can safely say that you've mastered making pillowcases. What else would you like to work on today? Still want to try to pin pattern pieces on fabric? Or, do you have any ideas?"

"A couple."

Before she could share her ideas, E.A. held up a darling apron. It was made of three different coordinating fabrics, each decorated in vibrant blue and yellow patterns. "What do you think about making one of these?" She smiled. "I think you'd look really cute wearing this in your kitchen."

Marta laughed. "No, I think *you* would look really cute baking in such a fancy thing. I, on the other hand, would simply look like myself: a plain-looking thirty-year-old woman."

E.A. frowned. "Marta, you are lovely. And, if I may say so, you have really pretty hair and eyes. And the kind of figure most women dream of."

Marta knew the right thing to do would be to deflect the compliment. But she'd had ten years of being told that she was too soft, too fat, too everything. Because of that, she looked at E.A. in wonder. "Do you really think so?"

"Of course." A touch of worry entered E.A.'s eyes. "Do you not see yourself that way?"

No. No, she did not. But maybe one day she would.

The kernel of an idea that she'd recently started thinking about was blazing inside her now. All she had to do was be brave enough to put it into practice.

Remembering Alan's morning tirade, Marta knew it was time. "Actually, E.A., I've been thinking that I'd like to make something else."

Her teacher smiled encouragingly. "Okay . . ."

Taking a deep breath, she plunged forward. "What do you think about me sewing a backpack?"

E.A. looked flummoxed. "You want to make a backpack?"

Folding her hands tightly together, Marta nodded. "Yes. I think it would be nice to have something I can put on my shoulders to carry things in case my hands are full." And in it, she could put some money and a change of clothes. The things she would need in case she ever decided to get brave and leave Alan.

Realizing that her little teacher was still looking confused, Marta shrugged. "I know it sounds silly, a woman my age wanting a backpack . . ."

"No, not at all," E.A. replied in a rush. "It doesn't sound silly at all. You just took me by surprise. And what's this talk about your age? You aren't even ten years older than me."

"You know what? You're exactly right." Marta smiled. "So, do you think it would be possible to make a little backpack? I'd really like to try."

"*Jah.* Of course." E.A. stared at the sewing machine—it was obvious that she was trying to figure out how to make a simple one. "I've never made a backpack before, but I could find a pattern and then modify it a bit. You know, make something fairly easy."

As long as it could hold some things and wouldn't hinder her running, Marta knew it would be fine. "Anything sounds good."

"It could have a drawstring," E.A. murmured. "Those aren't too hard."

Marta knew E.A. was talking to herself, but now that the project was out in the open, she knew she had to make the "right" kind of backpack. One that she could actually use. "If you don't mind, I'd kind of like it to have a zipper."

"Really?" E.A. bit her bottom lip. "Zippers can be tricky."

"I know, but I have you to help me, right?" Forcing herself to look more carefree than she was feeling, Marta chuckled. "You are very skilled, you know. And a very good teacher."

After another moment, E.A. threw up her hands. "All right. You're the student. If you want to make a backpack with a zipper, then that's what we'll do."

"Thank you so much." Impulsively, she reached out and hugged E.A. She'd done it! She'd made more plans for the day she would leave. She felt as big a rush as she'd felt when she'd first taken some of Alan's change and hidden it. One day, now sooner than later, she was going to be able to leave Alan. One day, she'd discover the perfect opportunity, find a place where she could get help easily and blend into the crowd . . . and then she would disappear from his life.

"No reason to thank me, Marta. It will be fun." E.A. stood up. "Now, you go look at fabrics and I'll go hunt down some patterns. Don't forget that you want something fairly sturdy. Backpacks are supposed to hold a lot of things, you know."

"I won't forget that," Marta murmured as she walked to the back half of the store, which was filled with bolts of all different kinds of fabrics. She walked right over to the bolts of thick cotton and denim. Running a finger down one particularly bright bolt of green, she imagined having it filled, zipped up tightly, and hidden in the house.

And though the image gave her goose bumps, it also made her feel even a little bit better. It was so good to have something fresh and hopeful to think about: something far different from what she had now.

TEN

"We later found out that Marie had been so mad and upset about her date abandoning her, she decided to wander around the school until I arrived. She'd thought she would have had thirty minutes or more until we arrived."

"That really is the truth," Marie called out.

FRIDAY

Over a week had passed since everything had changed between Will and E.A. But even though so much time had gone by, the whole episode consumed him. The way she'd felt in his arms was the first thing Will thought about in the morning and the last thing he thought about at night.

It had created a tension inside him that was both unfamiliar and unwelcome. He wasn't the type of man to feel uncertain or live with regrets, but lately, he was. He wasn't sure how to make things right with her. Or if there was even anything *to* make right.

As the days passed, instead of thinking about E.A. less, he began to think about her even more. Even at work, which wasn't a good idea.

Especially since people were beginning to notice that he wasn't acting like himself.

"So, are you ever going to tell me what happened between you and E.A.?" John B. asked as they left work together.

"Nothing to tell," Will lied. If he had to talk to John about it, he was going to have to come to terms with what was going on between them as well. And every time he thought about that kiss?

Well, it had him stumped.

"Are you sure about that?" John asked as they headed out of the warehouse and into the bright sunlight.

"Yep." Will pulled out his sunglasses and paused, enjoying the feel of the warmth on his skin.

John pulled the brim of his ball cap down further on his forehead. "Oh, come on," he said impatiently. "You can lie to me if you want, but I think you should talk to someone about what happened the other night. It might make you feel better."

What happened the other night? John already knew? Feeling even more rattled, he grunted. "And why do you think I need to talk to you about E.A. and me?"

"Because my wife has been having quite the conversation with E.A. and the girls about you two. That's why."

He could hardly believe what he was hearing. "All the girls?"

"Oh, *jah*. They had a slumber party . . . and you two were the chosen topic."

"I had no idea." Besides, weren't these women a little old to be having sleepovers?

John grinned. "That's because you ain't married. Since my marriage, I've discovered all sorts of things women do that men aren't aware of. Logan and Harley have said the same thing."

"Huh." Feeling so out of sorts, he kicked at a rock in their path. "And I have to tell ya, if the truth is even half as good as Marie made it sound, you two are in trouble."

Will had had every intention of acting calm and collected. But now he was feeling alarmed. "What exactly did Marie tell you?"

"Nothing much . . . only that you gave E.A. quite the kiss."

"I wasn't the only one kissing," he blurted before he could stop himself. "I mean . . . never mind."

"No way," John retorted. "There's no way you're going to take that back." Looking more amused by the second, he added, "And don't you start acting like we're strangers or something. We've shared plenty of things before. And you certainly weren't shy about giving me advice on Marie."

"That was different. You and Marie have always had something between you. It was only a matter of time before you got together."

"That is true. I sure can't say that I ever saw anything coming between you and E.A."

He hadn't, either. "Did Marie tell you that our kiss only happened because of David? It wasn't a case of us not being able to stay away from each other. It was me attempting to put that guy in his place." And . . . said like that? His actions were even more embarrassing.

Thankfully, John didn't look shocked. "*Jah*, I heard it was all a little bit of something like that."

"*Gut.* So, you understand what I'm trying to tell you about me and E.A.?"

"Um, not so much."

It seemed he was going to have to spell it out. "E.A. needed someone to lean on. I just decided to *pretend* to be her boyfriend so that guy would leave her alone."

"So that kiss didn't mean anything to you?"

Will couldn't say that. He wasn't ever going to be able to say that. But he was still confused. "I don't know exactly what it meant."

"Maybe you should figure that out, Will. And sooner rather than later, too."

"Because?"

"Because I'm thinking that E.A. might be thinking a little differently."

If that was true, it would make him feel even worse. What was wrong with him? He had never done something like this before. It was like he didn't even know himself anymore.

Stuffing his hands in his pockets, he confided, "John, I think I'm in the middle of a midlife crisis or something."

"At twenty-six?"

"I'm not saying what I'm going through is normal. Only that it's happening."

"What else is going on besides you pretending to be E.A.'s beau?"

"First off, I'm worried about work."

John's easy pace slowed as he turned to him. "Why? Everyone says you do a great job. I *know* you do a great job, Will. I've even heard Mr. Kerrigan tell other workers about how skilled you are. He really values you."

"But I'm still on the assembly line. And worse, I think I'm perfectly happy there."

"I don't understand what's wrong with that," John said slowly. "The majority of the employees at the factory work on the line."

"It doesn't seem very important."

"Sure it does. The whole place depends on every single employee doing his or her part. We're all a big team, Will."

"I know."

"*Gut.* Then you should know that your leadership on the line is really important. I've worked next to you, remember? You help all the new guys, help set the pace, keep up the morale." He waved a hand. "Everything."

"But shouldn't I be aiming to be a manager or something? I mean, look at you. You're designing the artwork for most of the trailers now."

"You know I always liked to draw. That's where my talent lies."

"Yes, but we started at the same time and now you are working in the front office. I know you got a raise, too."

John looked away. "I don't know why we're talking about this."

Because it mattered. At least, it did to him. "Can't you see how I might be wondering what I'm doing wrong?"

"I can see that you're entitled to your opinion, Will." But John's voice was full of doubt. It was obvious that he didn't necessarily agree with Will's reasoning. "So, is that the extent of your midlife crisis?" He grinned, obviously trying to lighten the conversation.

"No. I've been thinking I've been stuck in my personal life, too. The closest I've ever gotten to having someone serious in my life is what I'm doing now—*pretending* to be E.A.'s boy-friend."

John chuckled. "Come on."

Will did see the humor in it, but he also couldn't deny that it was worrying him. "What I'm trying to say is that I'm stuck while the rest of my friends have moved on with their careers and their relationships."

"You're only twenty-six."

"And you're working in the front office doing your dream job and going home to Marie . . ." Will let his voice trail off. Couldn't John see how his life paled in comparison?

After they walked another few yards, John spoke again. "I think God's timing is at work here."

"You know I am faithful to the Lord, but I think that's a bit of a cop-out."

"I don't agree." When Will got ready to interrupt, John said, "Just listen, okay?"

"I'm listening."

"A year ago, when everything was unfolding with Marie, I would have given anything to be you."

"I don't see why."

"Because you are one of the most positive, giving people I know. All of us in the Eight depend on your attitude to get us through hard times."

John's words were good to hear, and Will appreciated them. But he needed to be more than just a good friend. "I'm talking about my future here, John. Not just about being able to pat my friends on the back."

His buddy's expression flared. "You still aren't hearing what I'm saying. Will, your life is good, it really is. I'm glad you are still at home. You've got a good family and I know they appreciate you being there. I'm glad you do so well on the line, that everyone always puts the new guys next to you. Honestly, I admire your steadiness."

And now they were back where they'd started. Will blew out a breath of air. Why had he even brought his worries up? All it had done was make him sound whiney and ungrateful.

After they walked another half a block, John said, "Maybe your relationship with E.A. is the change you needed. Maybe that kiss wasn't a mistake. Maybe it was a sign that there is something between the two of you that is meant to be."

"I don't know."

"Buddy, no offense, but I think you'd better have a talk with Elizabeth Anne. I don't think the two of you are on the same page right now. And that's putting it mildly."

"I'll go over to her house tonight."

"Good. You know, if I were you, I'd tell her everything that you told me."

"Really?"

He nodded. "Absolutely. Lay your confusion out on the line. Things might be changing, but above all you're friends. She could help."

"That's true. She's really good at giving advice."

"*Jah*, she is. Even when we haven't wanted to hear it, she's given her two cents."

John patted him on the shoulder. "Maybe it's a good thing you don't want to jump into a romantic relationship with her. She'd always have something to say."

Will nodded. "Always."

But at the moment, he didn't think that was a bad thing. Not at all.

Three hours later, he called on Elizabeth Anne. After greeting her parents politely, he stood in the entryway, waiting impatiently for her to appear. When she did, he couldn't help but smile. There she was, dressed in a light blue dress, looking like summer itself.

"Hello, Will."

Aware that her parents were still standing nearby and watching them closely, he inclined his head. "E.A."

"Would you care to sit on the porch swing? It's rather nice out."

He followed her out, pleased that she was looking pleased to see him, too. When he sat down next to her, he almost took her hand but decided he needed to concentrate on what he came to say. But how to start? He just wasn't sure.

She noticed. "Will, is everything all right?"

"*Jah.* I . . . well, I'm just trying to figure out how to talk to you about something."

"You know you don't have to figure out anything when you talk to me. Just say it."

She had a point. They'd known each other too long to worry about finding the "right" words to say to each other. "So, I've been having a midlife crisis." He glanced at her from the corner of his eye, half-expecting her to stare at him incredulously. But instead, she only smiled.

"Do you find that amusing?"

"*Nee.* I was just thinking that I've been having one, too."

"Truly?"

She nodded. "When I was younger, I always had my goals

to accomplish. But now that I'm older? I'm at a loss for what to do."

"I've been feeling a lot of the same things."

She relaxed against him. "If that's the case . . . well, then I'd say we're quite the pair, Will Kurtz."

Yes. Maybe they were that, indeed. Liking their closeness, he took a big breath and then shared everything he'd been thinking. He told her all about his midlife crisis. About his job and his worries. Then, he apologized for kissing her in the first place.

But instead of looking sympathetic and relieved, she was staring at him like she was really confused. And, perhaps, a little put out with him.

That wasn't good. Not at all.

"E.A., what did I say?"

"Nothing." Looking increasingly uncomfortable, she kicked one of her legs out in front of her. "Will, um, while I do not regret our, um, kiss . . . I think you might be mistaken in what it meant to me."

"Perhaps you should tell me."

"It was nice, but I don't expect it to change anything about us." Looking frustrated, she said, "I'm not trying to make us into something that you don't want." She waved a hand. "I mean, it's not like I've been sitting around hoping you were about to propose or something."

"No. Of course not," he bit out.

Her voice rose. "I might have talked to the girls about what happened, but I never told them that I was upset with you, or that I blamed you for what you did. There were two of us on this porch."

"I know." He stood up.

"I mean, I could have pulled away from you or told David that you were lying about us being together. I didn't." Sounding even more defensive, she added, "I was just as much a part of that episode as you were."

Their kiss was her *episode*. "I understand," he said slowly, though he wasn't sure he understood that at all. "I mean, *jah*. Of course."

She folded her arms over her chest. "I'm a grown woman. I kissed you back because I liked kissing you. That's all."

She was lying. He knew it. No woman who had waited as long as she had for her first kiss was as world-weary as she was making herself out to be. That as much as she might like to remind him that she was independent and worldly, she also wasn't exactly full of experience. Neither of them were.

They stared at each other. Both of them were breathing heavily. Like they'd just finished running a race or were attempting to hold back a lot of emotion.

Seconds passed.

She sighed. "Do you want to sit back down? I'm not exactly sure what we were just arguing about."

"Me, neither." He returned to his place on the porch swing. Then, because it was a rather small space and he had rather long arms, he rested his right arm over the back of the swing. Over her shoulders. It felt good there. Right.

She tilted her face up toward him. "Will, about everything else . . ."

She smelled good. She was wearing some kind of perfume, something floral and expensive. "Hmm?"

"Please don't be so hard on yourself. Everything will work out all right for you. I know it."

"Don't worry about me."

"I can't help it, though. I don't think you are seeing how much I and all of our friends value you."

"I know you do."

She shook her head. "I don't mean just as a friend. We value your gifts. You've got a lot of them, you know."

"As do you, E.A."

"I hope so. I . . . well, I've been going through a bit of a mid-life crisis of my own."

"What's been going on?"

"Just a month or two ago I was ready to quit. You remember I told you that I don't really care for my boss."

"I do remember that."

"Well, then something happened. I got Marta, my sewing student."

"I remember you mentioning her. She's English, right?"

"Yes. She's as English as Marie, and a little bit older than me."

"And the lessons are going well?"

"They are. But, well, I can't put my finger on it, but I think there's something different about her." She stared straight ahead. "She's really tentative and shy." She tapped a finger. "Almost like Kendra was when she was ten or eleven."

Kendra had never been an "official" part of the Eight, but she had certainly been friends with all of them. She just hadn't been around much. They'd later learned that she'd been abused at home.

Will frowned. "Oh, E.A."

"I know. I have no proof, but I do have a bad feeling about her home life."

"I'm glad you're there for this Marta," said Will. "She could probably use a friend."

"Me, too." E.A.'s eyes glistened. "You know what? She acts like I am the one helping her, but I think that she's helping me just as much."

"That's how friends are. Ain't so? They're there for each other."

"*Jah.* That is true." She smiled up at him, and she looked so sweet, Will leaned down to kiss her cheek.

Except she moved her cheek, and his lips ended up touching hers.

And then, it was like his body didn't belong to his brain anymore. Next thing he knew, he was kissing E.A. again. Long, sweet, drugging kisses. Right there on her front porch. Muddling his mind and his good intentions until all he could scarcely think about was that he didn't want to stop. Not for hours maybe. Or, at the least, not anytime soon.

Which reinforced what he'd known all along. He wasn't pretending anything with Elizabeth Anne.

Not one single thing.

ELEVEN

E.A. couldn't help it. She smirked at the crowd of two hundred. "I bet all of you know what I'm about to say. As much as we all intended to get home really fast with no one being any the wiser, things didn't really turn out like that."

Another Tuesday, another day at work. Practically the moment E.A. arrived Lark had handed her a lengthy to-do list. Then, before she could hardly do more than clutch the sheet of paper in her hand, Lark announced that she had plans with her sister for brunch and that E.A. was left to do everything on her own.

Ten minutes later, she was gone.

Since the shop was empty, E.A. sat down in Lark's usual seat and read over her list of tasks. They were stupid, really.

- Put all the bolts of fabric back in their proper places.
- Unpack and display the box of patterns.
- Dust the figurines displays on the back shelves.

The list continued, naming off another six chores that were as obvious as they were unnecessary to give an employee of four years.

E.A. knew what needed to be done. She didn't mind doing all of the tasks, though she did find it irritating that her boss hadn't started a single one of them. Why hadn't Lark even attempted to clean up the fabric area? This was her shop, after all.

Just as she stood up to get to work, the front door jangled and two sets of customers wandered in. And so it began. E.A. knew that there was no way she was going to be able to get more than one or two of the tasks finished if more people came in.

And they did. But instead of getting frazzled, E.A. felt energized. She liked not only being busy but also feeling like she was in charge and capable of doing a good job.

And to her surprise, her mood lifted as she wandered down the aisles, helped customers, and returned a dozen bolts of fabric back to their correct places.

By noon, at least a dozen ladies had entered the shop. Almost every one of them had bought something. Though it would have been easier with two people working, she couldn't say she minded not having Lark's know-it-all attitude for company.

E.A. hadn't even complained when Lark came back from brunch and sat down behind the counter, interacting with the customers only when it was time to ring them up.

Because of that, E.A. had positioned herself in the back of the store. There she could cut fabric for customers and talk about patterns and fabric options.

Actually, she'd been just congratulating herself on not looking at the clock for almost an hour when an all-too-familiar voice spoke in a low tone directly behind her.

"I can't believe you were kissing him again last night."

She jumped. After making sure the two ladies nearby hadn't heard him, she turned to face David. "I'm working. You need to leave."

He shook his head. "Elizabeth Anne, we need to speak. You've given me no choice, you know. I've been trying to talk to you for days and you are avoiding me like the plague."

That was because he was her own personal plague. "Come over tonight and we'll talk."

"I'm not heading back to your house if I can help it. Besides, there's no need for me to go over there later. We can talk now."

"This isn't the place." Not that she wanted to see him any-where. David had his hands crossed over his chest and was glaring at her like she'd run over his cat. "You need to leave. You don't belong in here."

"Lark didn't seem to mind," he countered.

He knew Lark? "What is that supposed to mean?"

He lowered his voice. "My family is very upset with you, Eliz-abeth Anne."

David was an only child. His parents were older than hers. They were kind and never had a cross word to say about anyone. Especially not about their son. She used to think it was sweet.

Not any longer. "If that's true, then I'm very sorry to hear that."

"Of course it's true. What do your parents have to say about our breakup?"

His eyes were bright. She realized then that he wanted her parents to be upset with her. "They didn't say a word about it, David."

He stepped closer. Crowding her in the back corner of the

shop. "Not one word?" He looked incredulous. "Who's telling lies now?"

She'd never thought of him as a particularly forceful person. But now, since she could practically feel the heat roll off his body, she was beginning to grow uncomfortable. "I'm not lying to you. Now, you need to leave. We don't have another thing to say to each other."

"I'll leave if you come over to see me tonight."

Now he was bribing her. Or was it blackmail? "I'm not going over to your house." She couldn't think of anything worse.

"We need to speak together. Privately. I have things I want to tell you."

There was no way she was going to go anywhere alone with him. What she wanted was to put whatever had been between them to rest and never think about it again.

Considering hashing it out right then and there, she looked around. Hoping to see no one.

But two ladies were standing mere feet away. By the way they were watching her and David with alarmed expressions, it was obvious that they had been listening to every word exchanged.

And Lark?

Lark was staring hard at E.A. She didn't look pleased. In fact, she looked like she thought E.A. had invited David into the shop.

E.A. lowered her voice. "You are causing a scene. Leave right now."

David didn't move an inch. "If you want me to leave, then tell me when we can talk."

"David, honestly." When he simply stood there, panic set in. She had to do something to get him to leave.

Gritting her teeth, she made herself say the words. "Come

over tonight. We'll sit on the front porch and you can say whatever it is you want to say."

"You think I'm going to go anywhere near your porch?" he hissed. "After you and Will Kurtz were practically making love on that swing?"

"Oh. My. Word. You know nothing was going on that was even close to that. Will kissed me. I kissed him back. End of story."

"I saw where he put his hands on you when he kissed you the second time."

He'd been watching. David had been watching her and Will kiss on her front porch.

"You were spying on me?"

"I was *watching* you. There's a difference."

The eavesdropping women nearby gasped.

And she was sure she was turning beet red. "Get out now."

"Elizabeth Anne, please come up front," Lark called out. Oh, she sounded mad.

"David, stay if you want, but I have to get to work."

She turned abruptly and rushed through the aisle, hating that she was going to have to apologize to Lark for something that wasn't her fault.

"Lark, listen, I'm sorry about that."

Lark's expression was frigid. "Get him out of here or you will be forced to leave with him."

"I've been trying. He's being difficult."

Lark sighed. "You," she called out loud enough for the whole store to hear. "You, you young man in the back. If you are here to shop, then let me know if you need help. However, if you are only here to give my employee a hard time, I suggest you do that elsewhere."

At any other time, E.A. would have resented being called Lark's "employee," but she was certainly grateful at that minute. Feeling like she wasn't fighting with David alone anymore, she stood still, anxious to see what he would do next.

David opened his mouth as if to say something, then closed it abruptly and walked out the door.

Everyone in the shop watched as he walked down the sidewalk. Elizabeth Anne breathed a sigh of relief.

"Oh, my," one of the customers said. "He was surely in a mood." Looking at E.A., she asked, "What happened?"

This was getting worse and worse. "We broke up."

"I don't think he's happy about that, dear," an elderly lady said.

That was an understatement. "I don't think so, either."

Lark cleared her throat. "E.A., may I speak with you, please?"

"Yes, of course." After giving the kind lady an apologetic look, she crossed the shop. By now, she knew Lark well enough to not expect any expressions of sympathy. All she was hoping for was not to get fired.

The minute she approached the counter, she started talking fast. Maybe if the Lord helped her a bit she could calm Lark down enough so she wouldn't embarrass her in front of the whole store.

That would be a blessing.

"Lark, I'm so sorry," she blurted in a rush. "I promise, I didn't know David was coming over here."

"I should hope not." Lark sniffed. "He was really unpleasant, E.A."

"I agree." She paused, unsure of what to say next. Was Lark expecting her to apologize for him? That would feel kind of strange. "I don't know what he was thinking," she said. It wasn't a very good response, but it was the best she had.

Lark, all sleek blond hair braided neatly into a crown on the back of her head, perfect skin and cool disposition, frowned. "I don't think you'll ever need to know," she replied. "Are you going to get back together with him?"

"*Nee.*"

"*Gut.* You deserve better."

"I'm surprised to hear you say that."

"Well, it's not a surprise to me. I don't like men like that. He needs to respect you. And to respect my shop. He can't just go barging in here and disturbing my employees."

"Thank you for speaking up for me."

Lark clasped her hand in her usual brisk way . . . though E.A. was starting to realize that her usual brusque manner was simply her way. "No thanks are needed. What he was doing wasn't right."

"No, of course not." Okay, so it wasn't like Lark had just become her best friend or anything, but things had changed between them.

Or maybe it was Elizabeth Anne's attitude about Lark that had changed. Instead of seeing Lark as a rather self-centered woman, she realized that Lark was a woman who worked hard to create a successful business and didn't appreciate anyone messing with it.

Still feeling unsettled by everything that had just happened, E.A. gestured vaguely to the pair of women who'd been standing nearby. "I'm going to see if those ladies need any help."

"*Danke,*" Lark said in her crisp manner before turning away.

E.A. fought a smile as she walked back across the shop's floor. No, despite the moment they'd shared, Lark hadn't suddenly turned into a sweet and warm woman.

But, surprisingly, E.A. was okay with that. She was glad that something at the moment was exactly like she'd always known it to be.

TWELVE

"So that is more or less how seven out of the eight of us ended up wandering around the empty halls of the high school when we weren't supposed to."

"*W*ill, where are you?" Jake, Will's younger brother, called out from the downstairs landing.

Will was in his bedroom. When his brother called his name again, Will put down the book he was pretending to read. "I'm in my room," he yelled.

"Come on down and talk to me!"

"*Nee*." Knowing Jake, he wanted something, but right at that moment, Will felt like he had nothing more to give.

"Come on! I know you ain't doing nothing but sitting and stewing."

"Boys, stop yelling at each other across the *haus*."

"Sorry, Mamm," Jake yelled, then pounded up the stairs.

Hearing his brother's footsteps in the hall, Will put down

his book and went to stand by the pile of laundry on his bed. At the very least, he could pretend he'd been busy putting away his undershirts.

Jake opened his door without knocking. "Here you are."

"I've been here this whole time, which you knew. What's going on? What do you need?"

"Need?" Jake ran a hand through his hair. "Oh . . . nothing much. I was just wondering where you were at."

"Uh-huh." Will walked over to his dresser and started putting the shirts in the top drawer. While he and their sister, Nan, had always done their best to not make waves, Jake lived for those moments. He was as restless as a puppy who'd been stuck in a kennel all day, constantly ready to run out and do something exciting.

Jake had also been blessed with chestnut-colored hair, hazel eyes, and was built like a linebacker on a football team. It had been a running joke among their friends and family that Jake had been found on the doorstep. Actually, Will and Nan used to tease him that they remembered his arrival in a wicker basket until their parents put a stop to it.

But no matter how different he might have looked on the outside, he was the same as the rest of them. He liked home and stability and was fiercely loyal to their family. But that said, he wasn't the type of man to go running in search of Will for no reason.

"Want to tell me now what's on your mind?"

"All right. Fine." Jake plopped down on Will's bed, upsetting the pile of laundry. "I need to find a way to tell Mamm and Daed that I want to go to Pinecraft next month."

"Good luck with that." Pinecraft was in Sarasota, Florida.

He'd read once in a newspaper that *Englischers* called it the Amish Las Vegas, as in whatever happened there, stayed there. Will never cared much for that description. Though he'd never gone, a lot of his friends had, and the stories they'd told about their visit hadn't sounded very risqué or secretive. All they'd ever talked about was playing volleyball on the beach.

But all that aside, he now completely understood his younger brother's worry. His parents weren't fans of Pinecraft, or of their children going anywhere they didn't approve.

Which meant Jake wanting to go there wasn't going to be considered a good idea. Not at all.

After shifting a pile of socks, Will sat down beside Jake on the bed.

"You know how that idea will go over," Will said.

"Like a lead balloon." Jake slumped.

"Yep. So, what are you going to do when they say no?"

"I'm going to remind them that I'm eighteen." Jake's voice sounded confident. But the rest of him? Well, Jake looked just like the overgrown kid he was.

"Hmm."

"That's it?"

"Not much to say."

His brother practically rolled his eyes. "Did you swallow your tongue? Because you *always* have something to say."

Will was trying real hard to listen, which meant he wasn't exactly thrilled that his efforts to do that were being made fun of. "You know what's going to happen, Jake. The moment you say the *word* 'Pinecraft' Mamm and Daed are going to start listing all the reasons why being there is as dangerous as heading to the Amazon jungle."

"When they do that, I'm going to say that they're being old-fashioned and close-minded."

Ouch. If Jake said such things he'd better find a new address. Will changed tactics. "Who's going, anyway?"

For the first time since entering the room, Jake looked tentative. "Aaron, Evan, J.P., Lilly, and a couple of other people." His chin lifted. "There are a lot of us going."

"Lilly, huh?" Lilly was his brother's longtime girlfriend. Though Jake claimed they weren't at the stage where things were "official"—meaning that he wasn't courting on Lilly's front porch or anything—everyone in the family knew that it was just a matter of time before that was the case. "Her parents are letting her go with you?"

"*Jah*."

"Really? I thought they kept a close eye on her."

"They do. But they trust her." When Will raised his eyebrows, Jake sighed. "All right, fine. She hasn't told them that I'm going."

"You are going to be in so much trouble if they find out you encouraged Lilly to lie."

"She's eighteen, too."

"And your point is?"

"Fine. You're right, but I still want to go. And it isn't like we're going to share a room or anything. I'm pretty sure Lilly's sister Rachel is going."

"If you want this to work out, you're going to have to be up front with everyone: Mamm and Daed and Lilly's parents."

"If they know the truth, they aren't going to let us go."

"If they all find out you hid the truth, no one is going to let you two keep seeing each other."

Jake stared at him for a long minute, then fell back on Will's bed.

"Hey, you're wrinkling my pants."

"They're fine." He closed his eyes. "See, that's why I needed to talk to you. If I tell Mamm and Daed the truth they're going to accuse me of wanting to do all kinds of crazy and dangerous things with her."

Will smiled. Jake certainly had a way with words. "Trust me, *broodah*. They're not going to be worrying about you doing crazy or dangerous things."

"You don't think so?"

"Nope. Only that you two are going to be having sex."

His eyes popped open. "I can't believe you said that."

"I can't believe you didn't, Mr. *I'm Eighteen*." Will lowered his voice. "I hate to sound like our parents, but I'd be surprised if they didn't worry about that."

"I respect Lilly."

"Come now. You know what happened with Kyle Lambright. He and Gabby rushed things and now they're married with a baby on the way. Things can happen in an instant."

His brother's cheeks were flushed with embarrassment as he rolled off the bed and started pacing. "I don't want to go to Florida to have sex, Will. If that was all I wanted, Lilly and I could be doing that around here."

Will grinned. "There you go."

Jake stopped and stared. "There I go what?"

"When Mamm and Daed start saying things like that, that's what you need to do. Tell them what you just told me."

His brother sat up a little straighter. "I will. *Danke*."

"You're welcome. Now get off my laundry. I need to put it away and take a shower."

"Why? What are you doing tonight?"

"Going over to see E.A."

"So you really are courting her." Jake waggled his eyebrows, which was truly a bit too much, in Will's estimation.

"We're just friends. Don't make it into something it ain't."

"Uh-huh. And I'm 'just' friends with Lilly. I'm not that naive."

"What is there to be naive about?"

"I've heard about you kissing her on her front porch."

"Who told you about that?"

"E.A.'s sister told J.P.'s sister, who told Lilly, who told me."

"Sounds like you all need to go to Pinecraft just so you won't be sitting around gossiping about me."

Jake grinned as he stood up. "That's another good reason! I wonder if Mamm and Daed will let me go if I tell them that one."

"Don't you dare start talking to them about E.A. and me . . . They'll never let it go."

"*Jah*, that is true," Jake said over his shoulder as he walked to the door. "But if they don't, then that means they won't be as focused on me being in Pinecraft."

As his brother's parting words echoed in his ears, Will gaped at the open door. Somehow, his brother had just neatly turned the tables. Now he was acting like the self-assured and older brother.

Will, on the other hand, was starting to feel like he was now the foolish teenager, anxious to prove himself but too embarrassed to be honest about his feelings.

He hoped that wasn't the case.

What if he was messing everything up with him and E.A.

simply because he wasn't ready to admit what was actually happening between them?

That they'd actually become a couple, and maybe had been for quite some time.

And he'd simply been too blind to see it.

THIRTEEN

> "For those of you who don't know the Eight real well, I think it might be helpful to learn that none of us were unfamiliar with English schools. That said, we did get terribly lost."

$\mathcal{A}$s they got cups of coffee together after church at McDonald's, one of the few places in the area that was open on Sundays, Marta's good friend Elaine asked, "What are you working on in your sewing class, Marta?"

Though their restaurant of choice wasn't too fancy, that was okay. Coffee with Elaine was one of Marta's favorite parts of the week. Not only did she love going to church on Sundays, but she also enjoyed the chance to visit with Elaine without Alan nearby. Alan always chatted with two of the men from work after services. He liked using the time to strengthen his relationships with the men at work and always, *always* told Marta never to bother him when he was with them.

Other times, Alan got suspicious when Marta spent time with Elaine and made her tell him exactly what they'd talked about.

After adding a spoonful of sugar to her own cup, Marta shrugged. She loved her old friend but knew better than to reveal anything too personal. Elaine told her husband everything—and he, from time to time, shared whatever he learned with Alan.

"My sewing class has been going great. I'm not working on anything too exciting, just a pillowcase right now," Marta lied. In fact, her backpack was coming along nicely. But she was afraid to let anyone besides Elizabeth Anne know she was making it. She had too much depending on its secrecy.

As she hoped, Elaine wasn't too impressed. "A pillowcase doesn't sound very exciting."

"I suppose it's not."

"When do you get to start making something more interesting, like some clothes?"

She chuckled. Now, at least, she could be honest. "Not for a while, I fear. I'm still trying to get the hang of sewing straight seams."

"Boy, sewing sounds harder than I thought."

"Believe me, it is. But I am enjoying it." They walked over to a small sitting area. After exchanging pleasantries with several other women, they sat down in a pair of chairs. "I never thought I'd take up sewing at thirty, but I love learning something new."

"I should take up a new hobby, too. Do you think I'd like to learn to sew?"

Marta looked over Elaine's designer outfit. She had a feeling that the bright polka-dotted skirt alone cost more than Marta's whole outfit. "I think you should stick to shopping."

Looking down at her outfit and pocketbook, Elaine smiled. "I think you're right. I have a lot of fun buying clothes. I don't think I'd feel the same way about a bolt of fabric."

"You might appreciate a shopping trip to Nordstrom in Columbus a lot more than creating a well-finished seam at Sew and Tell."

Elaine grinned, though her smile faltered when she scanned Marta's simple outfit. "You know what? We ought to go shopping together one day soon and get you a couple of new things."

Looking down at her simple white blouse and black slacks, Marta frowned. "Why? Did I spill something on my shirt?" She hoped not. Alan would be so embarrassed.

Elaine quickly backpedaled. "No, not at all. It's just that you aren't dressed for the weather. It's going to be near a hundred degrees out today and you've got on long sleeves and slacks." She smiled encouragingly. "We could find you some pretty sleeveless blouses in bright colors. They'd be far cooler and add some color to your cheeks."

Yes, they would be far cooler. But that wasn't going to work for her. She needed sleeves to cover up her many bruises.

"I'm not hot," she lied. "The blouse is loose and cool."

"The slacks seem loose, too. Have you lost weight?"

"Maybe. I'm not sure." Again, that was another lie. She knew she'd lost weight, but that wasn't a surprise. Now that she was actually thinking about leaving, she was a nervous wreck.

Elaine smiled again, but this time the warmth didn't reach her eyes. Concern was etched there instead. After glancing around to see who was in hearing distance, she leaned close. "Marta, we've been friends for quite a while now."

"Years and years." Even though Marta and Alan had only moved to Walnut Creek recently, she and Elaine had grown up

together near Wooster. It had been a blessing when Elaine's husband had become one of Alan's clients. "Sometimes it's hard to
believe that we used to be little girls living next to each other on
our farms."

"I think a long friendship like ours means we can be completely honest with each other, right?" Elaine asked.

Marta nodded hesitantly. They'd both been children of modest farmers. They'd grown up living simply, both of them being
first-generation English girls, since their parents left the Amish
in their twenties.

They'd had so many things in common back then. Their
relatively old-fashioned names, the parents who spoke as much
Pennsylvania Dutch as English. They'd both felt slightly left out
when their classmates talked about computer games and television shows and bands they liked.

Then, right as they graduated high school, everything between them changed. Elaine had gotten a full scholarship to
Wooster and went to study hospitality and restaurant manage-
ment while Marta had ended up doing research for a number of
clients.

Two years later, Elaine had started dating Barrett right around
the same time Marta had gotten engaged to Alan.

Months later, Barrett had proposed to Elaine. All their friends
had teased them about being such good friends that they had gotten engaged at the same time. However, that was where their sim-
ilarities ended. Marta had loved Alan but was slowly becoming
aware of some of his idiosyncrasies and controlling nature. She'd
spent many restless nights wondering if she was making a mistake.

Elaine, on the other hand, had been head over heels for her
man—and bubbly about their plans together.

They'd been each other's maids of honor . . . and then had drifted further apart.

They'd both given the praise to the Lord that Barrett's work had brought them to Walnut Creek and he was one of Alan's clients—and that they belonged to the same church.

So, though there were many reasons for Marta to trust Elaine completely, Marta knew better than to trust anyone with the truth about her life.

But that didn't mean she wasn't good at pretending that she was content. Leaning back in her chair, Marta said, "Of course we can be honest with each other. Is something the matter?"

"Not with me, Marta." Her eyes darted across the room.

Marta knew Elaine was gazing at Alan. And though her back was to him, she could practically feel his irritation tingle at the back of her spine.

She needed to stop this immediately. If Alan thought she was talking about him, thought she was sharing any secrets about what really went on in their house, things might get so bad she would never be able to leave again.

She sat up straighter. "I'm sure I don't know what you're talking about."

Elaine didn't crack a smile. Lowering her voice, she said, "I think you know *exactly* what I'm talking about."

"Even if I did—which I don't—this isn't the time or the place to discuss it."

"There is no other time. You never want to meet for lunch. You don't even want to drive over to my house anymore." Elaine leaned closer. "Come on, Marta. You know I'm worried about you."

If Alan hadn't noticed them chatting seriously before, he

surely did by now. Marta stood up and pushed away every bit of softness in her voice. "I'm worried about you, too. I thought we were friends."

"We are, Marta." Standing up as well, Elaine pressed her hand on Marta's forearm, right where a particularly bad bruise lay under her shirt's fabric.

Marta tried hard to not flinch but failed.

Elaine noticed. Immediately, she lifted her hand. "We are good enough friends to share everything," she said, her voice rising. "You know we are."

A group of women standing a few feet away glanced at them curiously.

This was horrible. They were causing a scene. This conversation had to end now. Marta had too much to lose. Stepping back, she smiled grimly, hoping that she didn't look as awkward as she felt. "*Nee*, Elaine," she murmured in Deutch. "We *canna* talk about this."

"We can. But if not to me, then talk to someone. Please, Marta."

"Believe me when I tell you that this is something I can never talk about." Marta hardened her voice. "Not ever."

"But—"

"If you want to stay friends, you have to drop this. And promise never to bring it up again."

"I think you're making the wrong choice," Elaine said. "I think you know it, too."

"*Nee*—"

"What wrong choice are you making, darling?" Alan asked right behind her shoulder.

His voice was warm and slick. Stuffing a fisted hand in the

pocket of her slacks, Marta rolled her eyes. "Elaine was just telling me that I shouldn't be buying steaks from the grocery store," she improvised quickly.

His eyes narrowed. "That's what you were discussing? Where you shop for beef?"

"I know. It's silly, but that's what happens when two farm girls get together," she said quickly. She could practically feel Elaine's look of disapproval resting on her.

Desperate, Marta lifted her eyes and met Elaine's gaze.

Don't say a word, she said with a look. *Please don't.*

Elaine's expression pinched. But after a second, she chuckled. "Yep, that's exactly what happens," she replied. "I was just telling Marta that Barrett and I have been getting all our meat from the butcher in Berlin. It costs more, for sure, but the beef is better and without any harmful additives."

Alan narrowed his eyes before shrugging. "We'll have to give that butcher a try, won't we, Marta?"

"Of course, Alan. Whatever you want."

He smiled at her, but his eyes were still cool and calculating. "Well, I don't want to leave, but I think we'd better." He slid a hand down Marta's arm and then squeezed where her bruises were the worst. "Don't you think it's time, dear?"

"Of course," she said through gritted teeth. "But I need you to release me, Alan. My pocketbook is on the chair."

He lifted his hand and stepped away.

They both knew that his job had been done. He'd reminded her again of his power, though it hadn't been necessary. She never forgot just how much of a hold he had on her—physical or not.

After getting her purse, Marta walked back to his side. "I'm ready now," she said, smiling up into his face.

When he started walking, she stayed by his side, doing her best to ignore Elaine's troubled expression and some of the other women's questioning looks. Instead, she did what she always did: thought about something better. This time, she allowed her mind to concentrate on the little backpack she was almost done making.

And the back door to the shop that she'd discovered during the last class. It led to an alley. Maybe one day soon she would actually get up the nerve to trust someone to help her. If so, he or she could be waiting for her in the alley, and she'd be able to drive away.

Someplace so far away, Alan wouldn't be able to find her.

FOURTEEN

"That's how we ended up in a third-floor science lab. Unfortunately, it didn't explain why Katie decided to open up the cage of mice."

THURSDAY

"*There* you go," E.A. murmured encouragingly to Marta, though she wasn't sure if her student heard her or not. "You're doing just fine."

"I don't know about that. I seem to be all thumbs today," Marta said.

It was true. Marta's hands were shaking as she threaded gold cord through the opening of the backpack. Shaking more than usual. Threading cord could be an exasperating chore for certain. But her student seemed to be upset about something more than the task at hand.

When it looked as if she were about to dissolve into tears, E.A. intervened. "Marta, perhaps you should take a break, *jah?*"

"No. I need to get this done."

"Yes, but we're not on a time limit, right?" When Marta didn't so much as crack a smile, E.A. lightly touched her hand. "Forgive me, but I think it's obvious that you aren't yourself today. What is wrong?"

Her student jumped at her touch. "Nothing." Looking suddenly fearful, Marta glanced at the door. "Why do you ask?"

If Marta had been a good friend, especially one of the Eight, E.A. would have teased her a little bit. Honestly, Marta was looking so jumpy, she could have named a dozen different clues to give credence to her concern.

But she wasn't a good friend and she also seemed so skittish that E.A. was beginning to fear that she would inadvertently upset her so much that she would burst into tears.

"You seem worried today." Though she couldn't imagine why a simple sewing project would cause Marta to get so upset, she said, "The thing about sewing is that any mistake can be easily fixed. It might take time to pull stitches out, there might even be some snags or imperfections in the fabric . . . but nothing can't be undone. Besides cutting the fabric, of course." She smiled encouragingly.

Marta released her death grip on the cloth at last. Looking ashamed, she murmured, "Elizabeth Anne, I really am sorry. I guess I have been jumpy today."

"You certainly have. Almost as jumpy as a bullfrog," E.A. teased.

But instead of smiling at E.A.'s joke, Marta looked even more upset. "I . . . I well, I have something on my mind."

"Do you want to end early?" They only had another twenty minutes of their class, after all.

"No. I need to finish this."

She'd said *need* instead of *want*. E.A. felt a new burst of worry skitter up her spine. Something was really wrong. Both of Marta's hands were gripping the edges of the pack so tightly that E.A. knew she was going to have to iron the fabric before they did the next step.

"Let me show you something." She carefully took the backpack from Marta's hands and placed it flat on the countertop. "Do you see how easy it is to find the safety pin at the end of the cord?" When the other woman nodded, E.A. murmured, "I've found that if you simply move the pin with the edge of your finger in a slow, steady motion, like so, it moves rather easily." She demonstrated.

Marta was watching so intently, one would think her life depended on it. "I was fighting the fabric, wasn't I?"

"'Fighting' seems a little strong. I think you were simply eager to get it finished."

Some of the worry lines that had been present during the entire class faded from Marta's face. "Yes. I guess I was."

Hoping to lighten the tension that now seemed to be weighing the air between them, E.A. said, "I think you need to tell me what you're going to use this backpack for. Do you have a special vacation planned?"

"No," Marta blurted. "I mean, no, not really."

"Just a weekend getaway?" She knew she was grasping at straws, but she was determined to help Marta calm down. "Do you and your husband like to hike?"

"No. It's nothing like that."

"I see." E.A. sighed.

After glancing at the front door of the shop one more time, Marta pressed a hand to her chest. "Goodness. I guess I'm not making a lot of sense, am I?"

"No, I was overstepping. Your reasons for your projects are your own. You don't have to share."

"It's not that I don't want to share, it's just that I don't think I should."

What in the world? It was only a backpack. "I understand," E.A. said easily, not actually understanding at all. Just then, the safety pin popped out the other side. "There we go! Unfasten the pin and then we'll stitch the two ends together. And then it will be time to stop for the day."

Marta nodded as she followed directions. "Hey, uh, E.A.?"

"Yes?"

"May I ask you for a favor?"

"You may ask me anything you want."

"Sometimes my husband likes to check up on me."

"Check up? Do you mean stop by?"

"Yes. Um, if he does stop by when I'm not here, would you please not tell him about this backpack?"

E.A. noticed that every muscle in Marta's body was so stiff she looked like she was about to shatter. "I'll do whatever you'd like me to do," she said slowly. "Of course I will."

Marta exhaled. "Thank you."

"But what do you want me to say?"

"Anything but the truth."

E.A. wasn't sure she had heard correctly. "Pardon me?"

Reaching out, Marta grasped her hand so tightly that E.A. was sure she was going to have a bruise. "Tell Alan . . . tell him that I'm making an apron and that . . ." She paused. "And that you took it home to put on an appliqué patch or something and that is why he can't see it."

The sense of foreboding that had been present during their

last two classes increased. E.A. wasn't comfortable with being told to lie. It didn't make sense.

"Do you really think that is necessary?" she asked hesitantly. "I mean, surely your husband won't care what you make here, Marta."

"He's going to care, E.A. He cares about everything I do." Marta shuddered. "I'm sorry. I know this puts you in a terrible position, but it would mean a lot to me if you could keep my secret."

Marta looked like she was about to burst into tears or run out of the back of the shop. Now all E.A. wanted to do was calm the woman down and finish the class. "Like I said before, I'll help you in any way I can."

Marta relaxed. "Thank you so much." She smoothed the partially made backpack on the counter. "You don't know how much you are helping me. I really do appreciate it."

"Marta, do you need help with anything else?" E.A. asked, not really sure why she was asking or what she could even offer. But she felt like the Lord was guiding her words.

Standing up, Marta's expression was smooth and composed. Almost like the past forty-five minutes had never happened. "I'm sorry, I don't understand."

E.A. was fumbling now. "You know what I mean. If you are having a problem with your personal life . . ."

"I'm not. Everything is fine."

"Okay. Well, I'm glad."

Handing her an envelope, Marta said, "Thank you for the lesson. I'll see you next week." Then, before E.A. could say another word, she turned and walked away.

E.A. knew she looked as shocked as she felt. It was like the woman had just completely changed personalities. Gone were the furtive looks and the jerky movements. Instead, she strode out of the shop like she'd been merely browsing and hadn't found anything she liked.

And, to top it off, she hadn't even taken her project with her!

Feeling thoroughly irritated, E.A. carefully folded the back-pack in some white tissue paper and carried it to her tote bag in the employee workroom.

Then, realizing she was still holding the envelope Marta had handed her, she ripped it open, intending to put the cash that Marta usually paid her in her wallet.

Except there was a fifty-dollar bill inside instead of the usual thirty-five. And a small note.

Thank you for your help. I owe you.

Alarmed now, E.A. stuffed the whole thing into her purse. She wished she could tell Lark what had just happened, but she knew Lark would either tell everyone who came in about it or get mad at E.A. for accepting so much money for her services.

Instead, she vowed to talk to Will about her concerns. Hopefully he would know what to do.

Because now, she realized, she was going to be on pins and needles at work as she watched the front door.

Just waiting for Marta's husband to arrive so that she could look at him in the eye and spew lie after lie.

FIFTEEN

"Even though everyone got mad at me for opening the cages, I still don't think those twelve mice climbing off the table was my fault," Katie protested. "I had no idea they would be so anxious to leave their cage."

*B*ecause it had seemed like Elizabeth Anne's heart had been set on it, they'd gone for a walk instead of sitting on her front porch with cold glasses of lemonade.

Will had worked all day in a muggy warehouse. Then, after walking home, he'd spent an hour helping his father in the barn. By the time he'd showered and changed his clothes, he'd had to hurry over to E.A.'s house so he wouldn't be late.

When she'd suggested the walk, it had truly been the last thing on earth Will had wanted to do. But he wanted to make her happy, so he agreed.

Unfortunately, E.A. wasn't acting very happy at all. Instead of her usual chatty self, she seemed restless and distracted. She'd ignored his comments about the flowers, the pair of ducks in the pond they passed, and even how he'd gotten a pretty good cut from a piece of metal just before lunch. No, all she seemed to be interested in doing was racewalking down the road.

He was becoming sweaty. And yes, more than a little frustrated.

"My, it sure is hot out tonight," Will said. "I'm not sure where the wind is, but it feels like it took a vacation." He paused, waiting for E.A. to respond to his joke.

"Mmmm," E.A. murmured, adding a vague smile. The same vague, distracted way she'd been responding to pretty much everything he'd been saying for the last hour.

It was becoming a bit annoying. So much so, he began to wonder if she was really listening to him.

After pointing out a hawk in the field and getting only a "That's nice," he'd had enough.

He decided to give her a little test, just to see how much she was ignoring him. "E.A., you know what? I've actually been thinking about breaking into the factory and sleeping on the couch in one of the offices. Do you think I would get in trouble for that?"

"I don't know, Will."

"I guess I could always ask John B. to cover for me," he mused. "I mean, I could always say that breaking and entering was his idea. John probably wouldn't mind too much. What do you think?"

"I think that's a good idea. Maybe you should do that." She smiled tightly.

"Aha!" he said.

She stopped and stared at him. "What?"

"I caught you."

"Caught me how?"

"Caught you not paying attention to a word I said."

"Oh, Will. Of course I've been paying attention to you."

"Then tell me what I just said about the factory."

She rolled her eyes in the dim light. "That you wanted to . . ." Her voice faded. "Hey, did you just tell me that you were going to break in and blame it on John?"

"I did." He raised an eyebrow. "And you told me that I should do it."

"So that isn't true?"

"Of course it isn't. How could you have thought it was?"

She put her hands on her hips. "Will Kurtz, I don't think that's a very good joke."

"Elizabeth Anne Schmidt, I don't appreciate being made to racewalk around the backroads of Walnut Creek while being ignored."

"I wasn't ignoring you. And I wasn't walking that fast . . . was I?"

"You absolutely were." Before she could argue again, he reached for her hand. "Instead of ignoring me, why don't you tell me what's on your mind?"

Her blue eyes widened, then she exhaled. "I'm not sure if I can."

"Why not?"

"Because I think it's supposed to be a secret, but that's the problem, Will." Sounding even more worried, she added, "I'm not even sure what kind of secret I'm supposed to be keeping."

"Sounds like you've got a real puzzle, indeed."

"I do."

"You need to tell someone, E.A. Keeping it inside won't do you no good, I can promise you that."

"I know . . ."

"So, if you're going to tell someone, it might as well be me." He puffed up his chest. "I am standing right here, after all."

After walking a few more feet, she spoke again. "All right. It has to do with Marta, my sewing student."

"You've told me about her before, right?"

"*Jah.*"

"She's English, yes?"

"Yes." She looked up at him and smiled.

"So, what has happened?"

"She was acting really strange today. And then she asked me to do something that I'm not sure I'm comfortable with."

He looked at her in concern. "What did she want you to do, E.A.?"

"As far as I can tell, all her problems began when she started making a backpack."

"A backpack, you say?"

"Yes. Marta said she really wanted one. And today—well, it's not done, but it actually looks like a backpack now." She stopped and looked up at him, like that was supposed to mean something.

It did not.

"Okay . . ."

"But see, instead of being pleased about her project, Marta seemed really nervous."

This was what had gotten her so upset? An English lady and her backpack? "I think I need to sit down for this story."

Spying the remains of a stone chimney in the field, he tugged her to it. "Sit."

There were enough flat areas for both of them to perch on the stones and kick their feet out. Immediately, Will felt his body thank him for getting off of his feet.

"All right, now that we're comfortable, continue."

"Marta seemed really nervous today. She kept looking at the door like she was afraid of who was going to step through it. Then she asked me for a promise."

"What was it?"

"Oh, Will. It was the strangest thing. Marta said that sometimes her husband likes to visit places where she's been and check up on her. And then she asked me not to tell him that she's been sewing a backpack if he ever came by and spoke to me. I'm supposed to tell him that she's been making an apron."

Will didn't know why a husband would even care about such things. "But you won't have an apron, right? I mean, at least, she won't."

"You're right! She won't. I'm supposed to tell her husband that I have this made-up apron at home, putting on appliqué work."

"So she asked you to lie to her husband," he stated.

She wrinkled her nose, like saying the harsh truth pained her. "*Jah*. That's what she wants."

He didn't think anything about that sounded good. "What did you say about that?"

"What do you think? I said I would do it."

While he processed that statement, she waved a hand. "But it gets even worse, Will."

He was almost afraid to ask. "How?"

"She left the backpack and then overpaid me for today's session." She stared at him meaningfully. "I think it was a bribe."

"I don't know about that. Maybe she just made a mistake?" he asked hopefully, though he doubted it. The whole thing sounded fishy.

"I hope you're right. But I have to tell ya, Will, I have no idea what to do. I mean, it feels like I'm supposed to do something important. Like the Lord put Marta in my path in order to help her—but I'm woefully unprepared to help her in the way she needs."

Will wanted to hug her tightly almost as much as he wanted to nod in agreement. She was right. Elizabeth Anne was twenty-four, sheltered, and from a close-knit family—she had no experience dealing with such big things. This English lady was married, obviously frightened of her husband, and was spouting lies like it was her habit.

But he also knew the woman sitting next to him well enough to appreciate how much she could help others.

Feeling as if the Lord had placed him by her side this evening for a reason, he said, "At the risk of sounding trite, I think He would never give you too much to handle."

"Usually, I would feel that way, too. But I don't know, Will. At the moment, it sure feels like it's too much." She looked down at her feet. "I don't feel like I'm the right person to help her. But if I refuse, then I know I'm going to be letting her down, and that would be awful."

"What do you want to do?"

"I don't know!"

"Oh, E.A."

"That's why I'm telling you all of this. I'm afraid of what to do. I want to keep her secrets and help her in any way I can." She lowered her voice. "But I'm also afraid, Will. What if her husband shows up and I don't protect Marta enough? What if I mess up and say the wrong thing? What . . . what if he gets mad at me?"

Will could hardly bear to think about that. Though he was beginning to feel just as tense as she was, he tried to be her voice of reason. "You don't know that he'll show up. He might not."

"But what if he does?"

"Then you will do what you need to do," he said at last. "You'll help her as much as you can and decide how much you can lie."

"But what if I fail?"

Giving in to his feelings, he pulled her closer, close enough to practically set her on his lap. When she relaxed against him, resting her face in the nape of his neck, he rubbed her back.

After a few minutes, he tilted his head back so they were looking eye to eye. "You won't fail, because you're going to do your best. And that's all you can do."

"If I fail, something awful might happen to her."

"This is true. But we can't control the future, and you can't make your student happier or feel safer. All you can do is your best and to pray for help."

After studying his face for a moment, she exhaled, shuddering slightly. "Okay, then."

A lock of her auburn hair had fallen down from its pins with the action. He ran a hand along her cheek, liking how soft her skin felt. "You sure?"

"I think so. You know what's funny is that I always considered myself to be the most levelheaded of the Eight. I've always acted like I had all the answers, like I was so sure of myself. But now I realize that I was living in my own little bubble. I had all the answers because I had never been challenged before. I'd never asked too much of myself or moved out of my comfort zone. I feel like I should go to all our friends and apologize for the way I've sounded and acted over the years."

"Don't you dare. You've given all of us good advice. Said many things the rest of us wish we had. That's something to be proud about."

"You always say the right thing."

He laughed. "We know that's not true." He kissed her brow. "Now, try to relax for a minute, all right?"

She nodded, looking up at the stars. "I'm going to pretend I see God up in the stars, looking out for all of us. Protecting us." She smiled slightly. "Andy, too."

Will looked up into the sky as well. "I like imagining our Andy is up there with the Lord, keeping company with Him and reminding Him from time to time to look out for us Eight. I like that idea a lot."

E.A. closed her eyes and smiled.

And Will found himself gazing at her and deciding that she was something of a surprise. Maybe everyone was.

SIXTEEN

"The mice, obviously pleased to be set free, scattered," E.A. continued, anxious to move the story forward.

But Logan interrupted. "*Nee*, what E.A. is trying to say is that they ran in a group down the hall. And let me just say, a dozen suddenly free mice running in a pack is a fearsome sight."

"You were sure out late with Will," E.A.'s mother said when E.A. entered the house that night. It was after ten.

Elizabeth Anne was tired, ready to take a shower, and do nothing more than think about the conversation she'd just had with Will. But that wasn't going to be possible, at least not yet. Her parents expected her to chat with them for a few minutes. If she put off talking with them now, they would make sure they got some answers first thing in the morning.

Steeling herself for the conversation, she toed off her shoes and entered the den. Both of her parents were sitting on easy chairs with books in their laps. They looked anxious.

"I know it's late," she said with what she hoped was an apologetic smile. "We started walking and lost track of time. I didn't bring my cell phone so I couldn't call to let you know that we were fine."

"I figured if you were with the Kurtz boy you were fine," Daed said. "Will has always been a considerate boy."

Though she knew Will would have been amused by her father's description, E.A. relaxed. Perhaps this end-of-the-night conversation was going to go better than she'd expected. "I'm glad you weren't worried." She yawned. "I'm pretty tired, though. I'm going to go on up to bed."

Her father shook his head. "Not quite, Elizabeth." Gesturing to the couch across from them, he motioned for her to sit. "We want to talk to you about what happened while you were out."

"Oh?" Immediately thinking of Marta's husband, she sat down. "Is everything okay?"

Her parents exchanged looks.

"No one is hurt, or anything like that. But I'm not sure if everything is okay." Looking like she had just swallowed some bitter medicine, her mother sighed. "David came over."

E.A. felt like sighing, too. "What did he want?"

"To talk to us."

"About?"

"You," her father said.

After giving Daed a quelling look, Mamm said softly, "David has been worried about you, E.A." Crossing her legs, she added, "To be honest, some of the things he was saying were unsettling."

Unsettling. She gritted her teeth, already anticipating some of what he'd said. "I'm fine. There's nothing going on with me that he needs to worry about. He shouldn't have bothered you."

Her mother folded her hands on her lap. "His coming over wasn't a bother."

"But it wasn't necessary, Mamm."

"I know you two broke up, but we just assumed it was a temporary thing," her father said. "You two have been seeing each other for such a long time, we assumed that you would patch things up."

"We're not going to get back together, Daed."

Not. Ever.

"Are you sure you're thinking like yourself?" her mother asked as she leaned forward. "We thought David brought up something important."

"Which was?"

"That you might be still traumatized about poor Andy's death."

Just when she thought this conversation couldn't get worse, it had. "David brought up Andy and you listened to him?" She knew her voice had risen, but she didn't care one bit. "David never even knew Andy!"

"Now, don't get yourself all upset," Daed said. "David might have overstepped, but he made several good points."

"*Might have* overstepped?"

"All we're saying is that we know that Andy's death made you upset. You might be acting out and perhaps looking for someone to replace him."

"David came up with a convoluted story about how I am so upset that one of my best friends committed suicide so I dumped him and fell in love with Will?" E.A. stared at both of her parents. "I don't know if I'm more appalled with David for conjuring up such a horrible story or with you two for believing it."

Her mother's gaze hardened. "Daughter, based on the way you acted tonight, I can't deny that David did make a good point."

"How did I act?"

They exchanged looks yet again. "You know, staying out late, kissing in public . . ." Mamm said.

"It's ten at night. And we were kissing. Nothing more."

Her mother shrugged. "*Jah*, but still . . . it's worrisome."

"What's worrisome is that David feels comfortable coming over here to talk to you two about me when I'm not here to defend myself."

"That's why we wanted to speak to you." Daed straightened. "E.A., I think it would be best if you took a step back and spent some time reevaluating your actions."

"I don't even know what you're talking about. I spent time with a good friend, who I've known for years. And I broke up with my boyfriend, who is obviously not pleased about it. That's it. Neither should have concerned you."

"We're only trying to help you," her mother coaxed. "You know, every once in a while, we all need a helping hand. Someone who is willing to protect us from ourselves."

There was that word again. *Protect.* But this time, she didn't think they were offering protection at all. More like confinement. "I'm too old to be grounded."

"No one is talking about grounding you."

She grit her teeth. "But?"

"But we are concerned about you."

"I am grateful for your love. But I am not going to talk any more about topics that you discussed with David." Feeling even more sure of herself, she added, "I love you both and I know you love me, too. But I'm not okay with David discussing me in this room and you both siding with him. I may not do everything you wish I would do . . . but that doesn't mean I am wrong."

"David really cares about you."

"Does he? Because right now it sure seems like he cares an awful lot about himself."

"Watch your tone, E.A."

"I will. I think I'm going to be watching a lot of things from now on," she muttered as she stood up. Before they could reply, she walked upstairs, grabbed her robe and nightgown, and headed for the shower.

Turning on the faucet, she kept it far cooler than the usual temperature. She needed to cool off, she decided. In more ways than one.

The house was dark when Will entered. After grabbing a sleeve of crackers from one of the cabinets and pouring a large glass of water, he walked down the hall to his suite of rooms as quietly as possible.

He'd taken over his great-uncle's rooms about three years ago. It consisted of a bedroom, a small sitting room, and his own bathroom. About a year ago Harley had helped him add new cabinets and a better shower and replace some worn-out baseboards. Now, he reckoned it was as nice a place as he'd ever hope to have.

As he walked in, he felt guilty for wanting more than living at home. Here, he had the best of both worlds: a comfortable, private space where he could still see his family easily, enjoy his mother's cooking, and not have to pay rent.

He couldn't think of anyone who would feel ungrateful to have such a place to live.

But that, of course, was what he'd been feeling the past couple of weeks.

"You are ungrateful, Will," he muttered to himself. "You should be ashamed."

"Ashamed of what?" Nan asked from his doorway.

Will jumped at the sound of his sister's voice. "Don't do that to me no more. Knock."

Nan raised her eyebrows pointedly at Jake, who was standing next to her. "I didn't know we were supposed to knock on open doors in this house. Did you?"

"Nope. It's news to me."

Seeing the look of amusement on his brother's face, Will knew if he didn't put a stop to it, their teasing would get worse and worse.

"Is there a reason you two are standing there, or did you just stop by to give me grief?"

"Oh, I came for a reason, all right." Nan smiled as she wandered into his sitting room. "I'm here for information."

"About?" Immediately, he started thinking of the rumors that were probably swirling around him and E.A.

"About what we should do for Mamm and Daed for their anniversary."

He was so relieved, his mind went blank. "What about their anniversary? Since when do we start doing something for them?"

"Since they've been married almost thirty years. Their anniversary is in a month, Will. I think that means we're supposed to throw them a party."

Now he was embarrassed. He really should have remembered. "Sorry. You're right."

"I know we are," Jake said, doing that annoying thing he

did where it sounded like they were completing each other's sentences again. "But we don't know what to plan. Should it be a surprise party?"

Will loved his parents and he was mighty happy that they'd had such a long and successful marriage. But he sure didn't have time to start planning surprise parties.

"Maybe we should plan something simpler."

"Like what? A barbecue?" Nan asked sarcastically.

"I think that sounds great. Daed likes cheeseburgers."

She folded her arms over her chest. "*Nee*. We are not throwing our parents a cookout to celebrate their thirtieth anniversary, Will."

Jake looked smug. "Even I know we can't do that."

"If you two know everything, you shouldn't have come over to ask me."

"You have a point, but we can only do so much," Jake said. "You're the oldest."

And because he was the oldest, it was his job to help do the planning. "Fine. I'll ask around and see what I can do."

"*Gut*," Jake said as he sat down. Grinning, he said, "Now that that's taken care of, you can tell us all about your evening with E.A."

He started backing out his own door. "No way. I'm taking a shower and you two had better be gone when I get back."

Nan sighed. "Fine."

Will picked up his towel and walked to his bathroom, thinking that he needed to not only think about party planning but also about planning the rest of his life.

He felt like he was on the verge of something big—he just wasn't sure what it could be.

SEVENTEEN

"The mice raced down the hall that led toward the gym. And because we felt responsible, we ran after them."

TWO DAYS LATER

Still lingering over the last of her tasty pasta dish, Elizabeth Anne was content to simply listen to her girlfriends' comments about their meals at Rebecca's Café. Their comments were as familiar as her favorite quilt. It didn't matter where they were or what they were eating—Katie, Marie, and Kendra almost always said the same things.

"We always eat too much whenever we come here for lunch," Katie complained as she pushed her half-full plate another inch away from her place setting. "I'm stuffed."

"And after eating only half of it, too," Marie teased.

"I'm going to bring the rest home to Harley," Katie replied. "He will be happy to have such a treat."

"At least he won't be worrying about all the calories," Marie said with a frown. "I don't know why I always order Fettucine Alfredo. It's so fattening."

"Only you would complain about such a good meal," Kendra said with a satisfied look at her plate. "Rebecca's Café is wonderful. I haven't had a meal this *gut* in ages."

"You mean a meal this good that you haven't made yourself," Marie quipped. "You cook so well, you could be hired as a chef somewhere."

Kendra wrinkled her nose. "Slaving over a hot stove all day to make meals for strangers? No thank you."

"I wish I could cook half as well as you can," Katie said. "I can bake a decent orange bread, but not much else." Brightening, she said, "Hey, want to make a couple of meals for the inn from time to time?"

"You have Harley's sister Betty baking for you at the B and B. You don't need me as well," Kendra said.

Katie brightened. "This is true. Betty is a wonderful cook."

"I wish I could cook better," Marie said.

"Or at all," Kendra murmured.

Marie winced. "Poor John. Last night I tried to make meat loaf. It was just terrible. I burned it, too."

Swirling her pasta around her fork, E.A. smiled. And so it continued. Each of them able to hold a conversation about food, cooking, and their various successes and failures for hours. She wondered if their ability to play off each other was because they'd known each other for years . . . or that the Lord had simply placed them together and they were reaping His good judgment. She really wasn't sure.

Or, maybe it didn't really matter. What mattered was that she was feeling a whole lot better about everything, thanks to simply being around these women.

"E.A., eat," Katie said. "I've been watching you twirl that same pair of noodles around your fork for a full minute."

E.A. looked down. And sure enough, Katie hadn't lied. The two linguini noodles that had once been coated with cheese and cream now looked like bare limp things, barely clinging to her fork. Decidedly unappetizing.

She put her fork down. "Sorry. I lost my train of thought. I don't know why."

Marie winked at the others. "I do."

Alarmed by that sly smile, E.A. said, "I promise, my mind just went walking. That's all."

"I *canna* help but think that Marie is right. You have things on your mind other than this meal." Smiling broadly, Katie leaned forward. "Why don't you tell us how things are going with Will?"

Will, again. It seemed no one wanted to talk about anything else but him. "Things with us? Well, they're strange, if you want to know the truth."

Marie frowned. "Really? But Will is so easy to get along with."

"He is, but things are different now." E.A. hesitated for a moment, then continued. After all, it wasn't like anything the two of them were doing was a secret.

"I don't know how to act around Will any longer, especially now that my parents have decided to get involved."

"Uh-oh. How did that happen?" Kendra asked.

"David decided to pay them a visit and air his grievances about me." Still irritated, she added, "And apparently . . . he did so loudly and in detail."

"Ouch," Katie said.

"I hope they showed him to the door," Marie commented.

"My mother would have been horrified if an old boyfriend came over to talk about me."

"Your mother would have given David a piece of her mind, for sure. My parents? Well, they're currently mourning the fact that their dream of being related to their best friends through marriage is over."

Kendra coughed. "I'm sorry, but that sounds creepy."

E.A. chuckled. "I think it sounds creepy, too. They have their own life to manage. And Annie's life. They don't need to start telling me who to date, and they really don't need to be listening to David and taking his side."

While the server picked up their dishes and passed out dessert menus, Marie studied E.A. "So what are you going to do?"

"I don't know. There's nothing I can do. Not really, anyway. He's my neighbor, it's not like I can do anything to deliberately make things more awkward between us." Noticing the other girls exchange glances, E.A. sat up straighter. "What? You can't think I'm wrong."

"Not exactly," Kendra said. "But I think I should point out the obvious."

"Which is?"

"That David isn't thinking about keeping the peace between your parents. He's doing whatever he wants."

"And getting heard." Katie nodded.

"It does seem like he has the advantage," Marie murmured.

He did. That knowledge made her uncomfortable, but what could she do? "Until everything with Will gets straightened out, I'm not inclined to do much. I'd rather wait it out."

Katie looked sympathetic. "I'd do the same thing. I mean, I actually did that when I was worried about Harley's ex-girlfriend.

It's easy to 'say' one is going to do something big and dramatic in retaliation, but it's a whole other thing to act on it."

"Thank you," E.A. said with a grateful smile. Picking up the dessert menu, she said, "Is anyone going to get pie? I could split a piece if anyone wants to . . ."

"Sorry. I want my own slice of chocolate mousse," Marie said.

"And I was going to get cherry, which I know isn't your favorite," Katie said.

"Kendra, what about you?" E.A. asked. Seeing that Kendra was frowning at something across the restaurant, she put her menu down. "Kendra, what is wrong?"

"Hmm?" When she realized that they were all staring at her, Kendra shook her head. "Sorry. I just, um, well, I just saw this couple walk in."

"What about them?" Katie asked, turning to look where Kendra had been staring. "Which ones?"

"It's an English couple." Looking increasingly troubled, Kendra said, "The husband just grabbed his wife's arm in a way that you could tell pained her but she didn't say a word. Every once in a while I see something like that and it brings me back to things I try to forget."

Now all of them were trying to look over at the couple that Kendra had pointed out.

"I see what you mean Kendra," Marie said. "They don't look very happy together at all."

E.A. was at a disadvantage. She couldn't really see who they were talking about. Though she knew they were all being rude, she knew their minds were probably more on Kendra than on the pair of strangers. "I still can't find them."

"It's the brown-haired lady with the balding husband. She's

in a pale violet sweater," Marie said. "A strange choice, given that it's over ninety degrees out."

"She's likely covering up her arms," Kendra murmured.

"I wish I wasn't sitting right here," E.A. said.

"Oh, just stand up like you're getting something from me," Katie said.

E.A. stood up, pretended to reach across the table—which probably looked ridiculous and didn't fool anyone—when she saw a very familiar face looking back at her.

"Oh, *nee*," she whispered as she sat back down quickly.

"What?"

Feeling shaken, both by the sight of Marta and the fact she'd been staring at her in fright, E.A. felt her cheeks flush. "I know that woman. She's been taking sewing lessons from me."

Katie raised her eyebrows. "Goodness. Does she always look that worried when she's with you?"

"No. Not usually."

"She's afraid of her husband," Kendra said. "I know it."

E.A. was fairly sure Kendra wasn't wrong. But saying that felt like she was betraying Marta. She nibbled on her bottom lip.

"Girls, did you decide on dessert?" their server asked.

"We did," Marie said. "And I'll go first." As she'd said, she ordered the chocolate mousse pie. Next, Katie ordered cherry.

"E.A., did you want to split a piece?" Kendra asked.

"*Nee*. I think I need a whole slice of coconut cream pie to myself."

The server chuckled. "I guess you'll have to have your own then, miss. What will you have?"

"I'll have date nut pudding," Kendra said with a smile. "With fresh cream, please."

"Ugh. I should have known you would want that," Marie said. "You order it every time, Kendra."

"I can't help it. I love it," she said with a grin. "Besides, we have much to celebrate, right?" She paused then added, "We have *gut* friends and *gut* lives. Those are two blessings I never take for granted."

"Amen to that," Katie said.

"Yes. Amen," E.A. murmured. They were blessed, indeed.

EIGHTEEN

"We felt responsible because we actually were responsible," Harley said. Looking over at his wife, he winked. "I mean, one of us was."

*M*arta couldn't believe that Elizabeth Anne was sitting just a few tables away. When she saw E.A stand up and look directly at her and Alan, her heart had almost stopped. She'd been so afraid the girl was about to come over and say hello.

Alan wouldn't want for them to be disturbed at all, especially not by someone he didn't know. Now, he wouldn't cause a scene if E.A. came over. Marta knew he would smile at her and act all charming and pleased that his wife had a friend that he didn't know about.

But the moment they were alone, he would act far differently. Already feeling the ache in her arm, she knew that she was going to have a set of dark fresh bruises there. Her only goal was to make it through the rest of the day without another incident.

"Do you know what you would like?" their server asked.

Marta waited for Alan to answer. He'd been looking at his phone since the minute they sat down.

"Do you know, Marta?" he asked.

"Yes. Are you ready to order?"

"I will be." He smiled at her in a warm way. "You go first, dear."

The server smiled at Marta. "What will you have?"

"A salad, please, with Italian dressing on the side."

"And?"

"Nothing else for now, thank you."

"You sure?"

"I'm saving room for dessert." She smiled. While she never could eat much in front of her husband, she hadn't lied about that: savoring a piece of pie this afternoon would be wonderful.

Alan snapped his menu closed and handed it to their server. "I'll have the pot roast with vegetables and mashed potatoes. Bring rolls out, too."

"Yes, sir."

He nodded in a distracted way before looking back at his phone again.

She breathed a sigh of relief. If she was lucky, he would be so fixated on his email that he would ignore her for the rest of the meal. Going out to lunch wasn't anything they ever did. But when his boss asked him yesterday how his wife had liked this restaurant, Alan had felt cornered. He'd informed her at breakfast that she was to meet him here for lunch.

Though it was going to be a fairly long walk to it, she'd nodded. After all, it wasn't like she had a choice.

As the minutes passed, Marta sat still with her hands neatly folded on her lap and watched E.A. with all her girlfriends while she waited for her food. She couldn't help but smile when she saw all four of them had ordered dessert, each loaded with whipped toppings or ice cream. They were so cute about it, too.

"What are you smiling at?"

"Oh, nothing important. I just was watching some college-aged girls eat their dessert."

He looked over at the girls then grunted. "They sure are laughing a lot."

"Yes."

Looking back at his phone's screen again, he blurted, "I have a meeting tonight. I won't be home until late."

Just as it did every time she discovered she was going to get a reprieve, her body relaxed. Right on its heels came the quiet yet concerned look she'd perfected three or four years ago. "All right, Alan," she said calmly. "Thank you for letting me know."

He nodded, obviously not giving a thought that she could have said anything otherwise or complained.

"Here you two go," the server said with a bright smile, finally returning with their food. As she put their plates down in front of them, she looked from Marta to her husband. "Do you need anything else?"

"No," Alan said.

After giving an apologetic look at Marta, their server moved on.

Marta waited for Alan to start, then picked at her salad. While Alan went back to his phone, she occupied herself with watching the girls and the server and even the elderly couple sitting in the back of the dining room sharing an appetizer plate.

One day that would be her. One day she was going to be

doing what she wanted to be doing, talking whenever she felt like it, simply enjoying life.

"I'm done," Alan said as he stood up. Tossing a pair of twenties on the table, he said, "That should be enough for our meals and your dessert."

"Yes. Thank you."

"You are welcome." He pressed a palm down firmly on her shoulder until she lifted her head and looked at him directly in the eye. "Be good."

She smiled up at him, just like he liked for her to look at him when they were in public. "Of course, Alan."

He smiled back, then walked out the front door. The moment he stepped outside, she saw him put the phone to his ear and start talking.

As she watched him stride toward their car, she noticed that he was walking faster and his expression seemed lighter. She wondered who he was talking to.

"Are you done, too, ma'am? Would you like the check?"

Realizing the server was eyeing the money, Marta picked it up. Once again, Alan had given her too much money. "Not yet. I'll have a slice of coconut cream pie and a cup of coffee, please."

"Yes, ma'am."

Marta crossed her legs and carefully folded the cash into her pocketbook. Already doing the math, she figured she would have three or four dollars left over after she paid for the meals and gave the server a tip. It wasn't much, but she would be very pleased to add it to her stash.

Feeling optimistic yet again, she looked back at Elizabeth Anne and her girlfriends. They were now sipping coffee and talking nonstop. Giggling.

Enjoying their meal and their time together.

Yes, one day, she would be like that, too. She would have girlfriends again and be able to go out to lunch and simply enjoy it. Maybe even in another week or two. She almost had enough. Almost.

Until then? She would bide her time.

NINETEEN

"It was dark inside the gym, but there were lots of people congregating around the open doors. I'm not sure why those mice kept going, but they ran straight toward the open door. When the girls started screaming, it caused quite a commotion."

SATURDAY

The problem with only being a kind of–sort of couple was that it put one in all kinds of uncomfortable situations, E.A. decided.

Even though things between Will and E.A. had become far less pretend and far more real, neither had said anything about making their situation permanent. And when it was just the two of them alone together, E.A. was okay with that. She didn't need Will to make any professions of love or hint at marriage. Things were still too new for that stage.

But when they got around other people, their situation felt more precarious. It was like everyone was wanting them to put a label on their relationship. It made her feel incredibly awkward, and she imagined Will felt the same. She decided that the best thing to do would be to sidestep any questions that were asked.

But, of course, that was easier said than done.

E.A. continued to fret as Logan rolled the dice and moved three spaces on the Monopoly board.

"How much do I owe you, E.A.?" he asked.

"Hmm?"

"I landed on your railroad."

"Oh. Two hundred."

Logan passed two hundred-dollar bills her way. "For someone raking in all the money, you don't seem very excited."

"Sorry. I was just thinking about something else." She smiled. "You know I'm pleased about getting all your money. I never win at Monopoly."

"Today might be your lucky day," Will said with a wink.

She grinned. "This is true."

As Tricia rolled, Will leaned close. "You okay?"

"*Jah*. I was just thinking about some things," she whispered. "It wasn't anything important."

"Hey, you two," Katie teased. "No whispering during Monopoly."

"We ain't cheating," Will said. "We were talking about something else."

After Tricia landed in jail, Harley picked up the dice. "You don't have to explain to us," he murmured. "Katie and I have been there a time or two. Sometimes you can't wait to be alone."

E.A. felt like her face was flaming as much as Katie's. "Harley, that isn't what we were talking about."

Logan looked from E.A. to Will. "If you weren't talking about the game or, um, each other . . . what is on your minds?"

Just as E.A. desperately tried to think of something—anything—to say, Will spoke. "I've been trying to figure out what to do about my parents' thirtieth anniversary."

All of them—including E.A—stared at Will in surprise. Will was a lot of things, but a party planner was not one of them.

"Are you truly planning your parents' anniversary party?" Marie asked.

Will nodded. "Jake and Nan don't know where to hold it so they asked me to get involved."

"Uh-oh," Katie murmured.

E.A. hid her smile. "What are you all thinking of doing? Do you want a big party or something smaller?"

"Big. You know my parents. They know everyone and will want everyone to be there."

"They sure do, especially since your mother watched so many *kinner* over the years," Harley said.

"I thought about grilling burgers in the backyard, but Nan didn't like that idea."

"For a thirtieth anniversary?" Tricia asked. "Nan was right."

"What are your ideas, then?"

That seemed to open a can of worms. *Or maybe a jar of blessings*, E.A. mused as everyone surrounding them began to call out ideas. Will seemed to be mighty interested in everyone's suggestions, but she guessed that he was doing it to keep the conversation on that topic and off of the two of them.

"These are all good ideas. I should have pulled out a pen and paper so I could remember to tell Nan and Jake," he murmured.

"I'll help you remember them," she said with a smile.

"*Nee*, Will," Katie said. "You don't need to remember anything. You can have it here."

"Here?"

"*Jah*. I won't charge you for the space. You'll only have to pay for the food." Looking pleased, she added, "I know! We can pitch a tent in the back. There's plenty of room for up to two hundred people."

Will winced. "Boy, I hope there aren't two hundred people."

"You never know, though," Logan said. "These big parties end up having a life of their own."

"If you have it here, any out-of-town guests will have a nice place to stay," Katie added.

"My *frau* does have a good point," Harley said. "There's no finer inn around."

Will chuckled. "You're not going to get any arguments from me. It sounds perfect. *Danke*."

"You are very welcome," Katie said before looking back at the Monopoly board. "Uh-oh. I forgot whose turn it was."

"I don't think it matters," Logan said. "Trish and I better get home. It's late."

The rest of them agreed. Twenty minutes later, Will was helping E.A. into his buggy.

After he directed his horse down the back road toward her house, E.A. spoke. "I don't know if you mentioned your parents' anniversary on purpose or not, but I'm sure glad you did. I didn't want to discuss with other people our relationship."

He grinned. "I didn't, either. So, *jah*, the party planning worked like a charm. I'm glad we discussed it, though. Jake, Nan, and I had to make some kind of arrangements."

"The Loyal Inn is going to be perfect. I'll talk to Nan and Katie and see how I can help."

"*Danke*. I know me and my siblings will appreciate it." He stopped at an intersection and then guided his horse forward. "Hey, E.A.?"

"Hmm?"

"I think we should probably talk about us. Don't you?"

"If you want to."

"I think we have been doing everything backward. It's been confusing."

That was putting it mildly. "Are you confused now?"

He slowed his horse. "Not so much. I know I like you very much, Elizabeth Anne. I don't want to let you go. Um, what do you think about that?"

"I feel the same way."

"So . . . does that mean you are now my girlfriend?"

She couldn't help it, she giggled. "*Jah*, Will Kurtz. I do believe so."

He smiled as his horse picked up speed.

She scooted next to him and enjoyed the ride.

TWENTY

"Almost as much as the sight of a group of Amish kids scrambling after them."

"*W*ill, at your next break, Mr. Kerrigan wants to see you," Craig, his supervisor, said as he stepped over a collection of tools on the ground beside the trailer Will and his team were working on. "Can you do that?"

That was one thing Will had always liked about Craig. He valued their time and jobs and tried to stay out of their way instead of manage every bit of their days.

"*Jah*, sure," Will murmured as he looked up at the clock. He had a break coming up in fifteen minutes. "I'll go up at one forty-five."

"I'll let him know. *Danke*."

After Craig went on his way, Evan looked up at him. He was on his knees, fastening in bolts onto the floor of a trailer. "What do you think that's about?"

"No idea."

"Do you think there was a problem with one of the trailers last week?" he asked worriedly.

Will knew why Evan was concerned. As it sometimes happened, they'd had more orders than usual for their newest trailer model.

Craig had brought in five more men to help with the load but had put Will in charge of making sure they met their timelines and goals. The five men were good workers, but the addition had set some of the other men on the team off. They were used to their routines and didn't adjust as easily as Will had hoped. More than once he'd had to ask a team to redo a task that hadn't met the factory's high standards.

By Thursday, everyone was stressed and short-tempered. Will knew they were only human. Someone could have made a mistake that Will hadn't caught before the trailer had moved onto the next team. He hoped that wasn't the case.

"Let's not go borrowing trouble, Evan," he said. "You know how Mr. Kerrigan is. He could be calling me in for any sort of reason."

Evan's posture relaxed. "You're right. One time he called me in just to ask about Ruth's fried chicken. Knowing him, he could be asking about last week's lunch."

Evan was not wrong.

"I hope he doesn't ask me about the food I've been bringing in. I would have to tell him to ask my mother."

"Nothing wrong with that. Your mother is a mighty fine cook."

Will chuckled as he returned to work. Evan was right. His *mamm* was a fine cook, and he needed to take some of his own advice: whatever was going to happen would happen. There was no need to go borrowing trouble.

He wasn't quite so confident when he eventually stood outside of Mr. Kerrigan's office, however. He couldn't hear the exact phone conversation his boss was having behind closed doors, but it sure didn't sound good.

After another five minutes, he heard the call end and Mr. Kerrigan grumble under his breath. After another few seconds, he called, "Will, come on in."

Looking around the large room, with Mr. Kerrigan's desk on one end and a conference table on the other, Will half-expected to see John Byler working at the table. When John was promoted, he'd been given an office to share with Mr. Kerrigan himself.

Will had always thought that had to be uncomfortable, but John had never seemed to mind it. He'd often said that he liked being in the thick of things, plus he didn't have to go far to get computer help if he needed it.

"I heard you asked to see me?" Will asked as his boss glared at a large calendar on his desk.

"I sure did." He sighed again, then gestured to an empty chair. "I just got off the phone with one of our suppliers. They're running late, which means we'll get our parts late, which means we're going to have to make some hard decisions about how to deal with that."

Will sat down but was still confused about what that meant for him. He waited uneasily as Mr. Kerrigan turned, looked out the window, then at last seemed to come to a decision.

"Will, you've been with us for a while now. You not only come to work on time and always do a good job, but you also have a way about you that helps others." He sat down again. "There are only a few other employees here that are so well trusted."

That was quite a compliment. It was a balm on all the uneasiness he'd been feeling of late.

But it still didn't reveal why his boss had called for him. "Thank you, sir. But I'm not sure why you needed to tell me this today."

The older man's eyes crinkled in amusement. "I should've known that was coming. You aren't the type of man who enjoys receiving a lot of praise, are you?"

"I'm not sure if I am or I ain't," he replied. "I *canna* think of ever getting a whole lot of compliments."

"I think I better get to the point then. Will, these recent orders mean a lot to this company. We need to make sure the trailers ordered are built well and on time. That means we're going to have to change some things. Maybe temporarily. Maybe permanently."

"I see."

"What I'm trying to tell you is that we're going to need to add another shift, one that starts at two in the afternoon and ends at nine at night." He looked at him. "And I want you to lead this team."

Will blinked. "Me."

Mr. Kerrigan nodded. "I think you would be the right person we need to lead this new shift. People trust you, Will. They like working with you. More importantly, they like doing a good job around you. Your team rarely makes mistakes or has any problems."

The praise felt good, but he knew he didn't deserve it. "I've been fortunate to work with good people."

"You are right. We do have some really good employees. But as much as I believe in everyone, your success isn't based on mere chance, Will. Your example and leadership have played a part in this."

Not sure how else to respond, Will simply stared at him.

"What I need to know is how you feel about taking on this new position. It would mean a lot of changes. Changes to your schedule, to your teams, even to your personal life. You'd be giving up a lot of things." He leaned back. "Now, of course, we'll be wanting to compensate you. If you accept, it means a sizable raise."

"What figure are you talking about?"

Mr. Kerrigan pushed over a sheet of paper.

Reading it closely, Will was impressed. It was a big raise: over 20 percent. Though he didn't want to only be financially motivated, he was already imagining the changes that money could make in his life.

It was certainly more than enough for him to move out and live on his own. Or, perhaps, with a wife.

No, not with just a wife. With *Elizabeth Anne*. After last Saturday night, there was no doubt about their future anymore. At least, not for him.

Mr. Kerrigan was watching him closely. "I don't want to rush you, but I would like to know if you want to consider this. Do you need time to think about it?"

"I am interested, but I do want to think about it. Giving up my evenings would be a big change. And I'm not sure how many people would also be willing to move to a different shift."

"I know. After we find a shift manager, I'm going to hold a meeting. Then I think we'll get to see what the response is."

"If I do decide to do this, could I pick my team?"

"Of course. I know having the right team is going to make all the difference."

Will stood up. Though he was excited about the opportunity, he didn't want to make a hasty decision. "May I let you know tomorrow?"

"Yes. Tomorrow is fine." Mr. Kerrigan smiled, looking relieved. "I appreciate you getting back to me so quickly."

"If that call you were on is any indication, we don't have time to waste."

"We don't. But it can get done." Getting up to show Will out, his boss waved a hand. "I never imagined we'd have a plant like this. I figure if we can grow to a factory of this size after starting it in my barn, we can get through this hurdle, too."

"I'm thinking you're right. I'll see you tomorrow."

Mr. Kerrigan held out his hand. "Yep. I'll see you then. And thank you."

"Thank you, sir." After shaking hands, Will went back to work. Two hours later, he retrieved his lunch cooler, and started heading home.

It was early enough that the sun was still bright. He welcomed the warmth of the sun on his face, feeling like the brightness was a fitting companion to his spirits.

He had much to think about. And, yes, he had much rejoicing to do as well.

Mr. Kerrigan and the Lord had just answered his prayers. So had Elizabeth Anne. What a difference a month could bring!

It seemed he was in a rut no more.

TWENTY-ONE

"Well, between the mice, the screams, and well . . . all of us, things got a bit out of control. That was when the principal turned the lights on and stopped the whole dance."

*D*avid had found her again. Rather, David had found a way to invade her space again.

Sitting in her living room in the most uncomfortable chair in the world—the spindly, cane-backed chair that didn't seem to fit anyone over eighty pounds—Elizabeth Anne watched the clock on the wall slowly creep along.

It was only a quarter after eight, and David and his parents had now been there for forty-three minutes. Her mother, after a brief hesitation, had graciously invited them inside and offered refreshments . . . and had given E.A. a look that could not be misinterpreted. She was expected to put on her company manners and join them.

And so E.A. had, though she'd done little but bite her tongue and watch the hands on her mother's beautiful grandfather clock slowly move in a circle.

Elizabeth Anne had no idea how much longer their unexpected guests intended to linger. Probably until she started acting a lot happier to see them, she mused, somewhat sarcastically. If that was the case, she figured they would be there all night.

Or, perhaps, when Mr. and Mrs. Brennan finally got tired of bragging about David's newfound woodworking skills.

"*Jah*, David's new carvings have gained a lot of attention," Faith Brennan said. "For sure and for certain. Two stores in Millersburg are considering carrying them. Isn't that something?"

E.A.'s mother beamed. "That really is. Imagine that, David! Why, you'll be able to share your unusual gift with the world soon."

E.A. darted a look at her father. Though he was an awfully big fan of David's, she could tell that even he thought her former boyfriend's wood carvings were rather ugly. But to his credit, he still looked mildly impressed.

"Let us know when your carvings are in one of those stores," Daed said at last. "I'd like to see one in person."

"There's no need to wait," David said modestly. "I have one right here."

And then, to E.A.'s horror, he pulled out a piece-in-progress.

"Oh, my. Look at that. Why, it's *die katz*," Mamm said. "It is very detailed."

"*Danke*, Mrs. Schmidt." Smiling fondly at the figure in his hand, David continued, "I figured everyone loves cats, so it would be a good idea to carve some pretty felines."

Pretty felines. Whoever even said that? Just as E.A. smiled politely, more than ready to return to her clock watching, she caught a closer look at the figurine. It seemed to be on its hind legs. "I see that it is a cat, but I don't understand how it is positioned."

"You don't, Elizabeth Anne? Well, you see, it's like this." David balanced the piece of wood on his hand.

From what E.A. could tell, the feline was on its hind legs and its top paws were shorter and curved. Honestly, if the figure didn't have pointy ears and whiskers, she'd think it looked rather like a *Tyrannosaurus rex*.

David continued, "Arrow here is in a fight stance."

Some of her mother's peppy smile faded. "It's fighting?"

And her *daed*? Well, he sat up and stared at it intently. "Did you just call it Arrow?"

"*Jah*." David nodded. "I name my carvings." Rubbing a finger along the side of the cat, he added, "I thought his name was mighty fitting."

She was now staring at the cat intently, too. "Did you name it that because he's, um, standing so straight?"

"Oh, *nee*. It is because he is so lethal."

Her mother's eyebrows rose. "Lethal, you say?"

"Oh, *jah*," David said rather earnestly. "I envisioned this cat to be a fighter, you see. He's getting ready to defend his territory."

"Isn't that something?" David's mother mused. "David gives each of his creations so much personality. Why, they practically leap off the shelves, they're so lifelike."

E.A. could hardly keep a straight face. It was times like this when she really, *really* missed Andy Warner. He would be laughing right about now and whispering all kinds of comments to her under his breath.

When she noticed her father tilting his head, as if to envision a cat on its haunches, she couldn't keep her mouth shut. "Come now. Do cats even fight like boxers?"

"Elizabeth," her mother murmured.

But no way was she going to take that back. "I'm sorry, I'm not trying to be rude, but I've never seen a cat in that position. I thought when cats brawled, they scratched each other or something."

"That's because you haven't been around them very much," David said. "If you had, you would understand that each cat has his own way of defending his space."

"He is right," David's father interjected. "Cats are unique creatures. And my son? Well, he has a unique way with ears and whiskers."

"And with fighting cats, it seems," Daed said. When he traded an amused look with Elizabeth Anne, she felt her insides warm. At least she wasn't alone in thinking David's creations were peculiar.

As was this whole inane conversation.

Preening now, David leaned forward. "My father is very kind. But I do think these cats hidden in the sticks of wood are calling me. All I do is make their forms come alive."

"We get scraps from the lumberyard, you see," Mr. Brennan added.

"As a matter of fact, I just began another carving this morning. It's going to be Arrow's opponent."

"It's another fighting cat?" she asked.

"Oh, *jah*. I think they'll be quite popular in the stores."

Elizabeth Anne couldn't help herself anymore. Just the thought of two fighting wooden cats on some store shelf was cringe-worthy. She covered her mouth to prevent a snort, but it did no good. A burst of laughter escaped.

She slapped a hand over her mouth.

But it was too late as more laughter shot forth. She was now laughing so hard, she couldn't stop if she'd had to.

The whole room quieted—even her father, who had almost been on her side.

"E.A., *halt*," Mamm whispered.

At last she caught her breath. "I'm sorry," she said. "I just started thinking about a pair of fighting cats on a store shelf. The idea struck me as funny."

"I don't see why," Faith said.

"You're right," she said quickly. "I must be tired."

David snatched his carving from the coffee table and slipped it back into his pocket. "I don't think that's it at all," he said in a dark voice. "I think you've been losing the sweetness that used to be inside of you, Elizabeth Anne."

"I'm still sweet."

Okay, she might not have ever been *that* sweet, but she hadn't lost anything.

"Are you? I beg to disagree. You really have lost your way, Elizabeth Anne."

"David, my name is E.A.!" she bit out. "Stop calling me Elizabeth Anne."

David folded his arms across his chest. "You see? This is exactly what I'm talking about."

She'd had enough. "Once again, you are overreacting. All I did was laugh at your figurines. And I apologized for my rudeness."

David crossed his legs. "I wanted to marry you, but now I don't know if you'll ever be ready to be someone's wife. I think that's why all of your best friends have paired off with each other but you're left alone."

Daed set down the coffee cup he'd been holding in his hands. "I don't think such a thing is either necessary or correct to say, David. In fact, you are being mighty unkind."

"I must agree," her mother said, her expression cool.

"And . . . no one has paired off without me," E.A. said. "My friends fell in love."

David lifted his chin. "*Jah*. With other people."

"David is only speaking from his heart," Faith said. "He can't help but share his feelings."

"He is sensitive," his father said. "I've always thought he was more sensitive than most men."

"I'm starting to think a lot of things about him," Daed said simply.

David nodded. "I would have liked to have helped you, Elizabeth Anne. I confess I had even hoped that we could have straightened things out tonight. However, I'm afraid that time has passed. Now, I only feel sorry for you."

E.A. was just about to stand up and ask them to leave when there was a knock at the door. "I'll get it," she called out, anxious to escape.

And when she opened the door, she couldn't help but smile.

Because there was Will. Looking handsome, freshly showered, and oh, so normal.

Hearing everyone approaching the entryway, she blurted, "I'm going to hug you. Do me a favor and hug me back."

"Uh, say again?"

"I promise, this is important. Please, Will?"

His eyebrows rose but he complied. With a grin, he stepped forward, pulled her into his arms, and then pressed her close. Though she'd asked Will to hug her in order to prove to David that she certainly was desirable, the minute she relaxed against him, nothing else mattered.

She was wrapped up in Will Kurtz's arms. Will, who was so handsome and so kind. When she shifted and snuggled closer, enjoying the way his waist felt under her hands, he pressed his lips to the top of her head. And then she couldn't help herself. She smiled.

"Elizabeth Anne?" her mother said around a gasp. "What is going on?"

E.A. ignored her. Ignored the gasp that David's *mamm* released.

Even pretended that this hug wasn't just for show. Because right now, at that moment, she could feel Will's strong muscles, smell the soap on his skin, and knew without looking that he was absolutely perfect.

Perfect for her. She was so thankful that things between them had changed. She didn't need Will just to protect her from annoying David: she simply needed him in her life.

TWENTY-TWO

"I'm afraid I didn't make things much better when I announced rather loudly that we were all there to rescue Marie."

*W*ill was holding the pretty, slightly awkward, and very smart Elizabeth Anne in his arms again. Yes, because she'd asked him to, but Will knew that if they'd been alone he would have done it anyway.

"Well, now. Look who has stopped by," Mary Jean Schmidt said in an overly forced, bright tone. "Will Kurtz. Out of the blue."

"I'm so sorry. I know this feels odd," E.A. murmured into his neck. "Just, um, get ready." She pulled away before he could say that having her in his arms didn't feel odd at all.

He immediately felt her absence and found six pairs of eyes staring at him. "Hello, everyone."

"Ah. Hello, Will," Mr. Schmidt murmured. "I didn't know you were stopping by this evening."

"I didn't tell E.A." He took a deep breath. "I had some news today that I—"

"I can't believe that you tossed me over for *him*, Elizabeth Anne," David interrupted. "I would've thought you had more pride."

All of them stared at David. Will thought that even David's parents looked shocked by his rudeness. As such, he couldn't resist saying something. "I'm not real fond of you speaking to E.A. in that way."

"It's okay." Elizabeth Anne pressed a hand on his arm. He knew she was trying to defuse the situation, but he didn't like that she was the one trying to do it. Was everyone else simply used to David being so obnoxious?

"*Nee*, it isn't right," Will said. "I don't like David speaking to you in that tone." Turning to E.A.'s parents, he asked, "Is that how he always speaks to her?"

"No. This is new," Mr. Schmidt said.

"I am sure David is just shocked," David's mother said.

"Shocked by what?" E.A. asked.

"Come now. You two were just plastered together in front of the world. God, too."

David nodded.

"I could be wrong, but I don't think our Lord was that shocked." Will lifted his chin and looked David in the eye. "I don't appreciate you acting like there is something wrong with me, either. What is it about me that you find offensive?"

Mr. Brennan raised his hands in the air. "I'm sure he didn't mean anything by it."

"He's a grown man. I'm sure he did," Will countered.

"I can speak for myself," David said. "However, there is nothing more to say." And with that, David strode out the door, brushing past Will and E.A. on his way. The screen door slammed shut behind him.

Mrs. Schmidt inhaled sharply. Even Faith, David's mother, gave a little moan.

Will couldn't help but gape. David's actions were worse than an angry fifteen-year-old's.

"I think we had better leave," David's father said.

"*Jah*. I think it is time you did," Mr. Schmidt agreed.

David's mother turned to the group. "You know this isn't normal for him." Casting a dark look at E.A., she added, "He's obviously upset."

Before Will could say anything in E.A.'s defense, Mrs. Schmidt walked to the screen door and pushed it open. "Faith, we've been friends for two decades, but you know as well as I do that your son went too far. *Gut nacht*."

Without another word, Mr. Brennan reached for his wife's hand and tugged her out.

The four of them silently watched the pair walk down the sidewalk. When they were out of sight, Mr. Schmidt closed the door. Then, after taking a deep breath, he turned to face them. "Would either of you care to tell me what that embrace was all about?"

"It was my idea," E.A. said. "I asked Will to hug me."

"Oh, E.A.," her mother murmured.

"Mamm, you can't blame me. David drives me crazy! He hasn't been taking no for an answer, and his parents? They are almost worse. I know they are your good friends, but they've been far too pushy. I really don't like how they've put all the blame on me, either. It's like their son is perfect."

Will was glad she'd had her say, but he wasn't going to let E.A. take all the blame. "For what it's worth, I think it's obvious that I like having E.A. in my arms. We've become close."

The silence was so thick Will could have cut it with a knife. But then, to his surprise, Mrs. Schmidt started giggling.

"What a night. I couldn't have dreamed this up even if I tried." She looked up at her husband. "First that talk about fighting cats and now this?" She held up her hands. "I'm going to make some peppermint tea for myself and my husband. You two go sit and talk."

Mr. Schmidt looked like he was trying not to smile. "*Jah*. We'll see ya later, Will."

As her parents headed toward the kitchen, E.A. linked her fingers with Will's and guided him to the living room.

"Do I even want to know why you've been talking about fighting cats?" He chuckled.

"Oh, Will. I'm afraid if I told you I would start laughing until I couldn't stop. I'd much rather hear your news."

"Are you sure?"

"Oh, *jah*. I'll tell you another time. I promise." She plopped down onto the couch with a look of relief. Curling her legs under her, she smiled up at him sweetly. "So . . . what brought you over?"

You, he thought to himself. E.A. was becoming the person he needed when he had any news to share at all, he realized.

"I got asked to pay Mr. Kerrigan a visit in his office this afternoon," he said

As he'd hoped, she looked impressed. "What happened?"

"At first, I was worried that something went wrong with one of the trailers we'd been working on. Remember how I told you we got lots of orders all at once and have been scrambling?"

"I do. And I remember telling you to be careful."

"Anyway, even though I was pretty sure nothing bad had happened, I kept running through different possible problems in my head."

"And?"

"And, instead, Mr. Kerrigan asked me to be a shift manager."

"What? Oh, Will, that's wonderful! *Wunderbaar!*"

This was just the reaction he'd been hoping for, he realized. Her belief in him was making him believe in himself. Smiling at her, he reached for her hand and squeezed it. "It really is. It's really *gut* news. I can scarcely believe it."

"I'm so glad you came over."

"I am, too, but there is something else I wanted to share. This promotion will be bringing some changes with it."

As their eyes met, her full smile slowly ebbed. "What kind of changes?" she asked quietly.

"It's at night."

She frowned. "But, the factory doesn't run at night."

"It doesn't now, but Mr. Kerrigan thinks that if we start a second shift, one that starts at two o'clock and ends around nine, we'll be able to handle our workload."

"And he wants you to manage it."

"*Jah.*" Will blew out air. "I'm not going to lie. At first I was so relieved that I wasn't in trouble I felt like accepting right away. And then I'm afraid my pride got the best of me. He gave me a lot of compliments. That made me feel good, too."

"Will, of course it did. You work hard and are well liked by everyone. There's nothing wrong with people praising you for that."

"Mr. Kerrigan told me that I'd be able to choose the team.

That's a gift, you know?" As she nodded, he added, "This new job also includes a sizable pay raise."

Her eyes widened. "Congratulations!"

"The extra money would be a good thing. I would be able to get my own place easily."

"Do you even want your own house?"

"I will when I get married, E.A.," he said gently. He wasn't quite ready to speak of the two of them in that way, but he didn't want her to think it hadn't crossed his mind. When she blushed, he felt a surge of relief. He wasn't the only one who wanted to make things permanent between them.

He forced himself to continue. "But then, right when I was making all kinds of plans, Mr. Kerrigan reminded me of something else."

"What?"

"That a lot of men wouldn't want to leave their families every evening. And that, of course, reminded me that my evenings wouldn't be free, either."

"We wouldn't be able to see each other as much." She sounded as dismayed as he felt.

Meeting her gaze, he said slowly, "I'm worried that it might affect our relationship."

"Do you really think so?"

"Maybe."

E.A. swallowed. "Will?" Her voice was uncertain. It was obvious that she wanted to ask him to explain how he was feeling but didn't want to push him too hard.

He knew what she needed. His E.A. liked to be sure. She liked knowing what to expect and where things stood. Still holding her hand, he shifted to look her in the eye. "Because every time we're completely alone, I feel that it's never enough. Because whenever I hold you in my arms, I'm not ready to let you go." He leaned closer. "Because whenever we give into temptation and kiss, I realize that I don't want to wait another week until I kiss you again." He lowered his voice. "Is that clear enough for you?"

Looking a bit dazed, she nodded. "*Jah*. I mean, I think so."

After staring at her parted lips for a full second, he leaned back, reminding himself that the very last thing they needed to be doing was start kissing in her living room. She needed to be able to trust him, and her parents needed to be able to trust him, too.

"So, what do you think? What should I do?"

Looking down at their linked hands, she smiled. "You should take it, Will. It's a wonderful-*gut* opportunity. Too good to dismiss."

"But what about us?"

"I don't think there's a worry there. Everything you said was true for me, too. There's something between us that is stronger than schedules, I think. We'll make do."

"I hope so, because once I tell my boss that I'm willing to lead a shift, I won't be able to back out."

"I understand. Will, we've known each other our whole lives. Over and over, we've adjusted to changes. We can adjust to this one, too. We'll simply see each other on other days when you aren't working. Or in the morning. Or for lunch. We'll make it work."

Already, his mind was spinning, making plans. But he was so afraid of messing things up, he asked one more time. "You're sure?"

"If you're asking if I think what we have is worth changing our schedules around and making small sacrifices? Oh, yes. I think it's worth that. Absolutely."

When she smiled at him, he felt everything settle inside of him.

Perfectly.

TWENTY-THREE

"I don't think anyone knew what to say when Marie showed up, shocked to see us. Half of the school and faculty witnessed her running toward us ... as well as John telling her that he thought she looked mighty fine in her crown."

ONE WEEK LATER

*W*ill had known he'd have first-day-of-the-new-shift jitters, but he hadn't imagined that they would be this bad. From the moment he'd walked in the front door of the factory, he'd been a nervous wreck. Will had started doubting himself, doubting the team he'd put together, even doubting the company's ability to do what Mr. Kerrigan claimed was possible. Never before had he been under so much pressure.

All of this insecurity was something new. He usually approached every situation with a grin and a shrug. He wasn't one to second-guess himself, he just did his best, asked God for help, and continued on. But for some reason, none of that seemed enough.

Standing in the break room, he made a fresh pot of coffee and gave himself a silent pep talk. In fifteen minutes, all the men and women on his new team were going to arrive and he would need to give them a pep talk.

He needed to be the type of leader Mr. Kerrigan had thought he could be.

He needed to get his act together and fast.

"Hey, I'm glad I caught you before you started work," John B. said as he crossed the room to his locker.

"I walked in at the right moment, too. I just arrived." Pointing to the industrial-size coffeemaker, Will said, "I thought I'd make sure we had some *hays kaffi* for this evening."

"Good idea." John stuffed his hands in his pockets. "I won't keep you, but I didn't want to leave without wishing you well."

"*Danke*. I hope it goes well."

"I'm sure it will." John looked at him more closely. "Wait a minute. Why do you look so worried?"

Not wanting to share his insecurities, he shrugged. "Come on, you know how everything can go wrong."

"To be sure. But that's life, right? What's important is you know how to fix anything that can go wrong on those trailers." He grinned. "Boy, remember two years ago when our order came in wrong and there was a gap in the cabinets? You figured out how to attach the new piece of wood and made it look seamless."

Will had forgotten that. "We all worked together that day."

John nodded. "*Jah*, we sure did. But you led us."

He *had* led them. Until he'd carefully explained his ideas and organized the team, all of the men had been standing around debating choices. After he'd taken the lead, the cabinets had been fixed and installed in record time. "You know what? Maybe everything is going to work out after all."

"I know it will." Lowering his voice, John added, "Will, I feel certain that Mr. Kerrigan didn't make a mistake. You are the right man to lead this new shift."

"*Danke.*"

John smiled. "No reason to thank me for telling you the truth. Though, I am going to miss walking home with you."

"I'll miss it, too, though we didn't get as many of those walks as we wanted."

"Guess we'll have to make plans for the weekends, then."

Hearing some of his team walking down the hall, Will exhaled. "I better go."

John B. clasped Will's hand in a warm grip. "Good luck, buddy."

"*Danke,*" he said before turning and walking out to the large gathering space where his new team was waiting for him.

John's words rang in Will's ears when he stood up in front of all the men and women ten minutes later. When he'd walked in, the twenty-five team members were all looking at each other like they were strangers. The quiet, obviously stilted conversations drew to a stop when he strode to the front of the room.

"Do any of you feel like it's the first day of school as I do?" he teased.

Nervous laughter greeted him. "I thought I was the only one feeling like I wasn't sure what to do," Evan called out.

Will chuckled. "Nah, I'm certain you are in *gut* company, my friend." Looking around the room, he smiled. "I think all of this is going to take some getting used to, especially when it's near seven o'clock and we get tired." After a pause, Will raised his voice. "I want you to know that I have all the confidence in the world in each of you. Mr. Kerrigan told me to handpick the team, and each of you has graced me by accepting this new challenge. I am grateful."

He noticed that his words of encouragement were doing the same thing that John's words had done for him: each member of his team seemed to relax with each word he spoke. "Now, as I look around this room, seeing so many of you who I've worked side by side with over the years, I couldn't be more proud. You are some of the best employees in the company. I know we're all going to work well together and be one of the best teams in the company. We can make a difference, I feel sure of it."

Then, clear as a whistle, Frank Foley's voice rang out. "What you say, boss? Should we get started?"

"I say yes, Frank."

The other men chuckled.

Grinning easily now, Will said, "Let's get to work. Each of you knows your job like the back of your hand. Let's show Mr. Kerrigan that he was right to put his trust in us." When several of them clapped, Will felt a lump form in his throat. He'd believed in himself and had believed in these folks, but until that very moment he hadn't felt sure that they were going to be able to accomplish their goal. Now he was.

They exited the room. The team walked downstairs into the large warehouse, greeting a few of the other men and women before walking to the far left, where Will's team would be working.

He stood to the side, watching as each member strode to his or her designated spot, put on leather work gloves, turned on the machines. Then, just as he knew they would, they all got straight to work. He walked along the line for a few minutes, pausing at each station to make sure each person had what he or she needed.

Feeling better about everything, he pulled out his gloves and went to one of the first stations.

"You going to work with us tonight, Will?" Frank asked. "I thought maybe you were going to stand around and watch."

"*Jah*, I might do that tomorrow night. For now, though? I think I'll keep you company."

"In that case, stand right here," Frank said. "There's plenty of room for you."

Will nodded his thanks and got to work.

The moment not only felt right: it felt very fine, indeed.

TWENTY-FOUR

"Can anyone tell me why you all decided to share this particular story on our wedding day?" John interrupted.

WEDNESDAY NIGHT

*W*hen the front door slammed, followed almost immediately by the sound of Alan's car tearing down the road, Marta covered her face and wept. It had been a bad night. Worse than normal. Alan had been so angry.

So, so angry.

She'd known from the moment he walked in from work that he'd been in a terrible mood. Experience had taught her that she wasn't going to be able to do a thing about it, either. He'd come home looking for a reason to hit her, and Marta had known he would find it.

After giving into despair for a few more minutes, she wiped her face and forced herself to get to her feet. The kitchen was a mess, made worse by the splatters of spaghetti sauce that now stained the counters, walls, and floors. He'd shoved his dishes off the counter minutes after he'd hit her for . . . what was it again? She wasn't exactly sure.

Maybe it had been the fact that supper hadn't been ready the moment he'd gotten home. Or it could have been the fact that she'd gone on a walk when he'd called so she hadn't picked up.

Or was it her hair? He didn't like when she wore her hair in a ponytail.

At least she knew by now that nothing she did or didn't do was going to change the outcome. That understanding had saved her sanity . . . and propelled her to continue her plans. One day she was going to make dinner and simply enjoy it and then relax in front of the television. One day, things were going to be very different.

Grabbing a sponge, she ran the water in the sink until it was hot and then started cleaning.

Just as she was finishing the first pass of the countertops, she heard a knock on the back door. Before she could ignore it, the knob turned and Elaine poked her head in. "Marta?"

Elaine was there? "Hi. Um, I'm sorry, but now—"

Staring at her intently, Elaine's expression crumbled. "Oh, honey."

Everything inside of Marta wanted to lie, say she was fine . . . but she knew it would be useless. She'd recently come to the realization that the only person she fooled whenever she attempted to cover up her cuts and bruises was herself.

"Wh-what are you doing here?" she asked.

"I was out running errands and came across the cutest sewing basket. I thought I'd bring it over as a surprise." Looking embarrassed, Elaine said, "I heard him, Marta. I heard the things he said to you. I'm so sorry."

Marta was, too. But what could she say? Instead of speaking, she picked up her sponge and started wiping again.

Elaine let herself in, walked over, and pulled the sponge from her hand. "Honey, you need to get out of here. You need to put a stop to this." Her bottom lip trembled. "One day, I swear he's going to really hurt you even worse."

She was pretty sure he already had. "I know it looks bad."

"It is bad, honey."

Marta shrugged as she reached to take the sponge back. There was a part of her that ached to tell Elaine about the money she'd been putting aside for a year, how she was sure she had almost enough.

She wanted to tell her about the backpack, about how it was symbolizing the change inside of her and her plan to run away. She wanted to admit out loud how scared and angry she felt inside.

But she'd learned to keep everything inside. Sharing brought questions about things she didn't have answers for. Besides, what if Elaine told someone and Alan found out? She couldn't take that risk.

Walking over to a roll of paper towels, Elaine pulled a few sheets off. "I swear, it looks like a serial murderer was let loose in here."

The description wasn't that far off. Marta almost smiled. "Spaghetti sauce."

"I watched him drive off. Where did he go?"

"I don't know." Wherever he liked to go whenever he was angry and upset. Maybe to a bar. Maybe to another woman? She preferred to not know.

Feeling Elaine's pity flow over her in waves, she rinsed out the sponge and started wiping at the wall. "It doesn't matter. I . . . well, um, I'm sorry, but I can't talk right now. I need to clean this up."

Elaine looked under the kitchen sink, pulled out a spray bottle of cleaner, and walked over to the range. "I'll help you."

"There's no need."

"I'm afraid there's every need, hon. It's going to take a while to make this right. Plus, you need to get cleaned up and get some ice on that face."

Shame coursed over her again. "I don't know what to say."

"You don't need to say a word. Just let me help you, okay? And please answer me this: Do you have a plan? Do you ever plan on leaving that . . . that man?"

She nodded.

"Really?" Doubt laced her tone. "When?"

"Soon."

"Good." She scrubbed the oven range harder. "Now, go take a hot shower and put on some fresh clothes. After we get this mess cleaned up, we'll work on that ice."

Her face wasn't the worst of it. But she nodded anyway. "I'm going to change. I'll be right back."

"You take your time, honey. I have three kids. I can clean up spills with the best of 'em."

After giving Elaine a watery smile, Marta walked up the stairs, wincing with ever step. Then, as was her habit now, she walked directly to her closet, changing clothes as best she could without looking too hard at the welt on her thigh.

Then, when she couldn't put it off any longer, she walked to the bathroom and turned on the light to look at herself closely.

Her reflection would have scared her younger self. Her eye was bloodshot. Her cheek was already bruising. Spaghetti sauce was in her hair and on part of her face and neck.

After warming up the water in the sink, she carefully cleaned her skin. Dabbed it dry. Brushed out her hair and put it back into a ponytail.

Then she made herself stare hard at her reflection. "Ten days," she said to her reflection. "Only ten more days. Then you leave."

They were going to the county fair in ten days. His boss's son was showing a calf, and they'd invited her and Alan to go to the fair with them, and Alan couldn't possibly say no to his boss's request.

When he told her the news, she'd known then that this was her chance to escape.

Looking at herself in the mirror, she hardened her voice. "When you get to that fair, you're going to blend in with the crowd and find some help. And when you do, you're going to do whatever it takes to never be near Alan again."

Tears filled her eyes, but she swiped them away and made herself continue to look in the mrrior. "One day you are going to look in the mirror and like what you see. You're going to like it so much, you're going to have a hard time remembering days like this. Because soon, they're going to be just a memory."

With her words ringing in her ears, Marta walked back down the stairs and joined Elaine in the kitchen.

Looking up from where she was wiping at a corner on the baseboard, Elaine smiled at her. "You look better. Do you feel better, honey?"

"Yes, I do. I mean, a little," she said, realizing that she actually did. She had a plan now. And a date when she would make it happen.

Elaine shook her head. "I feel so sorry for you."

"Don't. Things will get better."

"Forgive me for saying this, but he isn't going to change, Marta."

"I know." But she had. And that was enough.

TWENTY-FIVE

"About that time, Marie's jilted date came forward. After they exchanged a couple of words, none of which were all that nice, we ushered her out of there."

THURSDAY

*E*lizabeth Anne supposed some days were like this. She was in hour five of her eight-hour day at Sew and Tell, and she was bored to death. Even Lark had given up thinking of tasks for her to do and had retreated to her office.

E.A. hoped she was reading a book behind the closed door so she would leave E.A. alone. She would love that. There was nothing worse than standing around, being bored—all while someone was critically watching her every move.

She looked at the clock and grimaced. Only seven minutes had passed since the last time she checked. If only Marta had shown up for her lesson!

Instead, she'd called and mumbled something about not feeling well. Then, she'd hung up before E.A. even had a chance to say that she hoped she felt better.

Because of that, the day had dragged something awful. She always looked forward to her lessons with Marta—maybe more than the woman herself did.

Finally giving up her position behind the counter, she walked over to examine the bolts of fabric. Kendra's birthday was coming up. Maybe she'd make her something special?

Fingering an especially pretty periwinkle bolt, she thought about making Kendra a fetching apron and matching dishcloths. Something silly and bright that she would hate to dirty but would still use when no one else was around. Kendra was like that—publicly practical but secretly one of the girliest-girls she'd ever met.

She'd just pulled out a pale yellow gingham and was wondering how it would look as a ruffle on the edge of the apron when the door opened.

A customer at last!

She hurried over to the man who had entered, her steps slowing as she got a good look at him. He was prematurely gray with light blue eyes and a ruddy tan—she supposed he could be handsome if his expression wasn't so cold. In his expensive-looking suit and tie, he also looked out of place. Not too many English men frequented the sewing shop. But no matter. "May I help you?" she asked as she got closer.

He didn't smile. "I'm looking for Marta."

Elizabeth Anne felt a shiver run down her spine. She spoke carefully. "I'm sorry, but no one named Marta works here. Perhaps I can help you?" She knew it was a sorry attempt at evading his question, but he was scary-looking.

He scanned the area, looking just beyond her. "She isn't a teacher here. She's a student." His eyes narrowed. "Don't tell me that you don't know her."

"Yes, I know Marta." Though she was starting to feel pretty scared, she said, "Who are you?"

"Husband."

"Ah." She folded her hands tightly in front of her. Boy, she hated the thought of sweet Marta going home to this man every night.

"Where is she? I thought she had a lesson scheduled today."

Remembering the backpack that was still hidden in one of the cupboards, E.A. said slowly, "Marta called the shop this morning and said she wasn't feeling well, so she couldn't be here for her class."

"She told you that?"

"*Jah.* I mean, yes. She called me soon after we opened today."

"Does she do that often?"

"Do what?" E.A. knew what he was asking, but she didn't like how he was speaking to her or how suspicious he was of Marta.

"Cancel at the last minute."

He was looking at her so intently, E.A. replied immediately. "No. This was the first time. I'm sorry, but why are you asking me all these questions?"

"That shouldn't matter to you."

Well, now it was official. There was something mighty bad going on with her student. E.A. suddenly didn't want anything more to do with him.

But because she had no choice, she simply stood there and looked silently back at him. Waiting but not offering any more information.

He didn't seem to know what to do next.

When the bell on the front door rang to announce another customer, he looked just as startled as she did.

"Elizabeth Anne! We brought you sustenance," Katie called out as she walked inside, followed by Marie and Kendra.

"Come here and see what Marie made," Kendra said. "Butterscotch brownies."

"Such a surprise they are, too. Why, they're almost edible," Katie added.

Stifling a giggle, E.A. looked over at them. "You all, hush. I'm with a customer."

"Oh! Sorry!" Marie said.

Marta's husband looked at her girlfriends and then back at her. He seemed to relax. "Looks like you're going to have a good lunch. That's nice."

"Yes. It's, um, very nice of them."

"I'll let you go then." He turned and walked out, pausing in front of Marie and tilting his head in her direction. "Ladies, have a good day."

"Yes, you, too," Marie said with a smile.

He smiled back before exiting the shop. E.A. stood and watched him walk away, thinking the man was much like a chameleon.

"Hey, isn't he the man we saw in the restaurant?" Kendra asked.

"Yep. He's my English sewing student's husband." *He is also very scary*, she added silently to herself.

"What was he doing in here? Did he want to buy her a gift certificate or something?"

"*Nee.*" She was tempted to share how he was checking up

on his wife, but it didn't feel right. She felt like she would be betraying Marta—after all, it wasn't like Marta had confided in her much at all. "He only came in to ask a question."

Katie wrinkled her nose. "That's all? Boy, you've surprised me. You looked so tense when we came in."

"Did I?" She shrugged. "Huh." Happy to concentrate on much happier things, she said, "I *canna* believe that you all brought me lunch! It's the best surprise."

"We came with ulterior motives, of course," Kendra teased.

"Uh-oh. What do you want?"

"Information about you and Will," Katie said.

"There's nothing to tell."

"Oh, yes there is," Marie said. "Will told John that he went calling on you the other night and walked into the middle of a David visit."

She slapped a hand over her eyes. "Don't remind me. It was awful."

"All of it?"

"David's visit with his parents? *Jah*." Suddenly remembering the whole cat conversation, she grinned. "Though I do have quite a story to share. But first, let me see if I can take my lunch now."

Just as she approached Lark's door, her manager stepped out. "Are those your girlfriends?"

"*Jah*. They brought me lunch."

Lark glanced at the clock on the wall. "It will be a late one."

"I guess so. Is it okay if I take my break now?"

"I can do better than that," she replied. "If you'd like to clock out now, it's fine with me. It couldn't be slower in here if it tried."

"Thanks so much. I'll go do that."

"Have a good time," Lark said. "After the day we've had, you deserve it."

Thinking about the conversation she'd just shared with Marta's husband, E.A. was inclined to agree.

In no time at all she'd signed out and had picked up her purse. Since Lark had already told them she was getting ready to leave, they were standing near the door.

"Come on," Marie said. "Let's go have a picnic at the park."

"Bye, Lark," she said. "See you tomorrow."

As Lark waved her off with a faint smile, E.A. was reminded again of how blessed she was to have her friends.

Thinking of Marta again, she hoped the lady had a group of close friends, too.

For some reason, she was pretty sure Marta would need them.

TWENTY-SIX

"Andy left with us, too. His date wasn't real pleased, but we later discovered she liked someone else anyway."

$\mathcal{N}$ow that another week had passed, E.A. wouldn't exactly say her parents loved the idea of her never being with David, but she did know that they were trying to make peace with it. David wasn't making things easier for them, however. Acting like a lover spurned, he'd begun making up tales about E.A. and telling those lies to anyone who would listen, which included his parents and hers.

Luckily for E.A., her parents weren't fooled by David's stories for a minute. They knew she had never drunk alcohol, would never try to encourage her sister, Annie, to do anything bad, and she certainly wasn't planning to move to another state.

"I'm beginning to hope David wants to move," her father had said last night. "I am real tired of him showing up at our doorstep with so many grievances against you."

"I told Faith on Wednesday that she should worry about her son instead of my daughter," Mamm proclaimed. "Enough is enough."

It was beyond strange.

At least she now had her parents and Annie on her side.

Annie had just wandered in, announcing she needed a break from studying for a test. Annie was a senior in high school. Like E.A., she'd done well in school. Unlike E.A., she had big plans for after high school. She wanted to go to college and study foreign languages and eventually do mission work.

But though she was driven and full of plans, she was still just a seventeen-year-old girl with stars in her eyes about her older sister's love life.

Plopping down on E.A.'s bed, she said, "When will you see Will again?"

E.A. had been halfheartedly reading a book in the chair by her window. Since she hadn't been able to think about much besides Will anyway, she set her book down. "Not until late tomorrow night or maybe even Saturday."

Will had suggested that they attend the county fair with John and Marie. It was still a little bit up in the air—Will hadn't wanted to make any definite plans until he got his first week under his belt. But she hoped it would work out. It would be wonderful to spend the whole day together and do nothing but wander among the tents and arenas.

Annie frowned. "I wish he wasn't working nights."

"Me, too. But we'll get used to it." She was determined to help Will be successful in his new position.

"I guess you will. I mean, it isn't like you've got a lot of choice." She paused. "Hey, E.A.?"

"Hmm?"

"If you marry Will, is he going to be Mennonite?"

E.A. blinked, a little startled by the change of topics, but she didn't mind too much. She'd been thinking about such things, too. "No one has spoken of marriage, Annie."

"But when you do?"

Annie was speaking like her future with Will was a foregone conclusion. Hearing that gave her a little rush of happiness. It felt good to think that she and Will would one day head to the altar. "If we do eventually get married, I'm sure I'll be his Amish wife."

"Really? Don't you think that's going to be hard?"

"A little, but it's not like it's going to be all that different."

"You won't get to drive."

"I know. But I don't like driving all that much anyway."

"You won't have electricity, either. Or your computer . . . that's going to be hard to give up."

"I know. But I can always go to the library and use their computers if I need one." She smiled at Annie. "Or use yours."

Annie nodded slowly. "At least you have a lot of Amish friends."

"That's true. I do. I've even gone to church with them quite a few times over the years. I like Will's church district a lot." Of course, it didn't hurt that Katie, Harley, Logan, and Tricia were already in it. She would have to give up a few creature comforts, but she would be in good company.

And then, of course, there was Will. He would make anything easier. That was the type of man he was, after all. So caring. So considerate.

Annie rolled on her side and sighed. "I'm so glad you broke up with David so you could start seeing Will Kurtz."

"It wasn't exactly like that," she tried to explain. "I just started realizing that David and I weren't a good match. Things with Will just happened at the right time." She smiled. "I guess the Lord had a plan in mind."

"I'm glad of that. David would've driven us all crazy. He is so full of himself."

E.A. couldn't resist chuckling. "*Jah*. He sure is." Especially lately.

"I like you better with Will. He really is so cute." Annie sat up and hugged one of the pillows from E.A.'s bed. "And nice."

"I agree. He's wonderful." He really was all of those things: handsome, kind, caring. Sometimes she could hardly believe that after all these years she now saw him in such a different way. Now, well . . . she loved him.

"You must really love him," Annie said, as if reading her mind.

"Annie, this is getting pretty personal."

"I know." She paused, then blurted, "But do you?"

"*Jah*." There was no reason to deny it.

"Has he told you the words yet?"

"No. But I haven't said I loved Will yet, either. So don't you tell him first."

"Don't worry. I won't."

"*Danke*."

Just as she was about to suggest they head down to the kitchen and get some ice cream, Annie blurted, "E.A., when do you think you'll tell him?"

"I don't know. The right time, I guess." And probably after Will said those words first. She looked at her sister curiously. "I don't mind talking to you about Will, but what's with all the questions?"

She shrugged. "I guess I was thinking that you're about to make a lot of changes. And your changes will make our life different here, too."

E.A. sat down on the side of the bed. "I don't think it's going to be that different."

"You'll be married to Will."

"I think we both knew that we each would marry someday," she said gently. "Who knows? You might even meet a special man when you're studying all kinds of things in college."

Annie giggled. "I can't even think about falling in love right now. I've got too much to do." She shifted, facing E.A. more fully. "I guess I'm just realizing that one day you won't be living next door. I always thought you'd be near Mamm and Daed."

Even thinking about marrying David, moving in with his parents and living next door to her parents, sounded awful.

Boy, had she ever really considered that?

"I think I needed something different," she said carefully. "Perhaps David did, too. Change is good, you know."

Annie got to her feet. "I think so, too."

"You want to go downstairs and get some ice cream?"

"Yep. Maybe we can find a movie on and watch it—you know, since you aren't Amish yet."

As they walked down the hall together, E.A. grinned. Yes, things in her life were certainly changing, but not everything.

She was glad about that.

Two nights ago, when Will had stopped by E.A.'s house after another shift, she'd been close to tears. Though at first she tried to tell him that nothing was wrong, he'd been persistent. Eventually, she'd revealed that David had tried to walk her home from work. And, when she'd told him to leave her alone, he'd spouted off a lot of innuendos about her and Will.

"Things have finally gotten better with me and my parents," she'd said. "Will, what if they hear some of the stories he's made up? They're going to be so disappointed in me."

He'd shaken his head. "They won't be disappointed because they aren't true."

"He can be convincing, though."

David was also a liar. Reaching for her hands, he bent down slightly to look her in the eyes. "E.A., we haven't done anything wrong. You haven't done anything to be ashamed of. Not one thing."

"But—"

"Listen to me. Even if we had taken things further than a few stolen kisses, that wouldn't have been his business. He has no right to be talking about you." He paused. "Do you understand?"

She slowly nodded. "I guess so."

"No, I know I'm right. Don't worry about him anymore. He can't hurt you. He *canna* hurt us."

At last, she'd relaxed enough to smile again. He'd ended up joining her, Annie, and her parents in the kitchen for apple crisp and homemade vanilla ice cream. They'd chatted about his job and Mr. Schmidt's garden full of tomatoes and Annie's classes. By the time he'd left her, E.A. was back to her usual self . . . but inside, he was fuming.

Instead of going right home after E.A. closed her door, Will walked over to the Brennans' house and rapped on the door. David answered.

"What do you want?" he asked.

"We need to talk."

The first bit of unease flickered in his eyes. "We don't have anything to talk about."

"*Nee*, that's where you are wrong. I just left E.A. and she told me about you harassing her this afternoon."

"I didn't do a thing," he said, looking smug. "All I was doing was walking."

"No, you were bothering her. Spouting lies about her and me."

"Are they truly lies?"

He'd never been a violent man, but boy, did Will have the sudden urge to shake some sense into him! Stepping closer, he lowered his voice. "I'm telling you they are. Not only would I never disrespect her that way, E.A. would never disrespect herself. You are hurting her, David, and it needs to stop. Do you understand?"

Will could practically see David debating about how to answer him. But then finally—at last—he nodded. "I hear what you're saying."

It wasn't the firm answer Will had been looking for, but he felt it was enough. "*Gut.*"

He turned and walked away, hoping that David had realized at last that his games had to stop. What he and E.A. had was too special to be tainted.

TWENTY-SEVEN

"I never found out what happened to all those mice."

ONE WEEK LATER

*M*arta began making definite plans for her escape when Alan announced that they were still going to the county fair on Saturday morning.

She'd been sipping coffee and nursing a bruise on her cheek when he'd stridden into the kitchen with a smile on his face—just as if the evening before had never happened.

"Looks like all of your country ways are going to finally come in handy. Frank Zook's son is showing a calf at the county fair."

"Oh?"

"Frank is so proud of his boy that I told him we'd go out to the fair for a few hours instead of just stopping by."

She knew that fair like the back of her hand. At least, she had eight years ago. "That sounds like a lot of fun."

"We're going to have to trudge around in the dirt, looking at cows and horses and pigs, but what can you do? I need Frank to approve my latest deal."

"I understand." Marta walked to the coffeemaker, poured a fresh cup of coffee, and handed it to him.

Taking a sip of it, he eyed her. "Your face better be healed by then."

It took everything she had not to cover the swollen bruise with her hand—the one he'd put there last night when he'd gotten mad at her because she'd forgotten to pick up his laundry from the dry cleaners. Instead she simply stared at Alan, silently daring him to blame her for his tirade.

It was a minor difference in her usual behavior, but significant. It was the first time that she wasn't cowing or apologizing for her looks. Thirty seconds passed. Maybe even a full minute. A new tension filled the air between them. And though her head cautioned her to not do anything to make Alan suspicious, the rest of her knew she needed to do this. She needed to remind herself that she was strong enough to leave.

Looking slightly uneasy, he put his cup on the counter and picked up his briefcase. "I won't be home until late. I've got to go get some jeans and a hillbilly shirt or something for the fair."

She relaxed, trying to make her voice sound caring and concerned. "Do you want me to make you a plate for supper?"

"No. I'll eat out," he muttered before walking out the back door.

After listening to the garage door open and shut, she peeked out the front window and watched his car roll out of sight.

Only then did she pour his coffee out, get a fresh cup for herself . . . and sit down at the kitchen table with a smile.

Alan wouldn't be home for hours, and they were going to the fair on Saturday. Even the image of her husband walking in one of the barns at the fair was laughable. Alan rarely even wore jeans, and the only thing he knew about cattle was how well done he liked his hamburgers grilled. In fact, he often made fun of her country mannerisms that sometimes surfaced from time to time.

But none of those things mattered now. All that did was that he was finally giving her the chance she'd been waiting for. The county fair would be crowded on a Saturday. Really crowded. And, if he was there for his boss, he wasn't going to be paying much attention to her. That meant that she was going to be able to walk around on her own.

And find a policeman or sheriff and beg him or her to help her escape. And then, buffeted by their protection and the money in her backpack, she was finally going to be free.

All she had to do until then was retrieve her backpack from the sewing shop, carefully sew her money into the lining, and plan an outfit to go with the bright yellow print so Alan wouldn't suspect a thing.

Yes, all she had to do was survive for three more days. Compared to everything else she'd been through?

Three days was practically nothing.

E.A. was feeling off, but she wasn't sure why. Maybe it was the disintegrating relationship with David. Yes, he was a jerk, but he'd been part of her life for years. It felt strange to now avoid his house and his parents after being over there all the time. Or, maybe it was because she had something new and unexpected with Will. She was a methodical girl, not an impulsive one. But everything with Will felt quick and out of her control.

Or . . . perhaps it was because she was keeping a secret from Marta. She'd never told Marta that her husband had stopped by the shop to ask a bunch of questions about her.

She was worried about her student. Marta had been acting so tense and nervous during their lesson that E.A. had come very close to turning off the Singer and asking how she could help her. But she hadn't.

Well, not until Marta had suddenly announced that she was going to take her backpack home.

E.A. had been caught completely off guard. And, perhaps, had felt more than a little left out. Marta had gone from needing her help to keeping her distance. Though she knew she was probably being too sensitive, she hadn't been able to accept Marta's request without commenting. The conversation still made her wish she'd kept her mouth shut.

"Are you sure about that?" she'd asked.

Marta's expression had turned wary. "I'm very sure."

But still, E.A. had not been able to let it go. Tracing a finger along one of the seams, she said, "I thought maybe we could redo this."

"Why?"

"Well . . . it's not perfect."

Hurt flashed in Marta's eyes. "I don't need it to be perfect, E.A. I just needed it to be usable, which it is. Right?"

"Yes. Yes, of course. It works just fine. I mean the zipper works perfectly."

"I'm going to take it home then," Marta said in a rush. Turning very businesslike, she opened up her pocketbook. "May I pay you now?"

Feeling terrible that she'd made such a mess of things, E.A. had nodded and walked her to the cash register. Five minutes later, she'd stood at the window and watched her student walk away, the backpack neatly folded in a paper sack.

And she'd wondered if she was ever going to see her again.

Ever since that moment, she'd been struggling, almost like she'd lost another friend. First Andy, then David, and now Marta. Though, of course, each of those circumstances didn't change the fact that she was feeling their loss.

Or that for each, she felt she hadn't handled the situation well. She hoped that eventually the Lord would help her find a way to make things right.

But until then? She was barely hanging on . . . and waiting for the other shoe to drop.

TWENTY-EIGHT

"Half of us piled into my parents' van, the other half into Andy's car. We decided to go to my house. It was the closest, and we knew my *mamm* wouldn't ask a lot of questions, only wonder if anyone wanted popcorn."

SATURDAY

"*E*.A., come on now. Stop worrying so much about work and David," Will said for what E.A. knew had to be at least the fifth time. "We're together, Marie and John are somewhere close by, and we have nothing to worry about for the next five hours. Let's enjoy ourselves."

They were at the fair, and everything Will said made sense. E.A. looked around at all the excited children running in front of their parents as they went from booth to booth, and smiled. Boy, being here sure brought back good memories. So did the brightly colored rides. Even after all these years, each one still looked more exciting than the last. She even enjoyed watching the great variety of people who were there. Everyone seemed eager to do the same things that Will and she wanted to do—to relax and have fun.

If only she could actually enjoy herself. It was just too bad that she felt more comfortable in the midst of strangers than she did on her street.

"You're right, Will, I do need to relax and enjoy being with our friends." *And Will, too,* she added silently. This outing was really the first time that she and Will were out together as a couple—not just two good friends. She loved the difference, too. He was so attentive and sweet to her, she felt taken care of and treasured. E.A. shook her head, trying to clear it. "This is a magical place. Being here is almost like taking a vacation."

Will laughed. "I wouldn't go that far, but it never fails to make me feel more lighthearted. After all, where else can we eat fried corn, frozen custard, and walking tacos?"

He certainly loved those bags of Fritos topped with chili and cheese! "Leave it to you to dwell on the food."

"Come on, there's a lot of good food, and we've hardly tried any of it." Reaching for her hand, he tugged her to a food stall.

She willingly followed, only pretending to not be as enamored about the thought of eating a whole ear of fried corn dipped in butter. That attitude didn't last too long, however. From the first bite, all her senses went on high alert. Had few things ever tasted so good?

Seeing her bliss, Will laughed. "Here. Take my napkin."

Feeling sheepish, she wiped her mouth before taking another too-big bite.

When Will did the same with his corn, she smiled at him, realizing once again that things between them had shifted. Yes, they still had their firm foundation of friendship, but there was something stronger pulling them together. She now was aware of every smile and frown on his face. Of the way his brown eyes darkened when he was upset . . . or when he gazed at her after sharing a kiss.

And her own body was responding to him in kind. Her stomach got fluttery when she waited for him to come over after one of his shifts. Her pulse certainly raced whenever he leaned close and whispered into her ear.

"Hey, are you okay?" he asked after throwing away their trash. "You got quiet."

"I'm fine." She smiled up at him. "I guess I was just thinking about how things between us have changed."

"They really have, haven't they? And to think, it all started as a game of pretend."

She nodded. "I'm not pretending at all, Will."

"Me, neither." Stepping closer, he lowered his voice. "This probably ain't the most romantic place to tell you how I feel, but I really like you, E.A." He stopped. "*Nee,* it's more than that. I'm falling in love with you."

"I'm falling, too." Hearing the words come out of her mouth felt almost shocking—like a dash of electricity that she'd been afraid would hurt but only woke her up.

She'd been so right to break things off with David!

Even before he'd gotten so crazy, she'd known that there had been something missing between them. She'd found it in Will.

"If we were anywhere more private, I'd give you a hug right now," Will said.

"If we were anywhere more private, I'd want you to. But, as you said, we have all day."

"*Jah*. And all night. Who knows? Maybe I'll even get you to ride the Ferris wheel with me."

"All you have to do is ask." E.A. smiled softly.

"E.A.? Will?" Marie called out. "What are you two doing? I thought you were going to go look at the lambs with us."

Elizabeth Anne smiled at her good friend. Marie looked as pretty as ever. She was wearing a bright green sundress, tan wedges, and her long golden hair was in a ponytail. In the midst of an ocean of *Englischers* all wearing jeans and shorts, she stood out like an exotic bird.

"Ah, we had to get something to eat," Will said.

"Already? What did you get?"

"Fried corn on the cob," E.A. replied.

"All those calories." Marie frowned but still looked at the booth longingly.

"And it was worth every one!" E.A. said as she walked to Marie's side.

"I'm going to get one later then." Linking her arm through E.A.'s, Marie said, "Come on. Let's go see the lambs first."

"Lead the way." She was tempted to tease Marie about her fondness for baby animals but knew her friend was perfectly justified in her love of them. No doubt about it, baby lambs were adorable. As they walked a few feet behind the guys, E.A. asked, "Are you having fun so far?"

"So much fun. Work has been so stressful—I needed to get away from everything. If John and I had stayed home, I would have gotten on the computer to work or done laundry or felt the need to get another ten thank-you notes written." She took a breath. "All of those things are good, I guess, but sometimes it's nice just to relax."

"Will was just telling me the same thing."

"Really? What has been on your mind?"

E.A. didn't really want to bring up either David and his lies about her or the stress she'd been continuing to feel at work, so she decided to skirt the question. "Just the usual, I guess."

Marie raised her eyebrows. "Which is—?"

"Nothing that I need to worry about today."

"Are you sure?"

"I'm sure. It's nothing out of the ordinary." She smiled tightly, trying her best to retain a hold on the optimism she'd been feeling just moments before.

Marie studied her for another moment then shrugged. "Good to know." After another few steps, she grinned. "Oh, look at that little girl. Isn't she sweet?"

E.A. looked to where Marie was focused and smiled. The little girl was Amish and was wearing a bright orange dress. Her white *kapp* practically sparkled in the sunlight. Little wisps of blond hair fluttered out of its confines. Best of all, she was holding a stuffed donkey. "She is adorable. Just like a ray of sunshine."

"Look how she is trailing after her brothers. That's how I always imagined Harley's little sister, Betty, being. Remember how all of his siblings used to follow him around?"

"I do. And I remember how you and I were always sad that we had such small families."

"Hey, at least you had a sister."

E.A. grinned. "Annie wasn't all that easy, so I don't know if I had the better situation."

"She wasn't that bad. Was she?"

Just as E.A. was about to answer, she caught sight of a man who was standing still in the middle of all the chaos. It took a few seconds, but then she realized who she was looking at: David.

She inhaled sharply as she realized he was staring directly at her.

"E.A.? What is it?"

"David is standing just behind that little girl. Next to the exit of that building."

She turned to look. "Oh, for heaven's sakes. He's glaring at you!"

E.A. felt a chill race up her spine. "I don't know what to think anymore, Marie. Practically everywhere I look these days, he's looking right back at me."

"What do you mean? Like he's stalking you?"

Stalking sounded so dramatic. But was it dramatic if that was what it was? "I don't know what it is exactly. All I do know is that it's starting to stress me out."

Marie grabbed her hand, and they started walking faster. "This has been happening for a while?" she asked.

"Yeah."

She frowned. "What have you done?"

"I've talked to him and told him that he needs to move on."

"And Will?"

"Will hasn't exactly said anything to him, but he hasn't been shy about letting David know that we're together."

"Maybe Will needs to say something to him, E.A. Don't you think?"

E.A. shrugged. "I don't want to make too big a deal about it."

"But it is a big deal, right?"

"I'm sure he'll get the idea sooner or later." She gave Marie a wry smile. "To be honest, I can't really figure out why he's been so intent on getting me back. I mean, David never acted all that excited about me when we were together." After a pause, she shared a little more. "I mean, it's not like I'm some kind of prize."

Marie frowned. "Don't say that."

"I mean it. I'm not like you, Marie. I'm pretty enough but not beautiful."

"I wish you could see yourself how the rest of us see you, E.A.," Marie said just as they caught up with John and Will.

Turning around and smiling softly at E.A., Will asked, "And how do we see Elizabeth Anne?"

"Oh my goodness! Don't say a word!" E.A. called out. She couldn't be any more embarrassed.

But Marie ignored her. "Like she's something pretty special. That's how."

Will took hold of her hand and threaded his fingers through hers. "Well, of course. I knew that."

John spoke. "When I looked back at you two, you girls looked to be in an intense conversation. Is that what you were talking about?"

"No. E.A. saw creepy David here," Marie explained. "You wouldn't believe the way he was staring at her."

John threw an arm around Marie's shoulders. "And how was that?"

"Like . . . like she was an ax murderer," Marie blurted.

The guys laughed. "That's a bit much, don't you think?" John said.

"Not really. E.A. was really creeped out. I was, too."

John's smile vanished. "Do you want us to go talk to him?"

"No," E.A. said. The last thing she wanted was another

confrontation with him. "I just want him to leave me alone. I'm really tired of him saying bad things about me."

Will searched the crowd, obviously looking for David. "I didn't know he was still bothering you so much. Why didn't you tell me?"

"I didn't want to make your first week in your new job any harder than it already was."

He ran a thumb along her knuckles. "E.A., you shouldn't worry about things like that." Looking like he had just made a decision, he said, "You know what? I'm tired of you being so afraid all the time." He scanned the area again. "Where is he? I'm going to go have a talk with him."

"You mean *another* talk with him," John said.

E.A. froze. "Will, what does John mean?"

"Nothing you need to worry about."

"Tell me the truth. Did you talk to David already?"

"*Jah.* I had to do something." He frowned. "It never occurred to me that he would act so contrary though. That ain't *gut.* E.A., you stay here with Marie and John. I'll come find you after I have a word with him."

"No way are you going to go by yourself," John said. "I'll go with." Scanning the area, he pointed to the livestock pens. "Marie, we'll come meet you over there."

Just as Marie nodded, E.A. shook her head. "John, Will, *nee.* I know you are trying to help, but I don't want you confronting David here."

"I'm not going to make a scene," Will said. "All I'm going to do is speak with him. Firmly."

"Please, no. Let's just forget about him."

"I don't see how that's possible."

"It will be because I'm going to put him out of my mind," she said in a rush. "And if I can, you all can, too."

"But you can't live your life looking over your shoulder and worrying, E.A.," Marie said.

"I agree, but we came here to relax and have fun. And I need this day. Can we just go look at the lambs?"

She knew she sounded desperate, and maybe she was. But something told her that she needed to encourage all of them to move on. She had the strangest sense of foreboding that something terrible was about to happen here on the fairgrounds. Looking at her three friends, she attempted to smile. "Please? I'd rather not let him ruin our day."

They all looked at her with strained expressions. No one said anything.

At last Will spoke. "Sure. Of course. We don't have to mention his name again."

"*Danke.*" She was relieved. Will cupped a hand around her cheek. "But you must promise to tell me if you see him again today. He's already made you upset. We're not going to let him create even more havoc in a place like this."

"If I see him again, I'll tell you."

"Promise?" His gaze was intent.

She nodded. "*Jah.* I promise."

But there was a part of Elizabeth Anne that was feeling on edge. No matter how hard she tried to see things another way, she was afraid that David had come to the fair for one reason only: he was determined to take his taunts and lies up a notch—which meant that she could lose everything she had with Will before their relationship had barely begun.

TWENTY-NINE

"About a half hour later, we were all gathered on the floor in my basement. Marie had borrowed a pair of my flannel pajamas, since I didn't have a lot of other options. After my mother brought down a pot of hot chocolate and two big bowls of popcorn, Marie—well, Marie burst into tears."

*L*eading E.A. into the covered pen where all the lambs were waiting to be judged, Will tried to relax, but he was finding it a difficult task. In truth, he was as angry as he'd ever been.

This David fellow was doing his best to make E.A. miserable, and he couldn't do anything about it. He hated feeling so helpless.

Worse, he'd thought he had put a stop to it when he'd knocked on his door and spoken to him that evening. He'd felt bad speaking to the guy behind E.A.'s back, but he'd hated seeing her so upset.

Will had been sure that David had only needed someone

to stand up to him. Bullies preyed on the weak, and it had been obvious to Will that David considered E.A. to be weak. Though E.A. was anything but weak, Will was happy to give her a hand.

David seemed to have taken him seriously. When Will had walked away, he'd felt that the situation was much better—at the very least, E.A. wouldn't have to worry about being harassed anymore.

Unfortunately, it looked like that conversation had made little impact on the guy after all. He wished he had talked to their friends about it more, or his father or even Jake. Maybe one of them could have given him the advice he'd needed to make sure David left her alone for good.

He was still stewing when they drew near a ten-year-old boy standing next to a pair of fuzzy black lambs on spindly legs. They had to be only a few weeks old, and were as sweet as anything he'd ever seen.

When the girls ran right over to coo over the lambs, Will was grateful for the chance to work out his plan to confront David. Maybe he should bring Harley or John? David needed to stop bullying.

"Hey." John pressed a hand on his arm. "Buddy, I know what you're thinking, but you've got to stop. This ain't the time or place."

"You wouldn't be able to stop, either, if some guy was practically stalking Marie."

John's blue eyes flashed. "I agree. But that doesn't mean it would be the right decision."

"John, I *canna*—"

"*Jah*, you can. Listen to me. If you continue looking like you want to strangle that guy's neck, E.A. isn't going to be able to do a thing but worry." He lowered his voice. "We all work too hard for you to ruin today with a bad mood."

Will knew John had a point. He needed to help make E.A.'s day better, not stress her out even more. "I hear you."

"*Gut.*"

Watching the girls squeal when one of the lambs nosed E.A., Will smiled. Then, he grimaced again, thinking that E.A. should have been enjoying herself the whole time they'd been there. He turned to his buddy.

"John, I just *canna* help but think that if I would have done a better job of protecting E.A., she wouldn't have had to worry about David at all today. Or ever."

"Look at her. She gave her worries to us and, hopefully, to the Lord. She's not worried now, she's playing with the lambs. You should do the same."

Will felt like grunting, but he also knew his buddy had a point. He needed to enjoy the day with his friends. He would sit down and get advice about what to do later.

He walked over to E.A. "Having a good time?"

"Oh, *jah*. Do you see how adorable this little one is?" E.A. called out. "His name is Blackie!"

John, who was now crouched next to Marie and petting another lamb, smirked. "Now there's an original name for a black sheep."

"Hey, their owner is only nine or ten," Will said. "I would have called him the same thing." Standing up, he shook the boy's hand. "Congratulations. That's a right good-looking lamb."

"Thanks."

"Are they both yours?"

"No, the other one is my brother's. He went to go get some nachos."

"I see. Well, when is judging?"

"Two hours. My dad is with my little sister now. She's showing a calf in the main arena."

"Sounds like your whole family has a lot to be proud of today," Marie said.

"Yep." The boy grinned, showing a missing tooth.

"Best of luck to ya," Will said kindly before walking with E.A. down the aisle toward the next stall. "You know what? I've never been a real big fan of sheep, but those little lambs are adorable. Want to keep looking at them?"

"I do." Smiling in Marie's direction, she said, "After that, Marie and I want to go see the pigs. Marie heard there are potbellied piglets!"

He laughed. Of course she wanted to see piglets. His sister, Nan, would have wanted the same thing. "Let's go see them then. I've a mind to see the calves, too. They're getting shown in the arena."

Looking excited, E.A. led the way. As they walked, stopping to pet the other lambs and chat with the boys and girls showing their livestock, Will forced himself to relax.

John had been right. This was what was important. Days like this came few and far between. He needed to remember that instead of dwelling on his problems.

Things were different now. Oh, not just with her and Will, but between them and Marie and John. They'd gone from simply being friends to being two couples. It was a slight shift in the way they acted toward each other. Sure, they all still joked around, but E.A. found herself smiling softly at Will when Marie or John made a joke. She stayed by his side when they walked up to a vendor or when they visited an exhibit.

Things had shifted to a new dynamic. Something not necessarily better, but very different. She was now not just part of the Eight, she was also part of a couple. It made her feel more stable. Maybe not as alone, though she'd never really considered herself to be alone.

"You sure look like you're thinking hard," Will said as they walked toward the next arena. Marie and John had left to get some iced tea with John's parents, and they'd agreed to meet back up in an hour. "Are you still upset by David?"

"By David? No, not at all. Actually, I was thinking about the Eight." Realizing that Will looked really confused now, she added, "This might sound strange, but I was just thinking that it feels a little different, going to the fair as a couple with John and Marie. I didn't expect that. Different in the best of ways," she hastened to clarify.

Will nodded. "I remember Harley telling me something like that soon after he married Katie." He smiled. "Guess what? Harley said he'd felt surprised about how different he felt. I guess he thought he wouldn't feel as protective over Katie as he did."

"That makes me smile." If there was a member who liked change less than she did, it was Harley. Both of them were late bloomers who had recently made a lot of changes in their lives.

Will leaned close. "You know I feel the same as you about us being here as a couple, right? I'm pleased as punch."

She chuckled at his old-fashioned expression. "*Gut.*"

"So, what would you like to do now? We have an hour all on our own. Are you hungry?"

"I feel like all I've done so far is eat." E.A. looked up at him. "Would you mind if we just walked around and maybe looked at a couple of the arts and crafts booths?"

"Not at all."

They continued walking down the packed dirt paths, stopping every so often for children to dart by or to say hello to various acquaintances. It was amazing how many people they knew there. Amish men and women. Mennonite friends from E.A.'s church. Customers from the sewing shop. Work associates from Will's work at the trailer factory.

E.A. would be lying if she said she hadn't felt a burst of pride the first time Will had introduced her as his girlfriend. She felt included and loved. Though she didn't want to think about David, she did find herself reflecting that she'd never felt as valued as she did now, when she was by Will's side. Whenever he introduced her, she heard a hint of pride in his voice. He really was pleased to have her as his girlfriend. In contrast, David had always acted as if he'd been doing her a favor by being her beau. She realized now that she'd become so used to that way of thinking that she hadn't allowed herself to envision being in a true romantic relationship.

When they eventually made their way to the arena, John and Marie were already seated on the back row of the metal bleachers.

"Hey, you two," Marie said as E.A. and Will scooted down the row toward them. "We were wondering when you were going to show up."

"Are we late? Sorry, we kept stopping and talking to people," Will said. "Then, of course, we had to get something to drink."

"It's really warm out," John said.

"How are your parents?"

"They're *gut*. They're planning a trip out west."

"Where?"

"Colorado."

"My aunt and uncle went to Estes Park two years ago," Elizabeth Anne said. "They said it was lovely."

When John started sharing his parents' plans, which involved being gone for three weeks on a Pioneer Trails bus, E.A. turned her attention down to the center of the arena. Boys and girls, roughly between twelve and fifteen or so, were showing calves. She loved seeing the pride shining in their faces almost as much as she loved watching some of the prettiest calves decide not to docilely walk beside them.

"Oh, Marie, look at that little girl trying to convince her calf to move."

Marie craned her neck and chuckled. "Isn't that how it always is? Animals have a mind of their own."

E.A. was just about to comment on how cute a little girl in a cowboy hat and boots was when she noticed Marie's expression had changed. "What do you see now?"

"It's nothing. I just hate to see a husband treating his wife that way."

"What?"

"Do you see that lady in the yellow print dress across the way? They're sitting almost directly across from us."

E.A. searched for a bright yellow dress and instantly recognized the woman wearing it. A whole wealth of emotions coursed through her. Happiness at the thought of seeing Marta again, curiosity, since she'd never thought of Marta as being particularly interested in farm animals . . . and dread, because she didn't want to see her husband mistreat sweet Marta. "I know her. She's my sewing student. What did you see?"

Marie frowned. "I noticed her because of that bright dress. But just as I was looking at her, thinking that she looked awfully familiar, I saw her husband grip her arm and say something harsh enough for her to look stricken."

Remembering that she'd witnessed that same kind of inter-action at the restaurant, E.A. felt her heart sink. "Her name is Marta. She's the nicest woman, but I tell you what, I don't think she's very happy. Her husband won't even let her have a car. She has to walk to our classes and is always worried about getting home on time."

"Marie?" John reached for her hand. "You look upset. Is something wrong?"

"Not at all." After sharing a look with E.A., she turned to her husband. "I was just telling E.A. how blessed I am to have you."

John raised his eyebrows but said nothing. Just looked pleased.

Just then the announcer began introducing the children and their livestock, and so there was no more time to talk. E.A. decided that was just as well. As much as she still enjoyed watch-ing the children, she now kept finding her attention drifting toward Marta and her husband.

There was something about her that E.A. couldn't ignore—and she couldn't help but wonder how such a different woman had made such an impression on her.

Lord, is there a reason You brought Marta and me together? she silently asked. *Was it to remind me to count my blessings, too? Or is there another, maybe more important reason?* Maybe it didn't even matter.

She and Marta were friends. Though they might never be

especially close, Elizabeth Anne definitely cared about her. That meant that her concern for Marta and her private life was growing. Just as her confusion about how she could help her was, too.

Time and again, even as the children showed their calves, her attention returned to Marta and her husband. She wondered what was going through Marta's mind.

"Hey," Will said as he leaned close. "What has you looking so glum?"

"My English sewing student is sitting across the way. I can't help but keep looking at her. She doesn't seem very happy to be with her husband."

"E.A., you know you *canna* judge any relationship simply by observing from a distance."

"I know." She lowered her voice. "But something just isn't right with them."

"I know it's not right for you to be staring at them so much," he chided. "You need to stop, *jah*? After all, there ain't nothing you can do."

She nodded, knowing Will was right.

But that still didn't stop her from wondering what she could do to help her timid student.

Or if she would simply be told to mind her own business if she said anything at all.

THIRTY

"I should probably add here that my parents weren't real happy when they learned that I'd not only snuck out of the house but also taken the car without asking. They said they'd talk to me about that in the morning."

Frank Zook was making Marta's life difficult. Instead of ignoring her and focusing only on Alan, he kept attempting to include her in the conversation. No matter how hard she tried to stay in the background, and yes, wait for Alan to say that she should leave the arena for an hour, the man kept asking her questions.

She knew he was simply being kind, and if she were anywhere else, she would have been grateful for his attention. He was treating her like a real person. But unfortunately, all of his questions about her life were difficult to answer. Alan stared at her so intently that she worried about every word she spoke. Suddenly, even sharing that she stayed home by herself most of the time seemed like too much information to share.

It made her a nervous wreck and made Alan irritated, especially when it was more than obvious to Mr. Zook that Alan knew next to nothing about his wife. He looked flabbergasted when she'd admitted that she'd actually made the backpack she'd brought.

And she thought she was going to faint when Mr. Zook looked as if he wanted her to take it off so he could admire her workmanship. That would have ruined everything. Her backpack was far heavier than it looked, thanks to all the money she had hidden in the lining.

Luckily for her, another gentleman caught the men's attention, and Frank took Alan over to introduce him. When they walked down the aisle left, she inhaled her first real breath of air in almost an hour. Knowing that she only had a few minutes before Alan would return, she tried to calm her nerves. It wasn't the right time to leave. Not yet.

When at last in the center of the arena the children were showing the calves that they'd been raising, Frank bid them good-bye and went down to the arena to be with his wife and their son.

As each minute ticked by, Marta felt her apprehension rise, and she could practically feel Alan's irritation emanate off of him. If he decided she was the reason for his problems, he could very well insist that they leave. Then her opportunity to escape would be gone.

He'd looked so appalled that she was wearing a handmade backpack she could even imagine him taking it from her. If that happened? Well, she couldn't bear to think about it.

She jumped when the announcer spoke into the microphone, introducing the next boy and his calf.

Alan noticed. "What's wrong with you?"

"Nothing." She smiled tightly. "I'm fine."

"Good." He smiled back at her. Almost as if he were actually concerned about her comfort.

Of course, they were both liars. She wasn't fine at all, and he didn't care. She actually felt like she was about to faint, she was so worried about getting away and finding help.

All she could think about was what would happen if she never left. For months she'd been saving money and dreaming about the day when she would be brave enough to leave her husband.

She'd felt like the Lord was finally giving her the perfect opportunity to break free. What if she never got another chance?

Another child entered the ring. This one was a little girl with a white calf. Its fur was so white and silky Marta knew the girl had probably been up early to give it a bath.

A pair of judges walked out, talking with the girl as they circled the calf.

The calf let out a little moo as it yanked on its bridle.

Marta tried to smile.

Each second passed like an hour. Instead of watching anything, she silently prayed for strength.

Another child entered the ring. As far as she could tell, Frank's boy was next. Then what would they do? Would Alan want to leave?

As the announcer started speaking over the loudspeaker, Alan leaned close to her ear. "Marta, I want you to leave us. He's never going to talk to me about business if you're here."

She looked at him, needing to make she wasn't imagining things.

He continued, "I'll tell Frank that you decided to meet some friends or something."

"Yes, Alan. I understand." Her heart was beating so fast she was sure he could hear it. Though every muscle in her body was screaming for her to get up and leave fast, she forced herself to speak calmly. "Where would you like me to meet you?"

"At the entrance." Alan looked at his watch. "In an hour. If I'm not there, wait." He glared at her. "Don't make me wait on you."

"I'll be there in an hour. I promise," she lied.

Just as she moved to get up, he pulled on the strap of her backpack. "Wait."

Her heart felt like it was in her throat. Was he going to make her leave her backpack with him?

"Yes, Alan?"

"Here."

Shock filled her as she realized he was handing her a twenty-dollar bill. "This should pay for a meal."

She got to her feet and carefully took the money from his hand. "Thank you, Alan. That is so nice of you."

"Can't have you telling anyone that I let you wander around empty-handed."

She smiled at him. "Goodbye," she said at last. Meaning every syllable of that word.

Forcing herself to walk slowly down the bleachers. Not to trip. Not to make a scene.

"Marta!"

Trembling, she turned. "Yes?"

He scowled at her. "Put that money away in your purse thingy. You might as well use it now. The moment we get home, I'm throwing it out."

Marta smiled tightly. "I will. I'll put it to good use now."

Carefully, she descended the rest of the stairs, waited for a group of teenagers to get by, then headed toward the open doorway.

The bright sunshine outside had never looked more welcoming.

THIRTY-ONE

"Anyway, back in the basement, we were all struggling with what to do about poor Marie. Andy tried to tease her about the night's events. That didn't go over real well, though. Katie and I tried to act like we knew what she was going through. We didn't, though, of course."

One day shortly after Christmas, around the time Will was seven years old, his mother had been watching Andy, Marie, and Logan for a few hours. Marie had been lugging around a new doll that she'd gotten from Santa Claus and had forbid any of them to touch it.

Now that he was older, Will couldn't say he blamed her. But back then, he, Andy, and Logan had simply been a bunch of little boys. Fun for them involved playing in the dirt and running outside in the snow. Marie's pleasure in playing with her doll was lost on him.

If he was honest, he'd also thought that Marie had been acting mighty selfish. He couldn't understand why she hadn't even allowed his little sister, Nan, to have a turn with her new gift. From the moment Marie had been dropped off, Nan had been eyeing that baby doll like it was the prettiest thing she'd ever seen. For some reason, he hadn't liked that one bit.

Because of that, when Marie fell asleep on a cot in his mother's sewing room, he'd crept in and taken that doll. Feeling pretty good about himself, he'd marched right over to four-year-old Nan and handed it to her. He'd even lied and said that she could play with it for a couple of hours. After all, Marie wouldn't be needing it while she was sleeping—and they all knew she took really long naps.

Of course, just like so many "good" ideas that quickly backfired, the doll had gone from Nan's hands to two-year-old Jake's hands. Jake had been eating peanut butter and crackers and he coated the doll's fancy purple dress with it good.

Jake, bored with the thing, had tossed it on the ground. Andy and Logan picked it up, tossed it around like a football for a while, then decided to hide it.

When Marie woke up and found the doll missing, chaos reigned. Marie cried and cried. Then Will's mother got involved. Then Nan and Jake cried after it was discovered that they'd played with the doll. Finally, Logan and Andy were sent outside to dig up one very ratty-looking baby doll. After they handed it to Marie—who cried again—they got a stern talking-to by his mother.

And he? Well, he had been told that he would get his lecture the minute everyone else went home for the night.

His father had given him a good swat on his rear end, which had hurt, though not nearly as badly as his feelings when both his parents lectured him for a good thirty minutes.

However the worst part had been his confusion. He'd told his mother that he didn't understand why he always had to share his things and his home (and yes, even his mother) with all of his friends, but they didn't have to share anything with him. He didn't think it was fair at all.

He'd thought it was a very good argument, indeed.

His parents had not.

"But Jesus didn't promise that life would be fair, Will," his father murmured. "You need to stop thinking that everything in your life should be."

Will hadn't realized it at the time, but his father's words had had an enormous impact on him. Through school and his hunt for work and even as he navigated his friendships, he forced himself to not expect too much or any recognition. Instead, he'd perfected the art of getting along with others.

Even through those dark days after Andy Warner's death, Will kept his faith and didn't ask why such a thing had happened. Instead he dwelled on the Lord's will and gave thanks for His blessings.

But now, as he walked by Elizabeth Anne's side and caught sight of her quick smiles—and, yes, some men's looks of appreciation sent her way—he realized that the Lord actually was fair, after all.

Elizabeth Anne surely was his reward for sharing so much when he was little. Her company had to be the reason he'd learned to stop complaining and started being happy for other people. Today, *he* was the lucky man who got to be called hers.

He knew he must have done something right to deserve that.

Today her long hair was in a mess of complicated braids away from her face. It looked shiny and healthy, just like the rest of her did.

And her heart. He was so proud of her for caring so much for everyone else. Even a visibly unhappy older woman who was her sewing student. Who else would care so much about the happiness of someone who was practically a stranger?

"Now you seem to be the one who is lost in thought," E.A. said as they sat down with Marie and John to eat some pulled pork sandwiches at a picnic table. "What have you been thinking about?"

"Believe it or not, I was thinking back when Marie and I were seven or so."

Marie put down her sandwich. "Really?"

"*Jah.* Do you remember that time you came over with your doll right after Christmas?"

Marie half covered her face with a hand. "Oh, my word. Jewel!"

E.A. grinned. "You named your doll Jewel?"

"Oh, yes. I thought she was the prettiest thing that I'd ever seen." Marie sighed. "Boy, I loved that doll."

"How come I don't remember it?" John asked.

Looking at her husband, Marie said, "You weren't at the Kurtzes' house the day I brought it over." Sounding bemused, she continued, "I'm afraid I begged Santa Claus for that doll for months. The moment I opened her package on Christmas morning, I would hardly let Jewel leave my sight."

John looked bewildered. "Any particular reason you've been thinking about Marie and her baby doll while we're at the county fair, Will?"

Will felt his cheeks heat. Put that way, it did sound mighty strange. "It's a convoluted reason, I guess. But I got to thinking about how much trouble I got in because I took that doll when Marie was asleep so Nan could play with it."

"I guess that was rude, but not that big of a deal," E.A. said.

"It wouldn't have been, except that Jake got peanut butter all over it before Andy and Logan decided to hide it in the snow by the woodpile."

"And I started carrying on like she'd been stolen and ruined forever," Marie admitted.

"I'm sorry I missed that day," John teased.

"I'm not," Marie said. "I'm very glad you don't have that memory of me acting like such a spoiled little girl in your head." Picking up her soda, she playfully glared at Will. "Thanks for bringing it up, Will."

"I promise, I didn't mean anything by it." Not wanting to bring up his father's fairness lecture, he said, "I guess I was just thinking about how we've all known each other for a long time. And, here we all are."

E.A. smiled at him. "I think the same thing all the time. I don't think we would trust each other or be as close if we hadn't gone through so many things together. You can't beat years of friendships."

"This is true." Deciding to wait until they were alone to admit how he was thinking of her as his reward, Will stood up to throw away his trash. "So, it's getting toward sundown. What does everyone want to do?"

"Go on a couple of rides," Marie said.

"Which ones?" E.A. asked nervously. "I'm warning you now that I won't go on anything that flips over."

"Me, neither," John said. "Especially not after this meal."

"Oh, you all are a bunch of spoilsports," Marie complained.

"Just because I don't have an iron stomach like you doesn't mean I don't like to have fun," E.A. said. "I know—how about we start with the Ferris wheel?"

Will thought it looked both rickety and boring. "Out of everything here, you want to go on the Ferris wheel?"

"Come on," John said. "It will be fun. The sun is going down and all the rides' lights are coming on. We'll be able to see everything."

"This is true." Realizing that he'd also be sharing a seat with E.A. and that they'd be essentially alone, Will grinned. "I say yes."

"Thank you, Will." E.A.'s eyes were warm and soft. "I can't wait."

"Me, neither," he said with a grin.

"Marie?" John prodded. "Even if it isn't the Tilt-A-Whirl, will you get on it with me?"

She slipped her hand in his. "You know I'm not letting you go anywhere without me."

Eyes shining, E.A. said, "It's official, then! A perfect way to end the evening."

As they started walking, Will thought he caught sight of David standing next to a food cart. He was watching them.

He paused, wondering if he should go over and give David another talking-to, this one a whole lot less kind and a whole lot more threatening. But if he did that, he knew he would ruin E.A.'s good mood. Maybe even the rest of their night.

There was a time and a place for everything. This wasn't it.

"Will, are you coming?" E.A. called out. She'd moved up and was talking with Marie and John.

"*Jah*, sure," he replied as he quickened his pace. "Sorry, I thought I saw someone I knew."

"Did you?"

After hurriedly throwing the can of soda he'd been drinking

in the trash, he dropped an arm around E.A.'s shoulders and motioned her forward. "Nah. I was mistaken."

Now all he had to do was hope and pray that E.A. wouldn't spy David for the rest of the night. If that happened, their good time might be ruined.

He couldn't think of anything worse.

THIRTY-TWO

"Logan said we should turn on the television. So, I did, and found some old Indiana Jones movie. Just when things started getting exciting, we noticed that John and Marie were completely ignoring the movie and whispering softly to each other. Marie, for the first time all night, looked happy."

*S*he was free. Walking through the fairgrounds, Marta kept her head down and her pace quick. She'd had only the faintest of plans for seeking help. All that had mattered was getting away from Alan—she hadn't thought beyond that.

She'd contemplated going to the entrance of the fairgrounds and calling for an Uber to take her to the police station, but she didn't want to spend the money or use her cell phone if she could help it. Alan could always call the phone company and demand to see its records.

Instead, she'd decided that it would be best to find a police officer or a sheriff, tell him or her about her situation, and then beg to be taken to a shelter. But when she saw a deputy in a light tan uniform right outside the livestock pavilion, she passed him and kept walking. He was too close to where Alan was, and she wanted to be out of her husband's direct sight.

Because of that, or maybe because she was so nervous, she kept getting turned around. Then, when she was finally at the far side of the fairgrounds, she couldn't find a single law enforcement official.

Was she going to have to head back toward the livestock areas to find someone?

Sweat began to trickle down the sides of her face and the back of her neck. As each minute passed, she began to doubt her chances to escape. Soon, Alan would be at the entrance and wondering where she was. His irritation would simmer into anger if she didn't show up. And then what would he do?

Marta closed her eyes. She knew the answer to that all too well.

Feeling a little dizzy, she forced herself to stand in the shade of a tent to calm down. Nothing had happened yet. Alan still thought she was fine. He wasn't going to realize she was gone for at least another thirty minutes. She no longer had to fear him.

She breathed a sigh of relief when she finally located a police-woman near a pretzel stand. She was talking to a pair of teenagers but seemed nice enough.

Marta's heart started to pound with relief . . . and trepidation. It was time to finally do what she'd been planning for a year: share her story. But what if the woman didn't believe her? Or what if she told her to simply go to the police station another time? Could she do that? She wasn't sure. Did she actually have another escape attempt in her?

No, she had to do this now, and make this woman understand that she needed help immediately.

Feeling more confident, Marta waited her turn to speak with the officer, mentally rehearsing her speech all the while.

But then the teens needed the officer to give them directions.

Marta couldn't help but glare at the teens. Didn't they see other people needed help? Unable to control her fidgeting, she tapped one foot.

The officer looked her way. "May I help you?"

"Yes, but I can wait."

The woman's expression turned puzzled. "Are you sure? Because this is going to take me a minute. Do you need directions, too?"

"I don't need directions. I can wait." When one of the teens snickered at her response, Marta felt her cheeks heat. She'd sounded like a robot.

Her hands fisted as she once again cautioned herself to calm down and stop fidgeting. Oh, this was not how she'd imagined things were going to go!

Another two minutes passed. Then three. Every couple of seconds, one of the teenagers turned to stare at her while the officer pulled up directions on her phone.

Marta felt sweat slide down the center of her back under her backpack. It was hot and dusty, but she knew it wasn't the heat that was getting the best of her. It was this moment. Everything inside her felt exposed and vulnerable.

Unbidden, a middle school science lesson came to mind— her teacher had been talking about animals' instincts to either fight or flee. She'd never thought about herself as being reduced to something so basic, but it seemed she'd been wrong.

Over the last year she'd decided to go into her own battle.

She'd saved money. Signed up for a sewing class. Developed a plan. Bided her time, even though there had been many days when she'd wanted to simply give up

She could do this. If she survived, she could.

Realizing that Alan was probably at the fairground's entrance now and scanning the area, Marta felt dizzy again. She felt herself sway.

"Ma'am?" the police officer said as she hurried to Marta's side. "Ma'am, are you all right?"

Marta blinked. Once again, she'd been lost in her thoughts. The teenagers who were still standing nearby looked her way and giggled before walking away.

Now was the time she had to fight the hardest. She had to do this. Going backward wasn't possible. No, it would kill her.

"I'm sorry, but no," she said at last. "No, I'm not all right."

The officer looked her over. "What is wrong?" Concern flared in her brown eyes. "Are you ill?"

She shook her head. "I'm not ill, but I need help." She looked at the woman beseechingly. "Please. I need help right now."

The officer stepped closer. "What's wrong? Are you lost?"

"I'm not lost." Grabbing a firm hold on herself, she said, "I need to get to a safe place as soon as possible."

"Because?"

The noise around her ceased to exist. She ignored the teenagers standing close, the squeals of excitement from the children on the rides. "Because if my husband discovers I'm trying to leave him, he's going to kill me."

The officer's whole stance changed. An alertness filled her expression. After looking around the area, she motioned with her hand. "Come stand over here. We need to talk about this."

No, she didn't need to talk about anything—she needed to get out of here. To hide. Bile stung her throat as a dozen frightening scenarios filled her head. She swallowed and told herself to remain calm.

"All right." She followed the officer to the side of a building under an overhang.

"Now, tell me again, ma'am?" She paused, looking irritated with herself. "I'm sorry. What is your name?"

"Marta . . ."

"Marta what?"

"I . . . can't. Not yet."

"All right," she said slowly, like Marta was a small child. "Marta, just to be sure I understand . . . Do you really believe your husband will kill you if you leave him?"

"Yes." Marta started feeling frustrated. She'd been naive to assume that as soon as she told someone in a uniform that she needed help her troubles would be over.

But now things were even worse. Her bright yellow dress and floral backpack stood out. She was a bigger target than before. Desperate, she did the only thing she could think of to spur some action. She unbuttoned the cuff on her left sleeve and slowly rolled up the fabric to reveal swollen skin and a dark set of bruises.

The officer flinched.

"This was from last night," she said, taking care to speak slowly and carefully. The officer had to understand what had been happening to her. "My husband pulled me down a set of stairs because he didn't think the kitchen floor was clean enough."

The other woman looked shaken and muttered something under her breath.

She looked into the officer's eyes. "If I undressed, I could show you the matching set on my left shoulder and a welt on my thigh. Please. I need your help right now."

Her expression full of compassion, she nodded. "Yes, you do, ma'am." She plucked at the radio that was attached to a utility belt at her hip. "Let me call for some reinforcements. I can't leave this area without getting coverage."

"Can't we hurry? My husband's going to realize I've left and try to find me."

"I'm hurrying, Marta. And don't worry, even if he does approach you, I'll stop him."

Marta nodded, but she didn't feel any better. The officer was wearing a uniform, but she didn't look that much stronger than Marta. Alan was a big man, over two hundred pounds. If he found them, Alan could hurt the officer and pull her away.

Standing against the wall of the building, Marta felt goose bumps rise on her skin as she heard the officer mumble into her radio to call for reinforcements. Seconds later, she put it back into her belt.

"Two deputies from the sheriff's office are nearby. They'll be here within ten minutes and then take you to their offices. There, you can fill out some paperwork and decide your next step."

Ten minutes? Her next steps? The policewoman was talking like she was trying to get rid of a parking ticket. Though she guessed the officer thought this made perfect sense, Marta was so panicked, she didn't want to wait another second to get out of sight. "Ma'am, I really need to go someplace where he can't find me," said Marta. "As soon as possible."

"To do this right, we need to follow protocol." When Marta was about to argue, the officer said gently, "I promise. These steps are in place for a reason."

"Yes." She exhaled. "All right."

Now that she was calmer, the officer looked relieved. "I know you're afraid, but I think you are being very brave. Hang in there."

"I will. Thank you." Marta smiled, feeling some of that same relief. She'd done it, she reminded herself. She'd actually walked away, sought help, and admitted out loud what had been happening to her in private. She wouldn't have been able to do any of those things two years ago. She really had been brave.

"So, this is what's going to happen next," the officer said. "When Deputies Consuelo and Japphet arrive, one will take my place, then you, me, and the other officer will be on our way."

"Okay. Thank you."

"Piece of cake." Just as the officer smiled at Marta, another woman about Marta's age came running up to her, a baby in her arms.

"We need an ambulance! My baby has a peanut allergy. I gave him a Benadryl but he's not doing well. I'm really scared!"

Without a backward glance, the officer got on the radio, calling for medical assistance and an ambulance.

The mother started to cry as the child visibly struggled to breathe.

The officer looked torn. But when the child looked to be having a seizure and his mother screamed, the officer rushed to help them. "Someone will be here in five!" she called out.

The next thing Marta knew, she was standing by herself again.

And looking into Alan's face as he strode over to her from thirty yards away.

She did the only thing she could—she started praying. She'd been as brave as she could on her own. Now she needed the Lord's help and His strength, too.

THIRTY-THREE

"After a few minutes, knowing one of my parents was sure to come down to check on us, I walked over to John and Marie. You know, to say that they better come sit with the rest of us. And that's when I overheard what John said to her."

"*E*.A., I *canna* believe you just screeched so loudly," Will teased. "Are you really that scared?"

"I can't help but be afraid. We're really high right now!" E.A. exclaimed as the ancient Ferris wheel came to a jerky, swaying stop.

While she wasn't truly scared—just a little nervous—she was still glad to have him to hold on to. She scooted closer.

Will laughed as he covered her shoulders with his arm. "Elizabeth Anne, you never cease to surprise me. I didn't think you could be so skittish."

"In my defense, I didn't know I was afraid of heights until now," she grumbled.

"But you've flown before."

"Yes, but that was different. I was in a sturdy plane being flown by a pilot. And I was buckled in my seat. I wasn't swaying in the open air in a metal box operated by a teenager."

Will chuckled. "You may have a point."

"I know I do!" She sucked in a deep breath as the wheel began moving again, this time making almost a whole complete circle before they jerked to a stop near the top so another pair could get off and a pair of children could get on. "This ride is never gonna end."

Will chuckled again. "Your problem is that you need to relax and enjoy it."

"Enjoy swaying in the sky?"

"*Nee.*" Pointing below them, to an older woman leading an Appaloosa whose mane and tail were beribboned with blue satin bows, he said, "You should look around at everything that's going on. Why, there are all kinds of things going on down there. This is the perfect spot to people watch."

E.A. did enjoy people watching, that was true. But people watching also meant looking down. "I'm trying . . ."

He lowered his voice. "Of course, if you don't want to enjoy the sights, we could always do what Marie and John B. are doing . . ."

"What?" Sitting up straighter, she craned her neck so she could see their cart just above them. Then she really wished she hadn't. "Will, they're kissing." Actually, they were practically making out.

"Indeed they are. They look like they are having a really good time, too." He grinned. "So, what do you say? Do you want to kiss me? It will not only stop you from being so scared, but it also seems like an excellent way to pass the time."

"Stop. You know I like our kisses, but I'm not ready to be quite so public with our affection."

He squeezed her shoulder. "For some reason, I thought you might say that."

Grinning to herself, she glanced down at all the people below, trying to look for the beautiful Appaloosa. Then she saw an ambulance parked just to the left of the horses. "Uh-oh. Someone must have gotten hurt."

"*Jah*." Will's voice was more somber. "I can't tell who it is, but there's no telling, ain't so? It's hot, there's lots of people, animals. Anything could happen, I reckon."

"I hope the person who is hurt will be okay," E.A. murmured. Just as their cart jerked upward again, a flash of yellow caught her eye. She gasped. "Will!"

"Hold on to me, E.A. I won't let you fall," he murmured.

"No, it's not that. I saw Marta down there."

"Your sewing friend? Hey, didn't you see her earlier, too?" Before she could interrupt, he continued, "I bet we're going to be able to see lots of people we know from up here." He leaned forward to point. "Hey, that guy kind of looks like Evan from work. I ought to try to call out to him. Do you think he could hear us from—"

"Will, listen to me. This is important. Marta—" She craned her neck and gasped. Marta's husband was yelling as he walked over to her. Then, he grabbed her arm and yanked her to his side. Marta tried to pull away but stumbled.

Feeling helpless, E.A. moaned. "Oh my word, Will. Marta is in trouble. Her husband is next to her and he's being so mean."

"Hmm?" He looked to where she pointed. She knew the moment he, too, spied what was going on because his whole body stiffened. "My Lord. He's practically twisting her arm. I think she's crying, but no one is paying her any mind because of the ambulance."

Unable to look away, E.A. winced. "She's really struggling now." Marta's husband was still gripping her arm but Marta was shaking her head and protesting. Scanning the crowd, E.A. waited for someone else to get involved, but no one seemed inclined to do anything but watch.

The Ferris wheel started moving again, this time bringing them to a stop near the ground. E.A. lost sight of Marta and her husband as they got closer to the ground. E.A. felt sick. "As soon as we get off, we have to do something."

Will's expression tightened as he nodded. "*Jah*. We do. I don't know what— Oh. Good. John and Marie just got off." Looking down, he exhaled. "John! Hey, John!"

John and Marie looked up at them. "Hey, you two," Marie called out with a sunny smile. "Don't worry. We won't leave. We'll—"

"*Nee*. Listen! There's a woman over by the ambulance in a yellow dress," Will called out. "She's a friend of E.A.'s and she's in trouble. You need to find the police."

"Please hurry!" E.A. yelled as the wheel stopped yet again. Both Marie and John stared up at them in confusion.

"Say again?" John said as they climbed higher.

"We're not kidding," Will called down. "Someone is hurting her!"

E.A. watched John pulled out his phone. "I think they're calling for help."

"At last." Will looked down into the crowd. "I'm trying to find Marta, E.A. She couldn't have gone far."

"I know." Worry suffused her. Each second that passed felt like an eternity.

Then, at last, the Ferris wheel brought Elizabeth Anne and Will to the ground. E.A. could barely sit still while the worker slowly unlocked the bar holding them in. "Did you have a good time?" he asked.

Ignoring him completely, Will grabbed E.A.'s hand.

She held on tightly as they took off across the fairgrounds, John and Marie behind them. All together, they ran toward the last place E.A. and Will had seen Marta.

Men, women, and children all scattered around them as they ran, trying to get out of their way. A couple of people yelled at them to slow down, but E.A. paid them no attention.

Only one thing mattered to E.A.: getting to Marta's side and helping her.

E.A. hoped and prayed that they would get there quickly. And that when they did, it wasn't too late.

THIRTY-FOUR

"John said that he would always be there for Marie. And for all of us. That no matter what happened in the future, we would all be there for each other."

*W*ill's father was one of the best men he knew. He was calm and patient and faithful. From the time Will was a little boy, his father had tried to teach him to be an upstanding man—and one who took their religion seriously. Because of that, Will knew that turning the other cheek was the best way to behave. He also knew that violence was never the answer to solving problems.

But as Will rushed through the crowd toward Marta and her husband, he knew he had no choice in the matter.

He couldn't stand aside.

As they charged forward, he heard E.A. call out to John and Marie, "We need your help!"

Thank the Lord, neither of their friends protested about getting involved, though he probably would've been shocked if they had. Though none of the Eight was perfect, each was a good person, and they trusted each other implicitly. If one of them asked for help, the others joined in automatically, even for someone outside of their tight group.

As they continued to walk quickly around a cart selling lemonade, he spied Marta's bright dress. Just as he was about to tell E.A., she inhaled sharply.

"Oh, thank goodness, I see them!" E.A. called out. "They're right over there. She dropped Will's hand and charged forward.

"E.A., wait!" he called out.

But she either didn't hear him or was ignoring his call. He weaved in and out of the crowd. "E.A.!"

When she turned around, obviously exasperated, he reached for her hand. "You can't just charge over there. We need a plan."

Looking obstinate, she shook her head. "*Nee*, we need to stop this, Will. I know you're going to think I'm crazy, but I am sure the Lord put me in Marta's life for this very moment. I have to help her. I have no choice."

"Of course, but—"

Marie, having caught up, stepped in. "Will, you, John, and E.A. go talk to them. I'll go speak to that sheriff and get him to join us."

Just as Will and E.A. stepped forward, John hesitated. "Are you sure you want to speak to him alone, Marie? I could stay with you."

"No, you go ahead," Marie replied. "I'll be fine. I promise. Since I've worked in the bank all these years, I've had a lot more experience speaking with law enforcement officers than you have."

"Come on, Will," E.A. said urgently.

After giving Marie a thumbs-up, Will turned to E.A.'s side.

"Hey, Elizabeth Anne, I know you're anxious, but don't forget that we can't chance making things worse."

"I know."

"Okay . . ." Just as Will was about to caution E.A. to be careful, he saw Marta's husband pull her by his side and start walking. If they hesitated a moment longer, they were going to lose them in the crowd. "Hey! Stop!" he yelled.

"Oh no." E.A. moaned. She took off, running directly toward Marta and her husband.

Will inhaled sharply as he and John took off behind her. As they ran he began praying as fervently as he could. He asked for His strength. Asked for His protection for Marta and E.A. Even asked the Lord to help him not make things worse.

"Almost there," John muttered by his side.

Just as they reached them, E.A. shouted, "Marta!" Her tone was loud and shrill. Loud enough for several people around them to stop suddenly and stare.

Marta turned her head and stared at E.A. Her husband pulled back his hand, obviously about to hit her.

Will knew then he couldn't just pray. He had to act. "*Nee!*" he yelled. "Let go!"

"Someone help us," John said to the growing crowd of people watching them and pointing at Marta and her husband. "That man is hurting her."

"Hey, now," a big, burly man said. "You ain't got no call to get involved—"

Marta cried out and stumbled as Alan yanked her arm.

Several people around them gasped.

E.A. was at Marta's side now. "Marta, are you okay?" Will heard her ask. "We're getting help. I promise."

"Get away from her," Marta's husband yelled. "This is none of your business."

"No. You stop!" Marta called out.

Before anyone could do anything, her husband kicked her.

That action seemed to be all the proof that the crowd needed to at last rush to help. Just as Will was about to pull E.A. toward him so she wouldn't get hurt, the burly man and several other men from the crowd grabbed Marta's husband's arms. On his heels, two other men, one of whom was John, practically wrestled him to the ground.

While they struggled Will helped E.A. lower Marta to the ground. She was ashen and looked about to faint. Tears were also in her eyes.

Will prayed again, asking for His help.

Just then, Marta seemed to settle down a tiny bit. He noticed then that the woman was clinging to E.A. with her good hand. "Thank you," she whispered.

Will knelt on one knee. "Marta, our friend went to get the sheriff. You do want our help, right? You do want the police to get involved?"

"Oh, yes," she whispered just as Marie, the sheriff, and two other police officers hurried over.

Two of them strode toward the group surrounding Marta's husband. A female officer moved toward Marta. Her eyes were sharp as she inspected her. Will could tell that the officer was taking in every bit of Marta, from the unnatural way she was holding her arm against her body to the bright red mark on her cheek.

"Oh my stars, Marta. I am so sorry," the officer said as she knelt down next to Will. "I turned around and you were gone."

"It's okay," Marta said in a low tone. "The little boy was sick."

"He was. But I feel horrible. I let you down."

"I was afraid, but it's okay now," Marta replied.

"It's going to be all right now," the officer murmured. "I promise." Looking up at Marie, she smiled. "Thank goodness your friends made sure we dropped everything and ran over here."

"They wouldn't take no for an answer," Will said.

Marta stared at Marie in confusion. "You argued with the police officers? But we don't even know each other."

"I'm friends with Elizabeth Anne," Marie said simply as she, too, knelt on the ground. "When she said you needed help, all of us"—she looked at Will and smiled—"well, we wanted to help as best we could."

"I've called for an ambulance and more help," the sheriff said as he walked over to join them.

Looking worried, Marta sat up. "An ambulance? Oh, no. I don't need that. I can walk."

"I'll help you stand up, Marta, but I think getting in would be a good idea," the officer said. "You need to get checked out. I'm afraid your arm might be broken."

Marta shivered as she stared down at her arm. "Oh. Yes. I think you might be right." She darted a worried look over at her husband, who was now standing handcuffed and silently glaring over at them. "What about Alan?"

"We're getting a squad car for him," the sheriff answered with a satisfied expression. "He'll go to the station for questioning."

E.A. spoke. "Will Marta have to worry about him coming over to the hospital?"

"I think we're going to have plenty of reasons for him to cool his heels in our jail for a while." The officer who had knelt by Marta smiled grimly. "Look at all these witnesses. Why, I think it's going to take several hours to get all of their statements."

Will stood up and hugged both John and Marie when he joined him. As more officers came and they heard the faint sirens of an approaching ambulance, John watched, heart in his throat, as E.A. whispered something to Marta and gently hugged her before walking over to the group.

"Don't go anywhere," the officer warned. "I'm going to need to talk to all of you."

"We won't," said Marie before hugging E.A. tightly.

As the crowd around them began to disperse, Will felt like he was finally getting his bearings. "That was incredible," he said to their group.

Marie looked exuberant. "E.A., I'm so proud of you!" she whispered. "You got your friend to safety! She's going to be okay now because of you."

E.A. shook her head. "No, it was because of all of us. You, Will, John, those strangers. Even Marta herself!" She smiled. "I think the Lord was on our side, too. We all protected Marta. And while we did that, our amazing Lord protected us."

Will kissed her forehead. "Amen to that. Amen to that."

THIRTY-FIVE

"I don't think John lied," she told the crowd. "We're an imperfect bunch, you see. We make mistakes and do stupid things and, um, often our best ideas don't always turn out that good."

*I*t was dark out. Riding home in the backseat of Marie and John's SUV, E.A. didn't know if she'd ever felt so tired yet so exhilarated at the same time.

After the female police officer—Officer Fuller—helped Marta get loaded into the ambulance, she'd taken E.A., John, Will, and Marie to a small office at the front of the fairgrounds.

Minutes later another police officer joined them. Then, with notebooks out, they asked the four of them an exhausting set of questions.

After they all recounted their run from the base of the Ferris wheel to Marta's side, John, Marie, and Will were escorted to a waiting room while E.A. was kept back for even more questioning.

E.A. had known the reason: she was the one who knew

Marta the best, and she'd also had that one previous interaction with the man she now knew for sure was Alan Miner.

She'd answered each question as thoroughly as she could, concentrating only on the facts of what happened and her instinctive need to help. She knew if she started imagining what could have happened if they hadn't been successful, she would break down into tears.

She still couldn't believe all that had transpired. Of how they'd been able to help Marta!

After E.A. had finished, she was led back to her friends. Then the sheriff asked a few more questions about what they saw Alan do to Marta, or how each of them had tried to help. Though each added what they could, E.A. found herself saying the most yet again. However, this time she had Will's hand wrapped around her own. He nodded encouragement when she paused in her story and added details whenever E.A. hesitated or faltered.

Finally, after giving the sheriff their contact information, they were free to go.

E.A. had no idea where Marta was or if she'd ever see her again. The sheriff didn't share anything with the group other than that Marta was "safe" and her needs "were being seen to."

It was hard for E.A. to realize that was all the information they were going to get, but in some ways, the respect for Marta's privacy seemed fitting. Marta had many secrets—and had obviously been holding a lot of pain and hurt close to her chest.

Riding home in Marie's Escalade, E.A. figured the four of them looked like they'd been put through the wringer. Each of them was rattled by what had just happened.

"Who should I drop off first?" Marie asked when they reached the outskirts of Walnut Creek.

"You have to pass my house first. You might as well drop me off then," Will said. "Is that fine with you, E.A.?"

"Hmm? Oh, sure. Whatever is easiest."

Five minutes later, Marie pulled into Will's drive. By mutual agreement, she stopped the car and they all got out.

Marie hugged Will goodbye and John slapped him on the shoulder. "Will, buddy, next time you ask us to come to the fair with you . . ."

"Yes?"

He grinned. "Remind me to tell ya that I have other plans."

"Don't worry. I'm not eager to go back again."

Turning to Elizabeth Anne, John said, "You know I'm joking, right? I'm glad we were there to help Marta."

E.A. knew John was being sincere, but she also knew that the whole experience had been traumatic for all of them. "Truly?" she teased. "Even though you had to spend the last two hours in a sheriff's office?"

He shrugged. "That was a new thing for me, for sure. But it doesn't mean it wasn't worth it."

Marie walked to his side. "I can't even joke about it, you guys. I can't believe that Marta's husband kicked her right in front of the whole crowd! He looked so mean, and she looked just like a cornered animal. Scared to death." She shuddered. "I would never want someone to think they had no choice in how to live."

John wrapped an arm around his wife's shoulders. "She has help now."

"I know, and I'm so glad." After giving John a sweet smile, Marie walked over to E.A. and pressed her hands on either side of her cheeks. "I hope you know how proud I am of you, E.A.," she whispered. "I'll never forget how brave you were today. I want to be more like you."

The praise was very sweet, but undeserved. "I wasn't brave. And it wasn't just me."

"No, it was," Will said. Looking at her intently, he said, "It's so easy to see something happening and say that it isn't our problem. Maybe it's even too easy for a man like me, who grew up Amish. If you weren't with me, I might have watched Marta and her husband and thought it was a sad situation but not done anything about it. Helping them? Putting Marta's needs in front of my own? It's made me stronger. Better, even. Never again will I be afraid to help a woman or child in need."

"They're right," John said. "You did good today, E.A."

"Thank you," E.A. said at last.

After Marie and John said they'd wait for her in the car, E.A. turned to Will. "I guess there isn't anything else to say."

"Nothing except that I'll see you tomorrow, and that I love you, E.A," he whispered.

"I love you back," she replied with a smile. When he pulled her into his arms, she relaxed against him, enjoying how cherished and secure he made her feel.

After kissing her lightly on the lips, he stepped away. "Good night. I'll see you tomorrow." Then he headed into his house.

Feeling like she was in a daze, E.A. returned to the car and got in the backseat, resting her head against the cushion as Marie backed onto the road.

Ten minutes later, when Marie pulled into Elizabeth Anne's driveway, both of her parents walked out to greet them. E.A. had called them from the sheriff's office and filled them in on the bare facts of what had happened.

Seeing their looks of concern, E.A. braced herself. She knew they wanted to be filled in on everything. And when she did that, she was going to have to admit that she'd been harboring some worries about Marta for some time.

"Good night, E.A.," Marie said as E.A. unbuckled her seat belt. "I don't think I'll get out again, since your parents are here."

"I understand. Thank you for driving. And, well, for everything." Including John in her gaze, she said, "I owe you both so much."

"You take care, E.A.," John said. "I'll reach out to everyone about what happened. I think it would be a good idea if all of us got together."

Marie smiled at her softly. "We'll have quite a story to tell, won't we? Who would have ever guessed that my John knew how to tackle grown men so easily?"

Smiling at them both, E.A. climbed out of the backseat and turned to face her parents.

"Hi."

Her mother walked forward. "You okay?"

Maybe it was her mother's gentle question. Maybe it was the way her father was looking at her with a new warmth in his gaze that she recognized as pride.

But whatever the reason, she released a ragged sigh she hadn't even realized she'd been holding and answered completely honestly.

"You know what? I just don't know."

"Come on in and have some peppermint tea," her mother murmured as she led the way inside.

"*Danke*, Mamm," she whispered, just as the tears began to fall. Tears for Marta and her fear, and maybe for the whole situation, a situation she wished had never happened in the first place.

But right as she sat down on the sofa, E.A. remembered one other thing. Just as Marta was walking away, her chin lifted. Her student, her friend, had been triumphant.

Now, that was something to savor, indeed.

THIRTY-SIX

"But I reckon what is important is that no matter what happens, we all have each other's backs."

*I*t had been a long night, and it was made even longer when Jake, Nan, and his parents shuttled Will into the family room and insisted he tell them all what happened.

So, after getting a fortifying cup of coffee dosed with plenty of cream and sugar, Will had done just that. But, of course, because it was his family—and because Nan could pull information out of a turnip—he wasn't allowed to skim over one bit of the event.

Though Will wasn't exactly fond of retelling the whole story close to midnight, he couldn't deny that being able to add his own feelings and commentary had felt cathartic. He hadn't realized until then just how conflicted he had felt about the whole event.

His mother noticed first. "What's going on, *boo*? You don't seem as pleased as I thought you would be."

He leaned back in his chair. "I am pleased—and proud of our efforts. Marta needed someone to help her, and I feel blessed that God gave me the opportunity to help as much as I could." Looking straight at his father, he said, "Daed, I believed all the stories you told us growing up—about how it is better to turn the other cheek. To be honest, I never thought I could be the kind of man who would enter into a conflict."

Jake grunted. "Well, I should hope you would be. You couldn't have just stood by and watched. Someone had to help that woman out."

"*Nee*, of course not," he said slowly. "But, for a moment there, I think I wanted that man to hurt. *Nee*, that's not right. What I'm trying to say is that *I* wanted to be the one to hurt him. He was hurting his wife so much, something inside of me wanted to put a stop to it right then and there."

His mother looked surprised. "My word, Will."

"I know." Looking at his father again, he murmured, "I'm sorry, Daed."

"Son, just because you used violence with good reason doesn't mean that you've become a violent sort. I think it just means that when your back is against the wall and you feel you have no choice, well, you are going to help as much as you can. And that's what you did. You helped E.A., and most of all, that poor woman."

Nan shivered dramatically. "I can't imagine being so afraid of my husband that I had to run away from him."

Jake folded his arms across his chest. "That's something to be thankful for. I hope you never have anyone treat you like that."

Nan smiled softly at him. "Thank you, Jake." She turned to Will. "Hey, Will?"

"*Jah?*"

"What do you think is going to happen to that woman now?"

"We learned that she was released from the hospital and taken to a women's shelter. I guess she'll meet with people there about pressing charges against her husband."

Nan's expression darkened. "I hope she can get a divorce, too."

Will nodded. He didn't believe in divorce, but there were times for exceptions.

"After she gets her bearings, I guess she'll have to start over," Mamm said.

Will nodded. "The whole way home, Marie, John, E.A., and I talked about everything. But to be honest, I don't think we ever really talked about how Marta is going to feel tomorrow morning, or even when she wakes up a month from now. I bet she's going to feel a little bewildered. Her life is going to be so different now."

"But she'll feel proud of herself, too," Daed said, surprising Will. "She must have been mighty desperate." He pursed his lips. "I don't hold with a man hurting his wife. What he did was wrong."

"I hope she knows she will still have a friend in Elizabeth Anne and all of you who helped," Mamm said.

Will liked the sound of that. He hadn't imagined he'd ever see the woman again. But if he did? Well, he would like to think that he could be her friend, or at least someone she could depend on.

"What are you and E.A. going to do now that you are a couple?" Nan asked.

Startled by the switch in topics, Will shrugged. "Hmm? I don't know."

His sister rolled her eyes. "Really? That's all you have to say?"

"What is that supposed to mean?"

"Come on, brother," Jake said. "You've been seeing E.A., you've been helping her rescue women in jeopardy . . . you've been friends with her forever. And . . . well, you've been seen kissing her, too."

"More than once," Nan said.

He was beyond embarrassed. "I can't believe you brought that up."

"It's kind of hard not to mention it," Jake said. "I mean, it's true."

Nan smirked. "Oh, Will. Don't look so surprised. It's been mighty obvious what's been going on."

"Oh?"

"Oh, please," she coaxed. "I don't think it's that hard to say the words. Come on," she singsonged. "Say 'I have strong feelings for Elizabeth Anne Schmidt.' I know you do."

He felt as cornered as a turkey on Thanksgiving Day. Looking at his parents helplessly, he waited for one of them to intervene. Weren't they going to step in here?

Instead, his mother only looked amused, and his father? His father looked directly at him like he expected an answer.

"Daed, what are you thinking?" he asked.

"What I'm thinking hardly matters."

"I think it does."

"Well, then. I'm thinking that it's all been decided. If E.A. is depending on you to help her and you like her well enough to be spending so much time together, then all that you need to do is make it official."

His mother stood up. "Not that you need to make anything official *right away*, dear."

"She's Mennonite and I've already been baptized." That meant she was going to have to become Amish, too. For most people, that would be a jarring thing—something that might take weeks or months to consider. But he knew E.A. had likely already thought about that.

"Perhaps we could worry about this another time?" Mamm asked gently.

"*Jah*," Daed said with a nod. "I think it's time we all went to bed. It's after midnight."

Happy to go upstairs, take a shower, and finally be alone with his thoughts, Will hugged his parents good night, then followed Jake and Nan upstairs.

"Night, Will," Nan said. "I'm glad you're all right."

"*Danke*. Have a good sleep."

She smiled. "You, too," she said as she entered her room..

Will and Jake walked a little farther down the hall. Will's room was next. At the far end of the hall was Jake's room.

Jake stopped Will as he was about to go in. "Hey, Will, why do you think God made you do all that tonight?"

Taking a minute, he gave some thought to his brother's question. The answer came to him immediately. Not as a flash, but as a certainty—an answer he knew that the Lord had supplied. "Because He knew I would help, I reckon. I think our Lord knew I would do my best for Him."

Jake smiled. "I like that idea."

"*Jah*. I do, too."

"For what it's worth, I'm real proud of you. Night," he added quickly.

Will watched his brother walk down the hall before replying. "*Danke.*"

After he walked into his room and shut the door behind him, he sat down on his bed and closed his eyes. Allowed himself to remember how worried he'd been about E.A. during their run toward Marta and her husband. How proud he'd been of E.A., John, and Marie as they'd all stepped up to help a woman they didn't know.

Then, finally, he allowed himself to remember his favorite part of the whole day and evening . . . when he'd told Elizabeth Anne that he loved her and she told him that she loved him, too.

Yes, that was the best moment of all.

THIRTY-SEVEN

"Just like the Lord does. We protect each other and
He protects us."

A week had passed since Marta left the fairgrounds in the
back of an ambulance: a crazy, stressful, amazing, and exhausting
week. First, she'd been taken to the main sheriff's office. There,
a victim's advocate had met with her along with the sheriff and
one of the deputies, who brought her a cheeseburger and fries.
They'd sat by Marta's side as she ate her meal with shaking hands
and told her story.

Admitting the abuse she'd experienced for years had felt both
empowering and embarrassing. She was a smart woman who'd
been raised by good people. She'd had lots of friends and had
even completed two years of college. She'd also been involved in
her church and considered herself to have a strong faith.

If she was all of those things, how could she have put up with
so much abuse for so long?

She wasn't sure what the answer was to that question, only that she had a feeling she was going to ask it of herself many times over the next few months.

Luckily, in the midst of all her self-recriminations, she'd also felt the warm rays of compassion. The victim's advocate had shaken off her doubts and guilt, and both of the law enforcement officers had shaken their heads whenever she tried to take some of the blame. The sheriff had even gone so far to say that if she took any of the responsibility, it would only give Alan more power over her.

That had been a hard lump to swallow, but it had also given her a measure of peace that she hadn't even known she needed. They were right: even though she had been strong, Alan had damaged her. He'd been able to convince her to take the blame for her abuse.

That was something she was going to need to stop.

After the difficult conversation, she'd been examined by a nurse and had pictures taken of her bruises. At first Marta hadn't wanted to put herself in such a vulnerable state, but when they'd explained that they would need as much proof as possible in order to press charges, she'd reluctantly agreed.

She couldn't say that the hospital visit had been easy, but when it was over, she reminded herself that it was something else that she'd been strong enough to do. Stronger than she imagined, certainly.

After the hospital visit—and the news that a restraining order against Alan had been issued—the social worker had taken her to a safe house for battered women. She'd been given a room, a pair of pajamas and a change of clothes, and told to rest. And boy, had she! Marta was fairly sure she'd slept most of the first two days she'd been there.

Now she was soon going to leave. At the urging of the women in the shelter, Marta had reached out to her parents and told them what had happened and what she'd been through. She'd been so embarrassed at first. And, yes, secretly afraid that they would be upset with her for losing touch with them.

But instead they'd reminded her of their love for her and said that they would arrive there the next day to drive her home. She was going to go home for the first time in years and heal.

Now, just a few hours before their arrival, Marta was receiving another visitor. Officer Fuller had arrived at the shelter with a shopping bag of items from her house and Marta's favorite treat: a latte.

Marta hugged her hello, thanking Jesus once again for bringing so many angels into her life.

"Are you excited to see your parents, Marta?" Officer Fuller asked as she handed Marta the coffee.

"Yes. I mean, I think so."

"You aren't sure?"

Realizing that Officer Fuller hadn't been in the room when she'd shared how she'd steadily distanced herself from her parents, Marta said, "The worse things got with Alan, the less I wanted them to know about my life. I was so ashamed, I kept a lot of secrets." She stopped, dreading the idea of seeing a look of recrimination or hearing a barrage of questions she wasn't ready to answer.

But instead of any of that, Officer Fuller simply nodded. "I can see how you might have wanted that."

Feeling relieved by the easy acceptance, Marta continued, "After I got here and realized that I was finally safe, I knew I needed to reach out to them."

"So you gave them a call."

Marta nodded. "I'm not going to lie. Those first couple of

minutes were awkward and felt scary. But before I knew it, everything was just how it used to be with us: comfortable."

Officer Fuller reached out and clasped her hand. "I'm proud of you."

"Thank you." Marta smiled at her. Then, seeing a look of resolve in her eyes in addition to the warmth that had been shining there, she added, "You didn't just come here to bring me a coffee and wish me well, did you?"

"No, I'm afraid not. I have some news."

"Okay . . ." Marta set her cup down.

Officer Fuller uncrossed her legs and leaned slightly forward. "So, Alan is home," she said in a matter-of-fact tone. "He got a lawyer, of course. And the lawyer discussed the restraining order with him."

"Do you think he's going to ignore it?"

Officer Fuller sighed. "Marta, I want to be truthful with you."

"Good, because I want the truth."

"All right then. Here's the thing. Unfortunately, I've met several abusers and stalkers over years."

"And?"

"And the majority do stay away. The consequences of ignoring a restraining order are serious. Alan would be a fool to think he's above the law, and he doesn't come across as a fool to me."

"He's not." But would he think he was above the law? She had a feeling that where she was concerned, that was a yes. Making herself tamp down the rush of fear that was threatening to overcome her, Marta looked the police officer directly in the eye. "Is there anything else?"

"He's pretty angry, Marta."

"That doesn't surprise me."

"Me, neither." She smiled at Marta before continuing. "Alan thinks you betrayed him. When the officers stopped by your house to get a couple of your things, it was obvious that he'd been searching through everything. We made sure to tell him that he had no right to be rummaging through your things."

Just imagining Alan hearing such a thing made Marta grimace. "I bet he didn't care to hear that."

"Not at all. He's even tried to say that you stole money from him."

"I did take some money, but it was only a thousand dollars that I scrimped together over a year." She promised herself she wouldn't cry anymore. Not for him.

Officer Fuller's expression hardened. "Don't you start over-thinking any of this. You did what you had to do. Not a bit of it was wrong."

"What did the sheriff say?"

"What you would think he would: he told your husband to stop acting so ridiculous."

Marta knew her eyes had widened, but she could hardly believe it. "Wow."

"I'm telling you all of this not to scare you, but to let you know that it's happening. Also, to share that though you have a court-appointed lawyer, you might see if your parents can help you find a good divorce lawyer."

"You think I need one?"

"Absolutely." Her voice hardened. "Your husband has already arranged for legal counsel. Marta, you need someone who is willing and able to make sure your ex doesn't hurt you again. And who is going to make sure you are taken care of."

"All right."

"All right? You sure?"

She was asking if Marta was willing to stay strong. "I'm sure."

"Good. I'm relieved to hear that." Officer Fuller smiled as she stood up. "Now, you already have my card and my contact information. I expect you to use it and keep in touch."

"I will. Thank you for everything." Just as they shook hands, she realized that they hadn't talked about the person to whom Marta owed the greatest amount of thanks. "I want to thank E.A. and her friends, but I'm afraid if I show up at the sewing shop I could put her in danger." She'd already told Officer Fuller about what a good friend E.A. had been to her.

"I don't want you going anywhere near Walnut Creek just yet. Why don't you do this: when you are ready, write her a letter. I'll pass it on. I'm sure E.A. will understand."

"All right. Yes. I'll do that." Realizing that it would be so nice to have that letter written, Marta asked, "Could I possibly write it now?"

"Of course. Take your time."

Feeling sure of herself for the first time during the conversation, Marta ran to her room and retrieved a pad of paper, pen, and an envelope. After seeing that the other woman had taken a seat and was focused on her cell phone, Marta sat down, took a deep breath, and thanked E.A. for everything she'd done. Marta kept the note short—after all, there was no way she could adequately convey how much she appreciated the girl's friendship. However, she was pleased to have taken the opportunity to do something for her.

When she was done at last, she sealed the letter, then also pulled out the small bookmark she'd hand-stitched over the last week. "Here you go, Officer. Here is E.A.'s note . . . and this is for you."

Looking visibly moved, Officer Fuller ran a finger along the stitching on the bookmark. "Did you make this?"

"I did. The folks here at the shelter have a box of donated clothes for the women who stay here. A lot of the things are real pretty, but there was a shirt that was in such poor shape I knew no one would be able to wear it. Charlotte, the lady who runs the house, said I could do whatever I wanted with it."

"This is beautiful." Officer Fuller's voice was filled with wonder.

"I wouldn't exactly call it beautiful . . ."

"I would. It's lovely. I'm very touched. Thank you so much."

"You're very welcome, though it's not a fair exchange for everything you've done for me."

"No thanks was needed. Helping women like you is why I became a police officer. I'm glad you are okay."

After Officer Fuller left, Marta went back up to her room and sat down next to the window to watch the police officer leave in her cruiser.

She knew that in less than an hour, she would see her parents again and she'd be heading back to southern Ohio.

She realized then that if she had her way, she'd never be in Walnut Creek again. She'd like to put it and her life there behind her.

Hopefully, it would actually be possible.

Feeling restless, she picked up the scraps of fabric from the discarded shirt and decided to make another bookmark or two. One she would give to her social worker and the other? Well, she might just do some thinking about what she could do with this new hobby.

Maybe she was going to be just fine, after all.

THIRTY-EIGHT

"So, that's our story for Marie. One night, we proved that she meant so much to us that we'd do just about anything to help her," E.A. finished. "Because we love you, Marie."

"You didn't have to walk over here, Will," Elizabeth Anne said.

"I walked over here so you wouldn't have to drive in the op-posite direction to pick me up."

E.A. smiled. "It isn't that far."

"You can drop me off later. Don't worry."

This wasn't the first time that they'd seen each other since "the big rescue," as Marie liked to call it, but it was the first time they were going to be around their entire group of friends as a couple.

"How was work today?" Will asked as she headed toward the Loyal Inn, Katie and Harley's B and B.

"Work?" She shrugged. "It was okay."

"Just okay?"

She shrugged again. "To be honest, I thought I would feel different after everything that happened with Marta. But instead, I just feel empty." She wasn't sure if it was because she was coming to terms with how ignorant she'd been of Marta's desperate situation or if it was because she had lost someone she was just getting to know.

Will's brown eyes were full of compassion, but maybe a little bit of confusion, too. "I don't exactly understand."

"I don't know if I do, either." Trying to figure out how to explain herself without rambling, E.A. drummed her fingers on the steering wheel. "Will, you know that I've felt like I was in a dead-end job."

He nodded. "And I remember that you aren't exactly fond of your manager, either."

"That's true. And things with Lark haven't gotten better. She and I still butt heads." She sighed.

"Are you trying to say that you want to look for another job?"

She shook her head. "No. I really just want to feel something more, you know? See, for a while, when I was helping Marta, I felt like I was at the sewing shop for a reason. Like I was doing something more than just selling fabric."

"Maybe you ought to look into teaching more students. Teaching sewing could be your calling. It's got to be a lot different from simply ringing up customers."

She loved how he was taking her concerns seriously. "I've thought about that, too. But now I'm starting to think that maybe teaching sewing itself wasn't what got me excited at all." She slowed down and turned on her blinker. They were almost at Katie and Harley's house.

"What do you think it was?"

"I liked helping people, Will. No, I liked being needed," she corrected. "For a while there, I knew Marta was hurting and struggling with something. And I knew that she was depending on me to help her get through it."

"You know she was. If not for you, her plan might not have happened."

"I'd like to think even if I wasn't there, Marta could have done what she did." She shook her head. "So, I liked helping a battered woman become stronger and help herself. But what do I do now?"

"I don't know."

"I don't know, either. I'm not trained to help women in abusive situations, and it's not like I'm suddenly going to be able to start helping them by teaching them how to sew pillowcases."

"You might, though. Women might be taking classes for other reasons. You never know." After a pause, he added, "E.A., think about all that we've been through these last couple of months. Andy's death hit us hard, some of our best friends moved back to town, others have gotten married . . . Why, even me trying to figure out my promotion had its challenges."

"And, we can't forget David."

"No, we sure can't," he said with a laugh. "It's a huge blessing that he finally decided to leave you alone."

"His *daed* told my *daed* that David didn't trust anyone who would speak to the police like I did at the fair."

Will smirked. "He's such a jerk." Looking earnest again, he softened his voice. "What I'm trying to tell you is that all of us have been privately going through some difficult times that we've kept to ourselves. I can't tell you the number of times I told people at work that I was 'fine' when I was still mourning Andy's loss. If you continue with your classes, you might be helping your students in more than just one way."

A lot of what he said made sense. Remembering the note Marta had sent her, she said, "Marta said in her note that she was staying at a women's shelter. Maybe someone at the police department could tell me about that place and I could volunteer to help some of them."

"I think that would be a wonderful idea."

As she parked the car, E.A. said, "Will, you always seem to know how to make me see things clearer."

"I think you've always seen things fairly clearly. All I do is help you get rid of some of the fog," he said just as a horse and buggy drove up behind them. "Look at that. Logan and Tricia are here."

It still caught her off guard. A few months before Andy passed away, his sister and Logan got together. Their relationship had its own special circumstances, least of all being the fact that Andy wasn't very happy about one of his best friends dating his little sister. But that worry paled next to the fact that Logan had been baptized and didn't want to leave the Amish faith. That meant Tricia had to make the decision to become Amish.

And, to the surprise of a lot of people, she had. She'd immersed herself in studies, both of Pennsylvania Dutch and their faith and way of life. Little by little, she'd eased into it, and Logan's family and friends began to see that she was earnest and ultimately supported their union.

Just a month after Marie and John married, Tricia and Logan had married as well. Now, E.A. reckoned anyone who met Tricia would be surprised to discover that she hadn't grown up in the faith.

Walking over to meet them, Will shook Logan's hand and smiled at Tricia. "Hello, Tricia."

"Hello to you, too," she replied in Pennsylvania Dutch before hugging E.A. "I'm so glad to see you. I've been worried about you."

"Nothing to worry about. I'm fine. How about you tell me how things are going as a real Amish wife?"

As she hoped, Tricia giggled. "Logan's *mamm* has been helping me sew my first dress."

"And, how is it going?"

"I think I'm going to need to take some sewing lessons from you," she said as they followed Will and Logan into the house.

"Anytime." She lowered her voice. "Or, just ask me and I'll come over and finish up the dress for you. I won't tell a soul."

Tricia hugged her. "*Danke*, but I'm determined to do it myself. For better or worse, you know?"

E.A. smiled. "*Jah*. I know."

"E.A., come look what Katie's been up to," Marie called out.

Entering the dining room, she was stunned to see a whole spread of beautiful-looking food arranged on the dining room table. Katie was pulling out a soup tureen just as E.A. walked into the kitchen. "Is all this for the B and B's guests or for us, Katie?"

"For us, of course. Harley and I decided to close the inn this week. We needed a break."

"Which for Katie means that she's going to fuss and clean and get everything ready for all of us," Marie said as she walked in the door.

"I tried to bring a side dish but she wouldn't let me," Kendra said.

Marie put a hand on her hip. "She wouldn't even let me bring cookies, and I can almost make decent ones."

"I'm sorry we missed those," Tricia murmured with a grin.

"Oh, stop," Marie said. "My cooking has improved. Kind of."

E.A. grinned, loving her girlfriends' silly exchanges as much as ever. "Just for the record, I'm feeling a little guilty. I didn't ask to bring anything at all. I'm sorry, Katie."

"Don't be, I would have told you no if you'd asked. This little get-together is for you and Will."

"Why us?"

"You don't know?" Before E.A. responded, Katie shrugged. "Well, you will. Now, grab a dish and bring it to the dining room. Let's eat while it's hot."

E.A. did as she was bid, but it felt like her body was on auto-pilot. Carrying a large casserole dish of delicious-smelling mac-aroni and cheese, she followed Katie into the dining room and carefully placed it on a hot plate.

But as she sat down, her mind was spinning. She had no idea about what their friends had cooked up—or how she and Will were supposed to react to it.

Will sat down next to her and sent a sympathetic look her way. She was grateful for it. No matter what happened, at least they were in this together.

After Katie sat down at last, Harley, who was sitting at the head of the table, smiled at the group of them all together. "No matter when we get together or for whatever reason, I am always glad that it happened. We have much to be thankful for."

Katie, sitting at the other end, smiled at her husband warmly. "Let us bow our heads and give thanks."

A sense of peace flowed through E.A. as she joined the others in silent prayer. Harley was right. All that really mattered was that they were all together. That was a blessing indeed.

Taking her time, she gave thanks for their friendships, the many hands that had made the food, and the constant faith that she held close to her heart. That faith reminded her that no matter what happened, they would emerge stronger on the other side.

When she raised her head, Tricia was looking at her strangely. Actually, most everyone was.

"What?"

"Nothing," Tricia said quickly. "I, well, you seemed to be praying so earnestly."

"I guess I was. Harley reminded me that there are still times when I take our group for granted. It encouraged me to give a lot of prayers of thanks."

"I've done that a time or two," Marie said as everyone began taking helpings from the serving dishes and passing them on. "Especially during this last year. I don't know how we would have survived if we didn't have each other to lean on."

"That is what brings us together tonight," Katie said. "I know that receiving gratitude and praise were the last things that E.A. and Will were thinking about when they helped that woman, but I don't think there's any harm in celebrating the fact that they stepped in and helped her."

E.A. had never thought about how her actions would be seen or judged by her friends. "We don't need to be celebrated for what we did for Marta. We did what any decent person would do."

"Oh, I think it matters a lot. I'm sure it mattered to her," Kendra murmured. "You saved Marta from an awful situation."

All of them knew Kendra spoke from personal experience.

She'd been abused as a child but had been too ashamed to tell them much of what she'd gone through until recently.

Will cleared his throat. "I feel the same way as E.A. I don't think we did anything that the rest of you wouldn't have done. And let's not forget that John and Marie were there, too."

E.A. shook her head. "If we give praise to anyone at all, let's honor Marta, who overcame a lot of odds in order to have a better life."

Logan raised a glass. "Here's to people who take chances and make changes, then . . . and to the One who protects us all."

Tricia cleared her throat. "Now that we've toasted John, Marie, E.A., and Will, I thought maybe we could get some information."

"About what?" Will asked.

"You two, of course," Katie said. "Are you two officially a couple now or not?"

All traces of humor vanished from Will's expression. "That's awfully nosey of ya, Katie."

"Oh, come now. It isn't like Harley and me didn't court right under your noses."

"But still . . ."

"I'm sorry, but I think you're being a little sensitive," Logan interjected. "It isn't like you two are the first of all of us to fall in love. So, put us out of suspense . . . are you two official now?"

Right as E.A. was going to "officially" declare them a couple, Will turned to her and gave her a look that was so warm, it made her feel like they were the only two people in the whole room.

"Here is your answer," he said at last. "Of course I love Elizabeth Anne Schmidt. I love her a lot."

While all of their friends started clapping, E.A. simply looked at her guy and smiled. Her heart was so full, there wasn't a single word that needed to be said.

THIRTY-NINE

Raising her glass of water, Elizabeth Anne smiled brightly. "Congratulations! May your future be happy and joyous. And if you ever need a helping hand? We'll all be there for you. For better or worse."

SIX MONTHS LATER

*B*ack when she'd been Lark's employee, E.A. had dreaded slow days in the shop. Lark had never wanted to talk to her or work on a sewing project. Usually, she'd just sat in her office or someplace in the back and played on her phone. She'd made sure that E.A. had known that she was supposed to answer the phone, dust, and simply be ready for customers.

Then, when people did walk in, E.A. would feel Lark's judgmental gaze on her back. It never failed to make her feel like she'd done something wrong. Even though she knew she hadn't.

But then, right before E.A. and Will's wedding, Lark had announced that she was moving to Florida. Elizabeth Anne's parents had helped her buy the shop, saying it was a good investment. Her mother also liked to come in to work a few hours a week now. She said she enjoyed having something interesting to do in her spare time.

Now that she was the owner of Sew and Tell, E.A. tried to make it a far more welcoming and fun place, where she encouraged her customers to come in and tell her about their latest projects.

Owning her own business seemed to suit her well. Her sales had grown, and more and more customers were bringing their friends in, just so they could see how cute the store was. That made E.A. very happy. So did the fact that she had more sewing students.

Actually, she was so busy that there was now always something to do. And because of that, she couldn't remember the last time she'd had a really slow day at work.

Yes, things had changed a lot over the last year. After a three-month engagement, she and Will had gotten married and moved into a small cottage on his parents' farm that Will's family, along with several other men in the area, had built for them.

Because Will was so wonderful, he'd paid an Amish carpenter to design their kitchen and a sewing room for her. It was beautiful.

And, so was her life.

Will was still working three evenings a week and one day shift. He and his manager, Craig, had dreamed up that schedule. Craig enjoyed the quieter nights and Will liked still being in touch with the rest of the employees.

E.A. had also made good on her promise to herself and now volunteered two days a month at a local women's shelter. Some days she did nothing more than serve meals and help watch children, but that was enough. She liked feeling that she was doing something good for someone else—kind of like how she'd felt with Marta.

But perhaps the greatest change was that she was living life Amish now. Just like she'd told Will, it wasn't a considerable change. Though it had presented some challenges—she didn't think she'd ever be able to actually drive a horse and buggy—she didn't mind living a simpler life.

Everything that had happened with Marta had reinforced her feelings that it was best to concentrate on what was important. Life wasn't about details and being safe. No, it was about helping other people and not waiting for the perfect time. It was about watching fireflies in the summer and laughing with their friends and being thankful for each day.

As if she'd conjured her up, the bells on the door at Sew and Tell chimed and in walked Marta herself.

E.A. couldn't help but stare. Her favorite sewing student looked so different! Her brown hair was longer. It now fell below her shoulders. She had gained a little weight, and the extra pounds looked good on her. Her cheeks were fuller and her skin was rosy. She looked healthy.

But the greatest change was the way she was holding herself. She looked confident and secure. No, she looked happy.

"Hi there," Marta said before E.A. could walk around the counter to greet her. "I'm looking for Elizabeth Anne Schmidt . . . wait, E.A.?"

E.A. rushed to her side. "*Jah*. It's me."

Her eyes widened. "E.A., you have on a *kapp*."

"I know! I'm Amish now."

Marta looked at her closely for another long moment. "I'm

sorry, I should have recognized you." Smiling slightly, she said, "I would know your blue eyes anywhere."

"I don't blame you for not realizing it was me. Believe me, you aren't the first person who's had to do a double take. Sometimes I forget that I look so different. A few months ago I married an Amish man."

"So you became Amish just like that?"

E.A. smiled. "I wouldn't say it was exactly that smooth, but it wasn't hard, either. Will and I were good friends for years. Falling in love just seemed like the right thing to do."

A line formed between Marta's brows. "Wait, did you say Will? Wasn't he the man with you that day?"

"Yes. Like I said, we've been good friends for a long time." Stepping closer, E.A. said, "I'm surprised to see you here! To tell the truth, I almost didn't recognize you, either."

"Really? Well, I guess my hair is longer."

"It's more than that. You look . . . well, you look happy, Marta."

She relaxed and her eyes sparkled. "I am."

"Come sit down and talk to me." She gestured toward the four padded chairs near the back of the shop.

Marta followed but she was looking at the office door. "I'm happy to sit and chat . . . if you're sure that's okay?"

"Lark left, so it's my shop now. That means I can do whatever I want."

"Wow, I guess we both have had a few changes." Sitting down in the chair next to E.A., Marta looked around the shop. "This is nice."

"Thank you. I wanted to make the shop a cozy place." Smiling at the pale pink walls and colorful animals drawn by children that were displayed in pretty frames around the shop, she said, "I wanted people to feel like Sew and Tell was a place where they could stay a while."

Marta crossed her legs. "It always felt that way to me, E.A. But that didn't have anything to do with how it was decorated. I felt that way because of you."

That was the sweetest compliment. "I don't know what to say."

"You don't need to say anything. It's the truth."

"Can you tell me what happened to you after the fair?"

Marta blew out a burst of air. "Boy, sometimes I wonder what *didn't* happen. Let's see. For starters, I reconnected with my parents and moved home with them. I live near Cincinnati now."

"Reconnected?"

Marta nodded. "I hadn't realized the extent of it, but Alan had wanted so much control over me that I slowly lost touch with most everyone else." Looking reflective, she continued, "First, I drifted away from my friends, then family."

"That is very sad. I'm surprised they didn't realize something was wrong."

"I think there's only so many times a person can cancel plans or not return phone calls before even the best of friends and family gives up." Marta clasped her hands in her lap. "Anyway, after I got settled back at my parents' house, they spoke to a lawyer and found a counselor for me. Those two people, along with my parents and a few loyal and patient friends, became my team."

E.A. smiled. "I like the idea that you have a whole team of people by your side."

"Boy, not as much as me! Over the last year, I had started to feel like I was completely alone." Her voice cracked. "Well, except for a few friends and you, E.A. You were there for me."

Overcome by emotion, E.A. swallowed. "Oh, Marta."

She shifted. "To finish up my story, at first Alan tried to get around the restraining order, and then he tried to contact me through our lawyers. But it was so strange. As soon as he realized that he wasn't going to get me back easily—and if he fought he was going to have to give me even more money than my lawyer originally asked for—he backed off." Looking a little smug, she said, "I have a feeling the charges against him had something to do with that."

"So then you got divorced."

"Oh, yes, I did. I'm not going to say it was easy or painless, but it just went through about five weeks ago." She straightened her shoulders. "I am now Marta Benson."

"You gave up your married name."

Marta's eyes lit up. "I couldn't do that fast enough. I really, really needed to get rid of any reminder of him. It was better for me not to have any ties to Alan. So, that's my story."

"I'm glad you are happier."

"I'm glad about that, too." She smiled. "I'm also working again."

"You are? That's wonderful."

"It turns out that I still love doing my research, and I'm still good enough at it to get work."

E.A. felt like a mother whose child had accomplished something difficult: so proud. "I'm so glad you came here to let me know. I've been worried about you! I've been praying, of course, but seeing how well you are doing makes my heart so full."

Opening up her tote bag, Marta pulled out the yellow backpack. "I also came here to give you something." She held it out to Elizabeth Anne.

"Your backpack?"

"If there is anything about the last year that I'm most proud of, it's this," she said, running a hand along the fabric. "You helping me sew it, keeping it here so Alan wouldn't know . . . never being anything but encouraging even when I got frustrated. I'll never forget it."

"Marta—"

"No, let me finish. Because of you, I was able to make this little thing. And it, in turn, became something pretty important. It gave me a lot of hope. I thought if I could make this, well, I could accomplish anything—even finally leave my husband."

E.A. was so touched she could hardly speak. "Don't you think you should be the one keeping it?"

"No. I have enough memories. I don't need a reminder of everything I did to leave. But . . . I thought, well, maybe you might need a reminder of the impact you made on me?"

Overwhelmed by emotion, E.A. took it from her outstretched hands. "*Danke*. I will treasure it, always."

Marta stood up. "I'm going to leave now. I only came back here to see you—and my friend Elaine. She testified in court about my bruises and the things she heard Alan say to me."

"Thank you so much for coming by. I've been wondering how you were doing."

"You don't need to worry about me anymore. I'm going to be okay." She smiled again. "Now I'm on my way to a weekend retreat."

E.A. walked her to the door. "A retreat?"

"It's with some women from my church in Cincinnati." She blushed. "Some new girlfriends, really."

E.A. reckoned that this was going to be the last time she ever saw Marta. It made her sad, but she understood. Being here in Walnut Creek no doubt brought back many bad memories. She knew she needed to be grateful that Marta had felt the need to even come back at all. "I'm happy for you, Marta."

"I'll always be grateful for you, E.A. Always." Quickly giving her a hug, she whispered, "I'll never forget what you and your husband and friends did for me that day at the fair. Never."

E.A. hugged her back. Then smiled at her. "I will miss you, Marta. God be with you."

Marta's eyes widened. "Oh, He already is, E.A. Of that, I have no doubt." She smiled softly before walking out the door, leaving E.A. alone with her thoughts. She felt a sense of loss as she walked back to the sitting area and carefully picked up the backpack to bring it to the front counter. Just as she was about to fold it and put it in a drawer, she realized there was something inside. After unzipping it, she found a card inside.

Opening the envelope, she saw it was a simple card with a verse on it.

> Blessed are those who believe without seeing me.
> John 20:29

Inside was a lovely silver cross with a slim pink ribbon with two words written on the fabric: HAVE FAITH.

Thinking about Marta, thinking about Andy, E.A. felt the strangest sense of loss.

But then the door opened and one of her regular customers came in, followed by two little girls.

She cleared her throat. "Hello, Rebecca. It looks like you have helpers today."

"I do! E.A., this is Pamela and Lauren."

E.A. walked around the counter and shook each little girl's hand. "I am Elizabeth Anne, but all of my friends call me E.A. It's nice to meet you."

Little Pamela, so cute with her dark hair in a bouncy ponytail, looked up at her with big blue eyes. "My mommy says you're a good sewing teacher. Can you help me learn to sew?"

"Of course I can. Teaching girls to sew is one of my favorite things to do. Come over and let's get started."

When the girls scrambled over to the tables near the sewing machines, Elizabeth Anne looked out the window just in time to see Marta get in her car and drive away.

She couldn't help but stand there a moment and smile. Some wishes really did come true. It was going to be a good day.

READER QUESTIONS

1. Who were some of the characters you connected with in *The Protective One*? Why?

2. Obviously, the theme of protection was represented many times in this novel. Characters were reaching out to protect Marta and each other. Other characters were hoping to protect their hearts. What or who have you protected lately?

3. Another theme in the novel was renewal. Both Will and E.A. yearned to renew their interests in their jobs. Marta was renewing her life. To an extent, all the characters were also renewing their faith. How might this theme be illustrated in your life?

4. I loved how Will was willing to give working the night shift a try and Marta was willing to learn to sew. Have you taken on a new hobby, relationship, or job lately? What were some of the emotions that you felt? How did your faith help you in your progress?

5. One of my favorite settings in the novel was the county fair. I asked one of my reader groups for some of their favorite "fair" memories and was enchanted by the stories. Have you ever been to a county fair? What was your favorite thing to do?

6. How did you feel about the outcome of the novel? What do you think will happen to Marta in the future?

7. I used the following verse from Psalm 61 to guide the writing of this book. "You have been my protection, like a strong tower against my enemies" (Psalm 61:3). How has the Lord been your protector?

8. "God adds to the beauty of His world by creating true friends" (Amish Proverb). As soon as I found this Amish proverb, I knew it would be perfect for E.A., Will, and the Eight. How have your true friends added to the beauty of your world?

Keep reading for a sneak peek at the next heartwarming
installment in the Walnut Creek Series

THE
TRUSTWORTHY
ONE

Available from Gallery Books in May 2020

PROLOGUE

$\mathcal{R}$ight about the time she'd discovered that mercurial, insidious emotion called envy, Kendra Troyer had been envious of the Eight. Though it shamed her, she understood it.

Why, just about everyone who wasn't in the famous clique envied them something awful. They were good-looking, loyal to one another, and led great lives. Their close friendship had already lasted a decade, and they were only in their early teens.

Above all that, just being around their group made a person feel better about the world. They constantly seemed to be in good moods, loved teasing one another, and always had something new and exciting planned.

So, sure, Kendra got why the group was popular with most everyone. But it didn't make sense. After all, they shouldn't have fit in anywhere, given that they were a combination of all the different groups in Walnut Creek. Some were English, some Mennonite, and others were Old Order Amish. Why, one member was even New Order Amish like herself.

The Eight were on her mind as she walked through the middle school parking lot on Friday afternoon. Two girls who sat behind her in choir had been talking about *Englischer* Andy Warner and his Amish best friend John Byler. Both boys were handsome as could be, and Mary Kate and Cassidy had seen them splitting a pizza together the night before. Instead of singing, they'd been whispering about the boys, wondering if they'd ever give a girl who wasn't part of their tight circle a second glance.

Kendra had wondered that a time or two herself.

She'd also wondered what it would be like to have a big group of close friends—or at least a group of friends who wanted to go have pizza with her on a Thursday night.

As she continued through the parking lot, each of her steps feeling like lead, Kendra half pretended that she was on her way to anyplace other than home.

She'd stayed late at school to help one of the teachers get ready for Saturday's science fair, not that she would be presenting a project or anything. Even if she had been smart enough to design an experiment, she couldn't have done it. Projects like the ones the other kids were showing cost money. That was something she didn't have. Something she'd never had.

She hadn't minded helping Mrs. Kline set up the table, though. She liked being helpful. More importantly, since this was her eighth grade, and therefore would be her last year in school, she wanted to do as much as she could. Next year she wouldn't be so lucky. No, she'd have to stay home to take care of her four younger siblings even more than she did now.

Realizing it was getting late, she sped up her pace. Their father was going to be home soon, and there was no way she would let her younger siblings be alone with him if she could help it.

Slinging her backpack over one shoulder, she pushed the crossing button at the intersection.

"Hi, Kendra!" E.A. Schmidt called out. "Are you walking home, too?"

"*Jah.*" She smiled at the red-haired girl with bright blue eyes. As far back as Kendra could remember, Elizabeth Anne had gone by E.A. It was rare to hear anyone ever call her by her given name, except maybe some teachers on the first day of school.

Most people did whatever E.A. wanted. She was pretty, one of the Eight, and most of all, she was probably the smartest girl in the whole school. It had always been that way. Every year, E.A. seemed to get smarter and smarter. She was always receiving awards for earning the best scores on tests or getting straight A's or tutoring her classmates or little kids.

E.A. didn't push all her gifts into everyone else's faces, either. She just went about her business, never acting like she was better than anyone.

But everyone in Walnut Creek Middle School still knew she was brilliant.

"Want to walk together for a while?" E.A. asked.

"Sure." Kendra smiled at her. Maybe she had a chance to be part of the Eight after all.

When the light changed, they crossed. "So, how come you were here so late today?" E.A. asked.

"I was helping Mrs. Kline set up the science fair in the gym."

"Really?" Her blue eyes looked incredulous before she quickly masked her surprise. "Why, that's wonderful. What is your project? Mine's on Newton's second law of motion."

"I don't have a project. I was just helping out Mrs. Kline."

"Oh."

And . . . there it was again. The confusion that wasn't quite masked. It wasn't E.A.'s, fault, though. "I, uh, saw your booth. It looks really good."

"Do you think so?" When Kendra nodded, E.A. smiled. "Thanks so much! It's taken me forever. My mother kept trying to tell me that it was good enough, but I wanted it to be really special, you know?"

What could she say to that? "Good luck. I hope you do well."

"Thanks! I know it's prideful to want to win first place, but I can't help myself. I'd love for that to happen," E.A. said just before her smile widened. "Hey, look who's walking toward us."

"Who?"

But E.A. didn't hear her. She'd already turned all her attention to the approaching boys. "Hey, Andy! Hiya, Nate."

Andy Warner grinned. Next to him, Nate Miller raised a hand.

Andy Warner! Kendra smiled cautiously at the boys, thinking that things really were changing. First, E.A. wanted to walk with her, and now, here she was, stopping on the sidewalk to talk to the leader of the Eight! If Mary Kate and Cassidy saw her, they'd be so jealous.

As the boys got closer, E.A. turned back Kendra's way. "You know them, right?" she whispered.

"*Jah.*" It was the truth, too. Their community was a small one, and most everyone knew everyone else, even if only slightly.

While waiting for the boys to catch up, Kendra pasted what

she hoped was a pleasant smile on her face. She feared she just looked desperate, though.

"Hi," Andy said when they all were standing next to one another. "What are you doing getting home so late?"

"I was tutoring. Kendra here was helping set up the science fair," E.A. replied. "What about you two?"

"Andy had baseball practice, and I stayed late to finish a history test," Nate said with a groan. "I *canna* wait until I'm done with school."

Andy grinned. "You only have a couple more months until you're done for good. I still have four more years of high school to get through." He shifted his duffel bag to his other hand as he turned back to them. "So, I've got a game tonight. Are you coming?"

"Of course," E.A. said. "Marie and I are going to cheer you on every time you get up to bat. You better hit a home run."

Andy laughed. "I'll do my best. Hey, afterward, my parents said I could have people over. Want to come?"

"I'll try," E.A. replied. "I've got to ask my parents, but it shouldn't be a problem."

Kendra could hardly believe it. He'd asked her over. It was happening! She wasn't just going to talk to E.A. and Andy on the sidewalk, she was going to get to go to Andy's house and hang out with all their friends! She'd sneak out if she had to, even though she would get in so much trouble for leaving the house.

She noticed then that his expression was a little sheepish. Maybe a little embarrassed. "Hey, Kendra. Um, you're welcome to come over, too. I mean, if you don't have anything else to do."

Time practically stopped.

Andy hadn't meant to invite her. He'd been talking to E.A. alone, as if Kendra hadn't been standing right there, too.

She'd been invisible to him.

"*Danke*," she said. "But . . . I've already got plans."

Looking relieved, Andy grinned. "Yeah. Sure." He turned to Nate. "Miller, you know Kendra Troyer, right?"

Nate looked at her and nodded. "We know each other."

Kendra had gone to the food bank once with her mother, and Nate had been volunteering there. Her mother had been sporting a black eye, and Kendra had felt as if every person in the facility had been staring at them.

Though that had been years ago, Kendra felt shame slide deep into her chest. She half expected Nate to tell them about that day.

She needed to get out of there. Quickly, she pointed to their left. "I'm headed that way. I'll see you later."

"See ya, Kendra," E.A. said with a smile.

"Yeah. Bye," Andy said.

Nate just stared at her.

But when she was about halfway across the street, she heard Nate say, "That girl is all right, but she's got a real messed-up family. And they're really poor."

"She can't help that. There's nothing wrong with Kendra Troyer," E.A. said.

"There's nothing good, either. I've seen them go to the food bank. And there's all kinds of rumors going around about her father, too. Like he drinks and is as mean as a snake," Nate added. "You got lucky Kendra ain't coming over to your house, Warner. Your *mamm* would have to hide all her stuff."

"Ouch. That's harsh," Andy said.

She didn't hear what E.A. said, but it didn't matter. Kendra felt like she was choking.

As she hurried home, she had a change of heart. From that moment on, she decided she wasn't going to be envious of the Eight. Not at all. No, from now on, she was going to be real glad that she wasn't a part of their group.

And as for Nate Miller? She hated him now, and probably would for the rest of her life.